I0788130

# Total Chaos

A LOVE & LYRICS NOVEL

USA TODAY BESTSELLING AUTHOR
# NIKKI ASH

It's okay to be a little broken.

# Author's Note

Like real life, the characters are far from perfect, make morally gray decisions, and deal with subjects that may be sensitive for some readers. If you are looking for a safe romance, this series is not for you. Trigger warnings (which contain spoilers) can be found on my website: Love & lyrics Trigger Warnings

# Playlist

"Love You Like That"- Canaan Smith
"Think a Little Less"- Michael Ray
"Marry Me"- Thomas Rhett
"Lonely If You Are"- Chase Rice
"This Is What You Came For"- Calvin Harris
"The Other Side"- Jason Derulo
"Bedrock"- Young Money
"Just a Dream"- Nelly
"Beautiful"- Akon
"That Should Be Me"- Justin Bieber
"Steal My Girl"- One Direction
"Like I Can"- Sam Smith
"Track Star"- Mooski

*Haven't touched a single drink all night*
*But I'm drunk as fuck*
*On your scent, on your touch*
*Hand it over, baby*
*And you'll never know what it's like to be without love*
- Declan, Raging Chaos

# One

## Declan

"THE LAST WE HEARD FROM RAGING CHAOS AFTER DRUMMER, GAGE SHARP, WAS TAKEN TO *the hospital due to a drug overdose is that they're taking some time off and requesting privacy during—*"

The bitch yapping on the screen is cut off by an incoming call from my mom. I hit ignore, but it immediately starts up again.

"Another, sir?" the bartender asks, nodding toward my empty glass.

"Yeah, and you can keep 'em coming," I tell him as my phone rings again. "As a matter of fact, if you could just bring me a bottle, that'd be great." Since the bar I'm drinking at is located in the building I live in, they have my card on file. Normally, I'd just drink in my apartment, but right now, it's empty and lonely, and I hate being there more than I have to be.

The bartender nods and grabs me a new bottle, opening and placing it on the bar top, along with a larger glass.

"If you need anything else, let me know," he says before he walks away to help someone at the other end of the bar.

My phone starts up again, and since she's clearly not going to stop until I answer, I hit accept and bring my phone up to my ear. "Yeah." I pour myself another double shot of Johnnie Walker Blue Label—my go-to—and throw it back.

"Hello? Who is this?"

"You called me, Mom," I say dryly.

"Declan, I wasn't sure if it was you. Is that how you answer the phone for everyone who calls? It's rather rude. I know you're in a band, but—" The word *band* comes out sounding like a curse word, and I sigh, already exhausted by this conversation.

"Mom—"

"What if it were someone important? A business—"

"Mom!" I bark, having zero fucking patience for her shit today.

"What in the world is wrong with you?" she asks, sounding as if I've offended her. "Have you lost all respect for your elders? I'm your mother, not one of your trashy friends. Don't—"

Fuck, I've had enough. "Is it an emergency?"

"Excuse me?"

"Your reason for calling incessantly. Is it an emergency? Because I'm really not in the mood to talk."

"Yes, it is, actually. Your father and I saw the news. That... *friend* of yours almost died, and they said your band is over. Why didn't you tell us?"

"Because one, you don't like my friends, so I didn't think you would give a shit that he almost died." Since the day I became friends with Camden and Braxton, who asked me to join their band—later, recruiting Gage—she and my dad have been negative as hell, trying everything in their power to get me to "stop messing around with the wrong crowd." It's been over ten years, and they still don't take my career seriously.

"And two," I add, "our band isn't over. We're taking a break, so if you're calling to gloat or whatever, save it."

I know I sound disrespectful as hell, and normally, I try a lot harder to be the son she and my father want me to be—the son I'll never fully be. Since I refuse to give up being part of the band, I make it a point to speak properly and dress nicely. I don't have any tattoos or piercings, but I do have long hair, which drives them insane—but in my defense, I had long hair before the band— so when I'm at home or at a function they've guilted me into attending, I make sure to wear it up and out of my face. But she's called me at the wrong time, at a moment when I just don't give a fuck about being nice or proper or respectful, especially to the woman who has done nothing but talk shit about the band since we started it over a decade ago.

"I don't know what's wrong with you, Declan, but I would appreciate it if you would not speak to me that way. I was simply calling to see how you're doing and talk to you about your future." And here we go… "You're only twenty-five years old, so it's not too late to go to college, and if you're in need of a job—"

I laugh. Fucking laugh. Because she's lost her damn mind. And if I don't laugh, I might snap at her because I don't have it in me to refrain from doing so.

"Mom, I am *never* going to work for you and Dad. I'm a musician, not a hotelier. I play the bass guitar and sing, and even if the band never produced another album, we're worth millions, so please fucking stop. I love you, but I can't deal with you today. Let's call this a loss and try again tomorrow. Goodbye."

Without waiting for her to respond, I pull the phone away from my ear and hit end on the call, throwing it onto the bar top, facedown. I pour another double shot and am bringing it up to my lips when a feminine voice, one I would recognize anywhere, says, "Drinking alone?"

"Got no one to drink with."

I swallow down my shot, set the glass on the bar top, and glance at the gorgeous woman occupying the seat next to me. Her naturally blond hair is pulled around to the side in a braid that would make most women look young and childish, but it looks sexy as fuck on her. With her hair swept up, leaving her face completely visible, the light makeup she's sporting makes her bright blue eyes pop and her lips look glossy and plump. She smiles softly at me while she removes her jacket, hanging it over her chair and revealing a long-sleeved white shirt that shows off the swells of her breasts, skintight jeans that, if she were to stand, would showcase her toned legs and ass, and those fluffy boots women always wear.

My gaze ascends back to her face, and I notice her eyes are a bit glassy and the area under her eyes a tad swollen, like she's been crying and did a good job of covering it up.

"You okay?"

Scrunching up her adorable button nose that, when she's not wearing makeup, houses a cluster of freckles, she waves me off while she grabs the bottle and pours herself a shot, slinging it back. "How's Gage?"

"Alive."

Her eyes flit over to me. "Because of you."

"No, he almost died because of me."

I reach for the bottle, but she pours the shot for me, then hands me the glass. "You saved his life, Dec." Her words are soft and matter of fact, but they don't change the guilt I feel about everything that went down.

"His life never should've needed saving in the first place." I down the shot and slam the glass on the table, glaring at her.

"It wasn't your fault," she insists.

"Yeah, it fucking was."

*Two weeks ago*

*"I love this. It's sexy and sweet and so perfect." Kendall reads over the slight changes to the lyrics and music I made and grins, nodding in excitement. "This is it. It's going to be amazing."*

*"Yeah? You sure?"*

*"Definitely. There's no way my dad won't be all over this."*

*Her dad is the owner of Blackwood Records, the label both she and I are signed with. Kendall is a pop princess—think Taylor Swift meets Ariana Grande—and I'm the bass guitarist for the rock band, Raging Chaos—think Maroon 5 meets OneRepublic. We couldn't be any more different if we tried, but that's precisely what Kendall wants—to shake shit up a bit. And since the band is on a bit of a hiatus, with our lead singer—her brother—Camden and his wife, Layla, having a baby, I had some time on my hands, so I said, fuck it, why not? We had written a few songs together while we were messing around, so all we had to do was figure out which one would be the best and make it perfect. Then we could pitch it to her dad, Easton.*

*When we first discussed it, we were both on tour, so it got thrown on the back burner, but now that she's living in New York, she brought it back up, saying it would make the perfect single—and I agreed.*

*The truth is, even if I didn't agree, I'd still say okay because I can't say no to Kendall. I've been in love with the damn woman for as far back as I can remember—even though she has no clue—and would go along with whatever the hell she wanted.*

*"We should totally record it, so he can listen to it when we pitch it to him."*

*"Sounds good."*

*We spend the next hour singing our hearts out until we agree it's as good as it'll get without having the professionals produce it.*

*"I'm going to play this for him tomorrow." Her stomach rumbles,*

*and she giggles, covering it with her hands. "We've been at this forever. I'm starved. Wanna grab some dinner?"*

*"You don't have plans?" I glance at the huge rock on her left-hand, trying to keep the bitterness and jealousy out of my words, but it's hard, so damn hard, wanting a woman I can't have.*

*"Kyle's working late." She forces a smile, and I want to ask if she's sure he's really the one, but I bite my tongue because it's not my place to ask. Because we're only friends. Because I've been friend-zoned.*

*"I'm not in the mood for being in the public eye tonight, but if you want to come over, I can cook us something."*

*She beams, and it takes everything in me not to beg her to dump the fool who'd rather spend his night at work than with the woman he's supposed to be in love with. "That sounds perfect."*

*Since it's late, we lock up the studio behind us and head out. Gage and I are renting an apartment just up the street, which was our goal when finding a place, but Kendall and I can't go anywhere on foot without security. So we jump into her waiting SUV, and her driver takes us to my place, leaving us at the elevator in the underground garage.*

*We're talking about the snowstorm that's supposed to be arriving in the next couple of days as we walk into my place. It's quiet, and I assume Gage is sleeping since I don't hear any of his loud music playing.*

*"I'm going to light the grill and see if Gage wants to join us. Want to pour us some wine?"*

*Kendall nods, and I hand her the bottle and opener, then search for Gage, hoping he'll agree. He's sunk low lately, and I'm worried about him.*

*I knock and, when he doesn't answer, crack the door open so I can check on him—make sure he doesn't just have his headphones on and can't hear me. Sometimes, unless I force him to eat, he doesn't give a shit enough to feed himself.*

*He's lying on the bed, and I'm about to assume he's sleeping as I originally suspected, but then the light hits him in such a way that I do a double take. He's still, too fucking still. The worst feeling comes over me, and I rush over to him, my heart pounding in my chest.*

*"Gage. Gage!" I shake him, but he doesn't move. "Fuck! Kendall!" I yell. "Call for an ambulance."*

*Everything from that point on is a blur. The paramedics, ambulance, hospital, doctors, nurses. They manage to save him but make it clear it was a close call. Too close. Had Kendall not been hungry... had we not gotten to the apartment when we did... had I not checked on him... He'd be dead.*

But she was, and we did, and I did, and he's alive... If you can call it that. Thankfully, there was no brain damage or long-lasting effects. He's been an addict since the summer after our senior year, and we've ignored it. We should've forced him to get help sooner, but he was functioning,  and when we brought up him getting help, he shot us down. We didn't want to push him away, so we let it go until he almost died.

Now he's agreed to get help, so that's where he is... getting help.

And Braxton's living with his girlfriend, Kaylee.

And Camden's married with two kids.

And that leaves me here, alone. Well, not alone. Right now, Kendall's here with me... But later, she'll go home to her fiancé, and then I'll be alone again.

"What are you doing here anyway?"

Kendall's gaze shifts, and she pours another shot. "Same thing as you." She throws her drink back and shakes her head, wincing as the whiskey goes down. "Trying to drown my problems at the bottom of a bottle."

My eyes stay trained on her for several seconds, and when

it's clear she isn't going to talk about whatever is wrong, I shrug because I know how she feels. The last thing I want to do tonight is talk. So instead of pushing the topic, I grab the bottle, pour us both a double shot, and raise my glass.

"To drowning our problems."

She clinks her glass against mine. "To forgetting the world exists."

We swallow back our drinks, and then I pour us another one. We do this a few more times before the bar music turns up—the game on the television has finished—and Kendall slides off the seat.

"Let's dance!" She's loud in the quiet bar, but since it's not too busy, only a few people glance over before minding their own business.

Nobody's dancing... There's not even a dance floor, but Kendall doesn't seem to care as she extends her hand and bats her long lashes at me, waiting for me to join her.

And that's exactly what I do... Song after song, we dance our drunken hearts out in the corner of the bar. Well, Kendall dances her drunken heart out while I watch her sway her luscious hips to the beat as she throws her head back, exposing her slim neck. The entire time she belts out the lyrics to each song like she's performing, I imagine what it would be like for her to be mine. To do more than dance with her. To be able to pull her closer, to kiss and touch her...

I'm lost in my fantasy, so I don't realize she's stopped dancing and is looking at me like she's waiting for me to say something.

"What?"

She cracks up laughing, and I join in, having no idea what we're laughing about but loving the sound of her laughter when she lets herself go.

"What?" I say again.

"I said, the bar is closing."

I glance around, and she's right. Everyone is gone, the music has been silenced, and the lights have been raised. "Well, shit…"

"I don't wanna go home yet," Kendall says. Stepping into my space, she wraps her hands around my neck. The smell of her perfume—Dolce & Gabbana Light Blue—mixed with the sweet scent of the whiskey on her breath sends my head into a tailspin.

"Let's take that bottle up to your place and continue drowning." She places a soft kiss on the corner of my mouth, and shivers, motherfucking shivers, race down my spine.

A throat clears in the distance, and I look over at the bartender, who's trying to silently convey he'd like to go home. His disruption is enough to help clear the fog clogging my drunken brain.

"What about Kyle?" She's engaged, which means she shouldn't be kissing me, and she most definitely shouldn't be giving me a look that says drinking isn't the only thing she wants to do once we're at my place.

"We're over."

This gets my attention. Kendall got engaged a little over three months ago, and their wedding is next month. She insisted on fast-tracking the hell out of it, so her saying it's over is a huge one-eighty.

"What happened?"

"I don't wanna talk about it." She drags her nails up my nape, stopping at my bun, and tugs on it gently. "I just…" She swallows thickly. "I just wanna forget." Her blue eyes, filled with so much sadness, bore into mine, begging, pleading. "Please, Dec," she breathes. "Help me forget."

I want to ask questions and find out what the hell's going on… But remember when I mentioned I would do anything for this woman? I wasn't kidding. So instead, I simply nod. "All right. Let's go up to my place."

# Two

## Declan


She's quiet on the elevator and stays that way when I unlock the door, and we go inside. I set the bottle on the counter and grab us both a water while she stands in the kitchen, looking around and not saying a word.

"Nobody's here." I hand her the water. "It's just me."

Her eyes meet mine, and she steps into my personal space, bringing her warmth into my cold, lonely existence. "You can't blame yourself for what happened. You didn't force the drugs down his throat."

"I knew he was struggling. I should've forced him to get help." It never should've fucking come to Gage almost dying. We should've done something, said something.

"He wouldn't have listened," she argues as if she can hear my silent thoughts. "He needed to hit rock bottom. Now he'll get the help he needs. And whether you want to believe it or not, he's alive because of you."

"I don't want to talk about it," I say, slinging her earlier words back at her. "Want another drink?"

She nods, so I grab two glasses from the cabinet and pour us each a shot. We throw them back, slamming the glasses on the counter. I'm about to ask if she wants another when I'm silenced… by her mouth.

Her supple lips glide against my own. Her tongue, coated with whiskey, delves into my mouth. My tongue swirls against hers, and then I capture it, sucking the liquor off and making her groan.

"Fuck me, Dec," she whispers against my mouth.

"You sure? We've been drinking and—"

"I'm sure." She palms my face, and I sigh into her embrace. "I want you to fuck me so long and hard, the rest of the world will cease to exist."

I stare into her eyes, making sure she means what she says, and when I don't see even the tiniest hint of uncertainty, I grab her ass and lift her into my arms. "You're about to get the goddamn fucking of your life."

The second we're in my room, and I drop her onto the bed, she starts peeling off her clothes. After tossing her winter jacket to the side, she kicks off her boots, each landing somewhere on the floor. When she grabs her shirt, I stop her, removing her fingers from the material. I want to take this slow, worship every inch of her, and memorize every second so when she's gone—and she will be gone because she's a runner—I'll be able to remember what it was like to have her in my arms, for her to be under me, to be inside her. When I'm alone again, I'll be able to close my eyes and remember everything about tonight.

"Dec, why are you stop—" Her soft voice snaps me out of my thoughts.

To keep her from finishing her question, I capture her mouth with my own, tasting her lips and caressing her tongue. I devour her, memorizing her taste, her scent. How soft her lips are and how strong her tongue is as it swirls with mine.

Her fingers delve into my hair, yanking on my hair tie. My hair creates a curtain around us when it falls, shutting the rest of the world out until it's just Kendall and me.

Breaking the kiss, I drag my lips across her heated flesh, suckling on her neck until I get to her collarbone. Then I pull back, admiring how beautiful she looks. Her lips red and puffy from being kissed. Her cheeks slightly flushed. Her eyes a bit glassy. And her hair fanned out across my pillow.

I take the hem of her shirt between my fingers and lift it over her head. Then I unbutton her jeans and tug them down her legs, pulling her socks off along with them.

Once she's undressed, I spread her legs so I can kneel between them, stopping for a few moments to soak her in. If I wouldn't look like a goddamn creep, I'd ask if I could take a picture of her just like this.

"I didn't plan for anyone to see under my clothes," she says, a hint of embarrassment tingeing her cheeks. I love that she's not in fancy undergarments, just a simple black and white polka-dotted bra and underwear set—both cotton and matching. It's the real her. The woman she doesn't let the world see. I follow her on social media and laugh when she posts pictures, acting like she just woke up, yet her hair and makeup are perfect. It's all part of the game. Only a select few get to see the real Kendall Naomi Blackwood, who loves to sing karaoke and bakes when she's stressed but enjoys eating the batter more than the final product. Who enjoys Sunday football, family get-togethers, and playing in the rain.

"You look perfect," I tell her, meaning it. I can't decide which part of her I want to taste first, so I start where her ample cleavage is peaking out the top of her bra. I place an open-mouthed kiss to the swell of her breast, then pull the cup down, exposing her dusty-pink nipple. Closing my lips around the hardened tip, I suck on it, tugging gently. I'm rewarded with the sexiest moan as her hands come around to the back of my head, silently indicating she wants more.

I bite down instead of sucking this time, and her moans get louder, reverberating straight to my dick. I bite harder, and the proof of her pleasure increases several octaves. Slowly, I swipe my tongue across the tip to soothe it, and she squirms under me. I do the same to her other breast, nipping and licking before I work my way down her toned belly, stopping at her navel ring—a multicolored music note. I give it a quick kiss and then continue my descent, kissing each of her hip bones and ending at the area between her thighs.

Lifting her leg, I slide one side of her underwear down, bending her knee so I can get it off, then lift the other leg, removing the other side, so her pussy is on display for me. It's trimmed neatly, and when I spread her thighs to get a better look, her lips are glistening with want.

My gaze flits from her pussy to her face, and our eyes lock. She's watching my every move, her bottom lip sucked between her teeth. I want to devour this pussy, but before I do, I need to make sure… "You definitely want this?" We've both been drinking, and the last thing I want is for her to wake up tomorrow and regret this.

She nods once, but that's not enough. "I need to hear the words, Kendall. Tell me you want this."

"I want this," she breathes, her eyes sad and pleading. "Please… today sucked. I need you to make me forget."

I'd like to think I'm a good man and that I wouldn't step into the middle of a relationship, but this is Kendall, and as much as I want to get the specifics as to whether they're really done, I don't have it in me to ask. I've waited years to be with this woman, for her to notice me, and when she finally did, she only saw me as a friend—as her brother's best friend and bandmate, and eventually one of her best friends. So while it might make me sound like a pussy, I'll take what she's willing to give, knowing this is all I'm going to get.

I drop to my stomach and part her lips, licking my way up her slit. She tastes just as I imagined—sweet with a hint of zest, just like her. I lick up and down slowly, inhaling her scent and memorizing her taste on my tongue. The more my tongue glides between her folds, the wetter she gets. I could do this all night, but she's panting, her chest rising and falling in quick succession. She's tugging on the strands of my hair and begging me to get her off. So I give her one last good lick, burning her taste into my brain, and then move on to her clit. The second my tongue lands on it, she jumps slightly, her hips jerking up. I tug it between my teeth playfully, sucking it into my mouth, then release it, so I can focus on getting her off.

With the flat of my tongue, I massage the swollen nub slowly, gently, giving it just the right amount of pressure to make it feel good. One hand ascends to her breast, tweaking and pulling on her nipple, and the other pushes two fingers inside her tight hole. The trifecta of pleasure is too much, and before long, she's flying high, her legs trembling as she comes all over my tongue and fingers.

"Oh, wow," she breathes, her eyes meeting mine. "That was… just… wow."

I smirk at the fact I've left her so sated that she's unable to form a complete sentence, and then pull off my shirt and unbutton my pants, needing to be inside her. She stays where she is, watching as I undress until I'm naked, and then, just before I'm about to drop over her, she sits up, taking my dick into her delicate hand.

With our bodies so close that our heat radiates between us, she darts her tongue out and runs it up my throat and over my Adam's apple. When she gets to my chin, she nibbles on it playfully, then presses her lips to mine as she strokes me up and down. The feeling of her touching me sends a rush of pleasure through me, and I have to force myself to calm the fuck down before I make an ass out of myself. In my defense, it's been a while… a long fucking while. And it's Kendall… touching my dick.

She falls back onto the bed, taking me with her—our kiss never breaking, her hand still stroking—and then guides me into her. The moment I enter her tight heat, I groan into her mouth, wondering if this is all a damn dream but praying it isn't.

Once she's stuffed full of my cock, I take over, slowly thrusting in and out, continuing to kiss her. Memorizing every moment of being inside her until we're both finding our release.

As we break apart, and I glance down at Kendall softly smiling at me, her lids fluttering open and closed, I have no idea how I'll ever go back to being without her. But I push the thought away, not wanting to ruin tonight. Tonight is all I have…

"What are you thinking about?" she asks, pulling my face toward hers for a quick kiss.

I consider lying, but then figure *fuck it. If tonight is all I have, I might as well give it all I've got.* At this point, what do I have to lose? "How I've been in love with you for years, and I can't believe you're finally in my bed, spending the night with me."

Her eyes fly open, popping her orgasm-induced bubble. "What? What are you talking about?"

"Just what I said… I've been in love with you for years."

"Why didn't you say anything?"

I laugh at that. "Until a couple of years ago, you didn't even know I existed."

"That's not true!"

"Oh, it definitely is…"

# Three

## Declan

NINE YEARS AGO

"GRAB ME A SODA WHILE YOU'RE UP THERE," CAMDEN YELLS AS I JOG UP THE STAIRS FROM his family's private recording studio to their main house. Usually, the fridge is stocked with drinks and snacks, thanks to Camden's nanny, Maria, but we've been down here all weekend, writing and fucking around—even though Camden's dad won't officially sign us until we graduate high school—so it's damn near empty.

"Me too!" Braxton adds.

"You want anything?" I ask Gage since he's the only one who hasn't said anything.

"Nah, I'm good," he says from behind his drum kit.

I'm grabbing several drinks and snacks from the fridge and pantry when a soft noise comes from behind me. When I turn around, Kendall is walking toward where I am, staring at her phone. She doesn't notice me until I close the fridge, and her head snaps up.

"Oh, God, you scared me." Her hand that's not holding her

phone goes to her heart, but my gaze is stuck on her face, on her red-rimmed eyes and blotchy cheeks.

"Sorry," I say, setting the shit in my hands down.

"Deacan, right?" she asks, slicing my heart in two. It shouldn't shock me that she doesn't even know my name. She's seven years older and mostly lives in LA when she's not touring. I might've been crushing on the woman hard for the past two years—since I came over for New Year's, and she was singing her heart out to old-school songs on the karaoke machine—but that doesn't mean she knows I exist.

"Declan."

"Oh, right. Sorry." She sniffs, sitting on the barstool.

"You okay?" I grab a tissue from the container on the counter and hand it to her.

She takes it with a watery smile and dabs the bit of makeup that's running under her eyes. "Do you ever feel… like you don't belong?" she asks, avoiding my question with one of her own—or maybe she's answering it… I don't know.

As she waits for my response, I can't help but see the vulnerability in her features. Every time I've seen her, she's always so put together. Her makeup and hair are done, and a smile is plastered on her face. But right now, something about her is different, like without everyone watching her, she's able to unveil her mask and simply be herself.

"Every day of my life," I tell her honestly.

She nods in understanding. "Did you know Easton isn't my real dad? It's why I have blue eyes, and everyone else has green and hazel."

"I didn't." I've been friends with Camden for a couple of years, but guys don't tend to gossip like girls do. Despite their age difference, I know they're close, but aside from me saying she's hot and him pointing out I don't stand a chance, she's not mentioned often.

"My real dad," she says softly as if she doesn't want to chance anyone hearing her, "was a piece of shit. A rapist and a corrupt politician. I never knew him, but from what I've read and heard, he was heartless." She sniffs and wipes her eyes. "Sometimes, I wonder if I'm screwed. If nature will win out over nurture, no matter how hard I try."

"You're afraid of becoming a rapist, corrupt politician?" I ask. "Because the last time I checked, you're a pop princess who sings about love and shit, and I don't think you'll be running for office any time soon." I'm half joking, hoping it'll cut some of the tension she's brought into the kitchen with her.

I know it works when she snorts out a laugh and rolls her eyes. "No, smart-ass. But…" She sighs and closes her eyes as if needing to get her thoughts together. Finally, she opens them, and her blue orbs lock with mine. "If you think about it, I don't *actually* sing about love. I sing about heartbreak because… I've never experienced love."

She swallows thickly, and it takes everything in me not to move toward her. "I'm afraid I'm more like my sperm donor. Cold, heartless, incapable of love. Every song I write comes to me once I've been hurt, or I've done the hurting."

Her words have me gravitating toward her—even though she couldn't remember my name a few minutes ago—and pulling her into my arms. Surprisingly, she lets me, dropping her head against my chest and releasing the sob she was holding back.

"What if I'm broken?" she whispers.

We stay like this for several minutes, in the kitchen, me holding her while she sits on the barstool crying into my chest, and every second that ticks by has me falling harder and deeper for her. Because every time I saw her, she was beautiful, talented, always smiling, and putting on a front for the camera and the fans, but now, she's real and broken, and in the world we live in, that's worth more than the fakeness we're surrounded by.

I lift her chin gently, forcing her to look at me, and then tell her the only thing I can think to say. "I think we're all a little broken, and that's okay."

PRESENT DAY

"YOU'RE RIGHT," KENDALL SAYS WITH TEARS IN HER EYES. "I DIDN'T NOTICE YOU… AT least not until that day. But that conversation was the only time I told anyone how I felt, and what you said glued several of my broken pieces together. I was so down. I had just broken up with a guy who told me I wasn't capable of more than a good time, and I was feeling low.

"And then I found out some stuff about my bio dad… And it all just hit me so hard." She reaches around and takes her bra off, and I'm confused about what she's doing until she lifts her arm, exposing a small tattoo covered by her bra.

I edge closer and read the words inked on her skin: *It's okay to be a little broken.*

"I got it that night after we talked. I cover it up in public, when I'm wearing something that could show it, not wanting the paps to psychoanalyze me, but when I'm standing in front of the mirror, naked, I look at it a lot… to remind myself what you said: we're all a little broken, and that's okay."

Finding out that she's been wearing my words for the past nine years has me grabbing her face and kissing her passionately.

I roll us over, caging her in my arms, and enter her smoothly, her legs locking around my waist. I've never been this turned on in my life, knowing that she looks at that tattoo every day and thinks about me, about what I said to her. If I wasn't already head over heels for this woman, this would've sent me right over the edge.

I kiss her the same way I fuck her, with slow, methodical movements, hoping to convey how much she means to me and how much I want her. Praying that tonight is only the beginning and not the end of what we could have together.

With my pelvis grinding against hers, she comes hard around my cock, moaning her pleasure into my mouth, and I follow, draining every drop into her.

When we've both gotten our breathing under control, I carry her into the bathroom, and we shower together. I wash her hair, and she washes my body. After two back-to-back orgasms, my dick shouldn't be able to stand at attention, but when she drops to her knees, wraps her fingers around the shaft, and licks my head, I'm a fucking goner.

My back hits the wall, and I watch as she takes me in as far as she can go, stroking and licking and sucking until I'm coming down her throat.

"Fuck, woman. I think you've drained me of my soul," I tell her as I help her to her feet. She throws her head back with a laugh, and I grip the curves of her hips, pulling her toward me so I can kiss her slim neck. I pepper kisses along her wet flesh and over to her ear. "Spend the night," I whisper, praying she'll agree.

When she looks up at me, our eyes locking, I hope I haven't pushed my luck.

"Okay," she breathes. "But I'll need something to sleep in."

I have no idea how the hell we got to this point—fucking and spending the night together—but I'm sure as hell not going to question it.

After we're showered and dressed, Kendall crawls into the bed, and I join her. For about a second, I consider giving her some space, but then I remember that tonight is all I have, so instead of keeping to my side of the bed, I tug her toward me, tucking her into my side. And that's how we fall asleep—with her snuggled against me and our legs intertwined.

PRYING MY EYES OPEN, I FIND THE OTHER SIDE OF THE BED EMPTY AND WONDER IF LAST night was a dream. And if it wasn't, does that mean she left?

I climb out of bed and go in search of her, hoping like hell she's still here. I find her in the kitchen, cooking. She's still wearing my clothes, and she's shaking her ass to the music playing on the living room television. Instead of alerting her to my presence, I take a few moments to watch her. Since she asked me to make her forget last night, I've spent every moment trying to memorize every detail, not wanting to forget a single second of my time with her. Knowing all too soon that our time will come to an end.

"Hey, you," she says, turning around. "Hungry?" She reaches into the oven and pulls out a pan. The scent is sweet, and my stomach rumbles. "I ran to the corner store early this morning and whipped up some homemade cinnamon rolls and bacon."

She baked. It's what she does when she's stressed.

"They smell delicious."

She smiles softly and turns off the stove, removing the pan. She lifts the lid, and the scent of bacon wafts in the air, overpowering the cinnamon.

"Try a piece," she says, picking up a slice and extending her hand.

I step toward her and lift her onto the counter, stepping between her legs. Her eyes go wide, but she doesn't stop me as I grip her thighs and lean in, opening my mouth so I can take a bite.

She feeds me the bacon, alternating between giving herself and me nibbles, and then she moves onto the cinnamon rolls, forking us each a bite.

"This is delicious. Sweet…" I kiss the corner of her mouth. "Just like you." I swipe my finger across the top of the rolls, scooping up some icing, and then run my finger along the seam of her lips. Once they're covered with icing, I dip my head and lick across her lips, making her moan.

"The rolls are good, but I think I'd rather have you for breakfast."

Food forgotten, she wraps her legs around my waist, and I take her back to my room, where I eat her until she comes, and then I fuck her until she comes again. And the entire time, I wish for time to freeze and for this moment, this morning, to never end.

"MY PHONE WON'T STOP VIBRATING," KENDALL GROANS, NUZZLING HER FACE INTO MY neck. "Make it stop." After I had her for breakfast, we fell back asleep for a little while, but the sound of her phone going off must've woken her up.

I reach over and grab her phone from the nightstand, ready to turn it off, but then I see the name Kyle on the screen and freeze.

"It's your fiancé," I tell her, moving her arm and giving myself some distance. With the bubble we created last night that continued this morning, it was easy to pretend that Kendall's mine, but seeing his name on her phone is enough to pop that bubble and throw my ass back into reality.

"He's not my fiancé," she says, taking the phone and turning it off.

"You're still wearing his ring," I point out, glancing at the huge rock on her finger. I was too distracted by the rest of her to notice it… until now.

She looks at it and grimaces. "I'm ending things with him today. I just didn't have a chance to take it off." She shrugs and rolls off the bed, standing. She's in nothing but my white shirt, and I can make out her perky tits through the thin material and the swells of her ass underneath. All I want to do is pull her back into bed and spend the day devouring her over and over again, but what she said stops me from dragging her back to bed.

"You're still engaged?"

"Technically, but only because he doesn't know it's over yet."

"And why is it over?"

She sighs and shakes her head. "I don't want to talk about it. It's embarrassing, and I'm just not ready yet, but as soon as I leave here, I'm ending things with him."

"And where does that leave us?"

Her eyes meet mine. "I'm a mess, Dec…"

"I don't care."

"You're best friends with my brother."

"Still don't care. You know how I feel about you, and nothing you say is going to change that, so stop fighting this."

"It would be irresponsible to jump from one man to another. People would think I'm a—"

"Life's too short to give a fuck about what anyone thinks. I want you." I grab the front of her shirt and pull her toward me.

"Last night, the chemistry was there, and this morning... still fucking there." I nip at her jaw, and she groans. "Tell me you felt it too."

"Of course, I did," she says softly. "I do... And I'd love to spend more time with you, to see where this could possibly go. But I have to end things with Kyle and call off the wedding first. It's all a clusterfuck, and I don't want to drag you into it. I just need a little bit of time. Tell me you understand." She palms my cheeks, and I nod.

"I get it. I'll be here. Take all the time you need."

Her shoulders drop in relief. "Thank you." She presses a chaste kiss to my lips. "I better get going."

I fist the back of her hair and crush my mouth against hers, coaxing her lips open and sucking her tongue into my mouth. My kiss is done with a dual purpose: needing to leave her wanting and remembering, so she'll come back to me, but also, if this is the last kiss I ever get, I want to make it count.

When I break the kiss, her eyes are glassed over, her lips are bee stung, and she looks as if she wants to climb on top of me— just how I wanted.

"I'll see you soon, beautiful," I tell her before I kiss her one last time, praying like hell she comes back to me.

# Four

## Kendall

**Kyle: Where are you?**

**Kyle: I'm sorry. Please let me explain.**

**Kyle: I've called everyone in your family, and nobody knows where you are.**

**Kyle: I'm worried about you.**

I ROLL MY EYES AT HIS TEXTS, THEN DELETE THEM ALL, WONDERING HOW I EVER ALLOWED myself to be fooled by him. I'm smarter than that, and the fact that I fell for his bullshit pisses me off.

Since I'm not in any rush to let him know I'm okay, and the only conversation I plan to have with him involves me chucking my engagement ring at his head while telling him we're over, I click into the family chat—since everyone texted me several times last night—to let them know I'm okay. Then I send a text to my parents only, asking if we can talk. They both respond instantly that they're home and I can come over any time.

After letting them know I'll be by in a couple of hours, I glance out the window of the Town Car I'm in, watching the city pass me by as I think about how quickly everything's changed in the past eighteen hours… Jesus, has it only been that long since I found—?

I push the thought out of my head, replacing it with Declan. Over the past couple of years, we've grown close. He's become someone I can talk to and have fun with. When we were both still living on the West Coast, we would have barbecues, go to the gym, and spend hours writing music together. And once we were both living on the East Coast, it continued—the hanging out, going out, writing music…

But not once did I ever look at him as anything more than a friend. Not because he isn't boyfriend material, because he totally is. The guys have been ragging on him for being a hopeless romantic for years. He isn't known for hooking up with random women, and he hasn't been seen with many over the years anyway. Still, when he is, it's clear he's spending time with them, getting to know them, and not just using them as a hole to fill like the other guys did before Camden and Braxton settled down… and Gage—my heart clenches when I think about everything he's been through. I hope he's getting the help he needs.

My point is, I never viewed Declan as being anything more than a friend, and I think it's because I knew he was boyfriend material. He's sweet and caring and selfless. Take last night—he asked me multiple times if I was sure I wanted to cross the line, knowing we'd been drinking. And when we crossed that line, he made sure my pleasure came first, something most guys don't consider—at least not the ones I've been with.

Which leads me to my very long-winded point. I never considered Declan an option because I think I knew deep down he would be the perfect boyfriend, and if my track record is anything to go by, I would mess it all up, like I always do… Because I'm not capable of loving anyone or being loved. At least not with anyone outside of my family. And even when I'm with them, I feel like an outsider, as if I'm missing a certain chromosome that allows me to simply feel happy and content.

But then I spent the night with Declan—and this morning— and for a little while, it felt like that chromosome wasn't lost. I wasn't the broken pop star, known for *stiffing* men—a stupid name I was given after a few—okay, a lot—of my relationships ended with me running, and then a few months later, releasing songs that may *or may not* have been about our time together.

I smile to myself, remembering the way my heart beat a bit faster in Declan's arms. The way I felt adored and cherished. And holy shit, the chemistry. I've been with quite a few guys in my thirty-one years, and none of them, and I mean none of them, could make me orgasm the way Declan did. But it wasn't just about the sex. It was the way he looked at me like I was more than Kendall Blackwood, pop princess.

When he told me he's had feelings for years, my first thought was nope, no way. I'm not going there. He's my brother's best friend and signed to the same label as me. He's been a family friend for years. But when he looked at me and said he didn't care what anyone thought, that life was too short and he wanted a chance to be with me, I couldn't help but imagine what it would be like to be with him. To be happy and content. To create a family, to love and be loved…

It's why I said yes to Kyle even though I knew he wasn't the one. I'm thirty-one years old, and the only thing I have to show for it is my musical success. But I want more than that. I looked up my shitty bio dad, and while he created a family, he wasn't a successful husband or father or human. And I don't want to be like him. I want to be like my mom: a loving wife and mother. I want to know what it feels like to be in love and love someone else. I want to have a family and create a life outside of music. One I can be proud of.

Before spending the night with Declan, I didn't think it was possible. I thought I was broken, damaged, and destined to settle or be alone. But now, everything looks different, like the sky is bluer, the sun is brighter. I'm capable of more with him.

But first, I have to break things off with Kyle and get my shit together. Once I do that, I can go back to Declan so we can see where this will go.

The car is about to pull into my condominium complex to drop me off in the underground parking lot when a loud siren rings out—a police car or ambulance. My driver is stuck in traffic—fucking NYC—and tries to get out of the way, but before he can, an SUV turns the corner like he's part of one of those reality programs that shows car chases. He's not paying attention to everyone trying to move over for the siren, and that's when the siren appears. Then it dawns on me that the SUV is in a car chase, and that siren is after him.

And before my driver can move out of the way, the SUV plows straight into the car.

Everything shifts and tumbles.

The car begins to roll.

And then there's a loud crunching sound.

And everything goes black.

# Five

## Declan

I STARE AT MY PHONE, PACING THE ROOM AS IF WILLING IT TO GO OFF WILL BE ENOUGH TO get Kendall to text or call. It's been hours since she's left here. She said she was going to end it with Kyle and get her shit together. Logically, I know that isn't going to take hours. It could be days or weeks, but fuck, I really should've asked for clarification before she left so I wouldn't be over here, wondering how long is long enough before I can contact her. A part of me knows it's because I'm scared. Because Kendall is a runner. It's what she does. She lets men get just close enough to fall for her, and then she runs. Where they all went wrong was when they saw this beautiful, wealthy pop star and didn't know what to do with her. But I do. I'm going to love the hell out of her, and when she tries to run, I'll catch her ass and drag her back. Okay, that sounds a little creepy, but you get my point.

My phone rings, and I jump since it's currently in my hand. The name on the screen says Camden, and I can't help wondering if maybe Kendall spoke to him and told him about our night together. "Hello," I say cautiously, preparing for anything.

Well, I think I'm ready for anything until he speaks. "Kendall's been in an accident. We're all heading over to the hospital now. New York Medical."

And with those words, my entire world implodes.

Having zero patience to call for a car, I throw on some clothes and rush downstairs to flag down a taxi. Thankfully, there's already a car available, so I hop in and tell him I need to get to New York Medical. The twenty-minute ride feels like it takes hours, but finally, he pulls up to the entrance. Camden had texted that the hospital gave them a private room to wait in so they didn't draw attention. I head straight toward it, finding Simon, one of our bodyguards, standing outside the door.

He nods at me and opens the door to let me in, where I find Kendall's entire family. Her brother, Camden, and his wife, Layla, their baby daughter, Marianna, and son, Felix, are on the couch huddled together. Her sister, Bailey, and her wife, Cynthia, sit together on another couch. Her other sister, Phoebe, cries softly in the corner with her mom and dad holding her.

And then I lock eyes on the final person in the room: Kyle Sanford. His presence means either she never got a chance to break it off or he cares that much he's here even though they're no longer together.

When the door opens and shuts, everyone glances over, expressions hopeful for information, but then shut down when they see it's only me. Camden texted me on my way over that they don't know anything yet. Sophia is her emergency contact, so they called her when Kendall was brought in, but the hospital hasn't given the family any information about what happened yet.

"This can't be good," Phoebe cries. "If it weren't that big of a deal, we would be able to see her. Why can't we see her?"

"Shh, stop," Sophia coos. "We don't know anything. All we can do is think positive thoughts and pray. The nurse said as soon as they've finished assessing her, they'll be back to let us know what's happened."

I walk over and give Camden a hug, then go around hugging everyone else, avoiding Kyle, and just as I'm sitting on the couch next to Bailey, Braxton and Kaylee burst through the door. Kaylee hugs everyone while Braxton asks if there's any news. They tell them the same thing they told me. And then we wait for what feels like hours.

Finally, there's a knock, and in walks a young man, who looks no more than thirty, wearing a white lab coat, along with a woman in blue scrubs. "Good afternoon, my name is Dr. Babki, and this is Dr. Kerns. We're the doctors who assessed Miss Blackwood."

Introductions are quickly made, and then he continues telling us about Kendall. "When the vehicle flipped, she wasn't wearing her seat belt, and her head hit the ceiling, causing a transient disturbance to her brain, creating a—"

"Doctor," Easton says gruffly. "Can you please tell us in layman's terms? Is our little girl okay?"

The doctor winces. "Sorry, this is a teaching hospital, so we tend to use medical terms. When Miss Blackwood hit her head, a blood vessel burst, causing bleeding in her brain. We were able to go in and stop the bleeding before any severe damage occurred. It helped that she was brought in immediately."

"So she's okay?" Sophia asks.

"She's stable. We'll keep her in a medically induced coma to give her time for the swelling to go down while her brain heals. We'll monitor her closely, and once the scans come back clean, we'll decrease the medication to slowly wake her up."

"And what about side effects?" Easton asks.

"Unfortunately, we won't know until she wakes up. I won't scare you with all of the possibilities, and I suggest you don't google them as it won't do you any good. Once she's awake, we'll reassess and take it one step at a time. But for right now, she's doing okay. The bleeding has stopped, and she's stable. All very good signs, especially for the hit she took."

"What about the driver?" Sophia asks. He's been with the family for years, so it makes sense she would ask.

"I can't give out any information to non-family," the doctor says, but the way he frowns tells me it's not good. "His family has been contacted and should be here shortly."

"When can we see her?" Bailey asks.

"I'll have a nurse come and get you once she's been situated."

"We would like a private room," Easton says. "I don't care about the expense. Whatever it takes to make sure she has the best medical treatment and is comfortable."

"She'll get that here," Dr. Babki assures him. "If you have any questions, I'll be on for another few hours. I'll find out who'll be treating her once I leave and let you know."

"Thank you," Sophia says, shaking his hand.

The moment he leaves, the girls all fall into a fit of cries, and their significant others hold them. I watch, wishing I could hold Kendall, wondering if I would've pulled her into my arms and made love to her one more time… if I would've insisted that we eat the cinnamon rolls she baked… if this never would've happened.

While we wait for the nurse to let us know Kendall is ready for visitors, a pair of police officers come in and introduce themselves, telling Easton and Sophia that they were two of the officers on the scene and called the ambulance.

"What happened?" Easton asks.

"A convenience store robbery gone wrong," one of the officers explains. "He was armed and when the owner refused to give up the money, he shot him. The panic button was pressed, and the perpetrator took off. It turned into a car chase, which took them into the city. Not wanting to lose him, the officers followed him until the helicopter could take over, but by the time it arrived, the man was in the thick of traffic. Tire tracks indicate he tried to slam on his brakes, telling us he must not have been expecting the traffic to be at a standstill, but it was too late. He hit the driver-side of the vehicle your daughter was in, but luckily, she was sitting on the opposite side in the back seat, so she didn't take the brunt of the impact."

"We want to press charges," Kyle says, finally speaking up like the lawyer he is.

"He didn't survive," the officer says. "And, off the record, neither did her driver. We're waiting for the family to arrive to tell them. A few others were injured when the vehicle rolled, but nothing serious."

Everyone goes silent at that, realizing the weight of the officer's words. Out of the three most affected, two of them died. Kendall could've died. But she lived. We could've been having an entirely different conversation with the doctor and police officers, but somehow, an angel was looking down on Kendall, and she survived.

"Mrs. Blackwood," a female nurse says. "Your daughter can have a visitor now."

Sophia and Easton glance at Kyle, unsure who should go first, telling me they either have no idea that Kendall has broken the engagement off, or she never made it to tell Kyle. Either way, I have to keep my mouth shut. The only important thing right now is concentrating on Kendall's healing. Everything else can wait.

"You should go," Kyle says. "You're her mom. Please… umm,

give her a kiss for me." I could be wrong, and maybe it's just me overthinking shit, but he sounds off. The words make sense, but his tone is weird, almost as if it's riddled with guilt. Could she have been coming from seeing him when she was in the accident? Did something happen from the time she left my place to when she was hit? At this point, it doesn't really matter, but it also doesn't stop me from wondering what the hell happened.

Sophia nods, then kisses her husband quickly and follows the nurse out.

"Should we tell Gage?" Braxton asks, breaking the silence after a few minutes.

"No," Easton says. "The last thing he needs is unnecessary stress or to feel like he should be here. He's where he needs to be." He glances around the room. "I appreciate everyone coming, but as the doctor mentioned, Kendall won't be awake for some time, so if you want to go home and get some rest, I can text everyone and keep you updated." He walks over to Layla, who's rocking her sleeping baby girl, and tears fill his eyes. "Life is so damn precious," he murmurs, bending slightly and kissing her forehead.

"I'm going to take Layla and the kids home, and then I'll be back," Camden says to his dad. "If anything changes…"

"I'll keep you informed."

One by one, everyone hugs Easton, telling him if they need anything, to let them know, until it's only Kyle, Easton, and me left.

"I left without showering," Kyle says awkwardly. "I'm going to go home and shower and change, and then I'll be back up. Do you need anything?"

"No, I'm good," Easton says, giving him a small smile, "but thank you."

With a nod, Kyle leaves, and it's just Easton and me.

"If you want to get going…"

"Actually, I think I'll stay, if that's okay," I tell him.

He nods. "Of course, I know you and Kendall have grown close. She's been so excited about recording that song. She made us all listen to it over a dozen times at dinner."

"It's going to blow the hell up," I say with a small laugh to lighten the mood. "It's a side of Kendall her fans haven't seen… raw… real."

Easton chokes out a watery laugh. "She's an expert at putting on a good front, isn't she?" He laughs a little harder, fresh tears filling his eyes and falling. "I remember when I first met her. Her mom was soft and sweet, but Kendall… She was all mouth and sass." He chuckles softly. "We argued for hours over the lyrics of 'I'm Looking for a Love.'"

It takes me a second to place the song, but once I do, I give him a brow up in confusion. "Isn't that your song?"

Easton full-blown laughs. "Yeah, but she swore the lyrics were *looking for a dove,* and nobody could tell her any differently. 'Doves fly, so obviously, it flew away, and he's looking for it,' she argued, hand on her hip, brows dipped in determination. 'Why would anyone be looking for love?'"

I can't help but think about the irony in his words—Kendall's spent half her life looking for and running from love…

A few minutes later, Sophia comes back, looking a mixture of relief that her daughter is alive and distraught that she's in a coma.

Since Kendall's been moved to a private room, they're both able to go visit with her, so while they do that, I go to the gift shop to pick up a couple of things for her room. I pass on the flowers since they're cliché as fuck, and instead, I grab some candy since she has a huge sweet tooth, playing cards since she loves to play solitaire when she's alone and Rummy with her family when they're hanging out and bullshitting, and a stuffed puppy holding a huge heart. It's cheesy as fuck, but I've been in Kendall's room and know she loves stuffed animals, especially dogs. She would love to have a real one, but with her traveling, she can't. She once told me that she wants to get a puppy whenever she finally settles down.

I'm waiting in the private waiting room when Camden returns, saying his dad texted and said the room is big enough for a few more people to go in.

When we walk in, my eyes go straight to Kendall. I imagined she'd look rough since she was in an accident, but aside from the monitors attached to her chest and arms, and the bandage covering her head, she looks like she's simply asleep.

"She didn't break or bruise anything," Sophia says. "It was just horrible luck that she wasn't wearing her seat belt and her head hit the ceiling."

I place the stuffed dog on the nightstand, along with the candy and cards. I glance over, and her parents and Camden are talking about something the doctor said, so I take the moment to lean over and kiss her forehead. "Come back to me, Kendall," I plead softly. "We haven't even gotten started yet."

# Six

## Kendall

THERE'S A *THUMP, THUMP, THUMP* IN MY HEAD AS IF SOMEONE WITH THE WORST RHYTHM is drumming against my skull. I attempt to open my eyes, but they're heavy, like a pair of weights have been set on my lids. A constant beeping has me questioning where I am and why I feel like death warmed over.

Inhaling, the scent of antiseptic assaults my nostrils. *What the…?*

"Kendall, you can do it. Wake up, sweetheart. Just open those beautiful blue eyes and come back to me."

The sound of Declan's soothing voice has me sighing in contentment and wanting to open my eyes so he knows I'm awake. *Where does he think I went? I'm right here…*

With all the strength I possess, I take a deep breath and pry my lids apart. At first, it's blurry, and with the constant drumming, it hurts. But I can see. White walls. A whiteboard with writing on it. A sink… cabinets… machines. *What the hell? Why am I in a hospital?*

I swallow thickly and wince when it feels like sandpaper is being shoved down my throat. I glance over at Declan and take in his appearance. His brows are knitted together in worry, there are dark circles under his eyes, and his hair is up in a messy bun. He looks how I feel: like he's been to hell and back. But even as distressed as he appears, he still looks delicious, with his blue eyes that have the ability to see beyond the bullshit, his full lips, pouty and pink and kissable, and his face full of scruff that I have no doubt would leave burn tracks between a woman's legs.

*Whoa, where the heck did those thoughts come from?*

With more effort than it should take, I part my lips to ask where I am and what's going on, why he looks so upset and was just begging me to *come back to him*, when the sound of a door swinging open and then voices speaking distract me.

My gaze flits over to where the noise is coming from, and my eyes land on my parents and… Kyle—my fiancé.

"Oh my God!" My mom gasps. "She's awake?"

"She was just opening her eyes," Declan explains as he stands and steps back so my mom can take his spot. "We were so worried," she breathes, a watery smile spreading across her face.

"I'll, uh, go tell a nurse she's awake," Kyle says, glancing at me oddly.

"How are you feeling?" Mom asks, running her fingers gently through my hair. "You gave us quite a scare, Sunshine." She takes my hand in hers and threads our fingers together.

Confused and disoriented, I don't say anything. It feels like everyone is talking in riddles. It's clear I'm in the hospital, but I don't know why. I want to ask, but my throat hurts, and I'm too tired to speak. I try to smile at her to let her know I'm okay, but the action is too exhausting, so instead, I squeeze her hand the best I can and close my eyes, wanting to rest them for a few minutes.

"Miss Blackwood." With my name being called, I force my eyes back open, and standing in front of me is an older gentleman dressed in a suit with a white jacket. "I'm Dr. Oswald. You're in New York Medical because you were in a car accident and hit your head pretty hard."

His admission has me trying to recall the accident he's referring to, but when I think too hard, the drumming in my head switches to downright banging, and I stop trying to remember.

Dr. Oswald has me go through various exercises to test my sight and touch, and then he asks if I can speak. The room is quiet—the only sound coming from the incessant beeping—and I want to say something to break the silence, but I can't find it in me to speak. It should be so easy... I've been speaking for over thirty years. All I have to do is part my lips and release the words, but I can't.

"It's okay," the doctor says. "You've been through quite an ordeal. Would you like something to drink?"

I nod, suddenly extremely thirsty, and my mom rushes to the counter to pour me something to drink.

She brings the cup to my lips, and I open my mouth just enough to swallow down the cool water. It feels like heaven sliding down and softening the feel of sandpaper in my throat.

Once my throat isn't so dry, I release a deep breath and attempt to speak. "I..." I croak out.

"Take your time," Dr. Oswald says gently.

"I don't know what happened."

In my peripheral, my parents both frown, and Kyle raises his brows.

The doctor smiles softly. "That's okay. Sometimes when we hit our heads, our brains go a little haywire. Can you tell me your name?"

"Kendall."

"Good," the doctor says. "Do you know the people in this room?"

I nod, then clear my throat. "My parents, Declan, and Kyle."

"Good," the doctor repeats. "And do you know what year it is?"

I think for a moment, but it's a bit fuzzy, so I go with the year that pops into my head.

"That's right. Now, I want you to tell me the last thing you remember."

I think for a few moments, trying to remember this supposed accident he mentioned, but my last memory is… laughing, drinking… "Declan and me…" I try to place where we are, what we're doing… And then it hits me. "Dancing on New Year's Eve." I glance at Declan, and his features are etched with concern. "We were talking about the song we were working on, and then you asked me to dance. We danced to…" I think hard, trying to recall the details. "I can't remember." I shake my head, then wince at the pain radiating into my skull.

"It's okay," the doctor says. "So New Year's Eve is the last memory you have?"

I nod. "Did something happen?" A flash of Declan and me getting into a limo has me looking at him. "Did we get into an accident?" I rake my gaze over him, but he looks okay. No bumps or bruises. "Are you okay?" I ask, just to be sure.

Declan clears his throat. "I'm okay. No, we didn't get into an accident. You did a few days ago, but I wasn't with you."

"Oh," I breathe. "That's good." But then I'm confused. "Where were you? You were with me in the limo, right?"

"I was. The limo dropped you off first and then me."

"Okay, so then what happened?"

"Kendall, can you tell me what month it is?" the doctor asks, ignoring my question.

"Umm…" If my last memory was on New Year's, and the accident, as Declan said was a few days ago, that would make it… "January?"

Declan curses under his breath. "What?" I ask, getting annoyed. "What's going on?"

"You were in an accident a few days ago," the doctor begins, "but it wasn't on New Year's. It's February sixteenth."

I think about what he's said, but I don't remember anything past New Year's. Declan and me dancing, the ball dropping, and him kissing me softly, me wondering where Kyle was. After several texts, he replied, apologizing that his emergency meeting ran late but that he would meet me at my place. The limo took me home, and I fell asleep waiting for him.

"I can't remember anything after New Year's," I tell the doctor. "What does that mean? Is there something wrong with me?"

Dr. Oswald shakes his head. "Losing your memory isn't uncommon with brain injuries. We'll need to run some tests now that you're awake to make sure you're healing properly, but I wouldn't worry about it. You also just woke up, so your brain is still fuzzy." He pats my shin. "I'm going to put an order in for those tests. Take it easy and let the nurses know if you're in any pain. I'll be by with the results to discuss this further."

With a gentle smile, he exits the room.

"We were so worried," Mom says.

"What happened?" I ask, wanting to know since I can't remember.

"There was a car chase in front of your building," Dad explains. "Your car was hit and rolled, and because you weren't wearing your seat belt, you hit your head."

"Is my driver okay?" We use a car service, so it could be various people, but the same handful tend to rotate.

"It was Greg," Mom says solemnly. "Unfortunately, he didn't make it."

My heart sinks in my chest, a contradiction of emotions hitting me hard: sad that a good man lost his life yet grateful I'm still alive.

"Can you please text Marcia and tell her I want to make sure his funeral is covered and his family is taken care of?" Marcia is my assistant back in LA. Since I moved here after my tour ended, she works remotely. With my brother and Layla having a baby, I wanted to spend some time at home and take a little break of sorts. With Kyle and me getting married in a few months… Oh, shit! "It's February sixteenth?"

"Yes," Mom answers, her brow popping up in concern. "What's wrong?"

"Well, we're supposed to get married in a few weeks," I say to Kyle, who flinches. "How are we supposed to do that if nothing is planned? Maybe we should postpone it," I blurt out.

"Actually," Mom says, smiling softly, "it's all planned. You can't remember, but you've only been out for a few days."

"Oh, right," I breathe. "Yeah, okay…"

My head throbs, and I'm suddenly tired. "I think I need to rest," I mutter.

"Okay," Mom says, giving me a kiss. "We'll be by tomorrow. Camden, Phoebe, and Bailey have been coming by every day. I texted them you're awake, and they wanted to come by, but I told them to wait until tomorrow, so you're not overwhelmed."

"Thank you," I tell her. "I love you."

"Love you more, Sunshine."

"Your phone was recovered," Dad says, pulling it out of his

pocket and setting it on the nightstand. "I made sure it's charged. If you need anything, call or text us."

Declan says goodbye next. He looks at me oddly, like he wants to say something, but instead, he sighs and kisses my forehead before retreating and leaving Kyle and me alone.

When a sharp pain radiates through my skull, causing me to wince, Kyle asks if I'm okay.

"I think I need more pain meds."

"You can press the button here, and the nurse will come," he says. A few minutes later, the nurse has upped my pain reliever, and we're alone once again.

"I can—"

"You should—"

We talk at the same time. I have no idea why it's so awkward between us, but something feels off.

"You go first," I insist.

"I was going to say I can stay if you want."

I nod. "I'm just going to sleep. I'm sure you have tons of work to do. Have you been here this entire time?" Kyle works for Berg, Weiss, and Ross—a law firm specializing in creative professionals and businesses. He's a junior partner and is working hard to make partner. One of the partners has announced he's retiring soon, and Kyle hopes to fill his position. This means he works more than he's home, something I can understand since I've spent the past thirteen years working my ass off to get to where I am.

"Of course, I've been here," he says. "I had these delivered for Valentine's Day." He points to the beautiful red roses sitting in a vase on the bedside table. "Once you're out of here, we'll celebrate properly."

"Thank you." My eyes move from the roses to the adorable stuffed puppy, and I reach out and grab it. "I've always wanted a puppy," I say, petting his soft fur. If it weren't for how busy I am, I would already have one. But I can barely take care of myself most days...

"Oh, uh..." He clears his throat. "That's actually not from me."

"Oh, who's it from?"

"Declan."

At the mention of his name, butterflies try to attack my belly. But before I can think too hard as to why that is, Kyle scrapes a chair across the linoleum floor and has a seat next to me, changing the subject. "So, uh, you really don't remember anything after New Year's?"

I shake my head. "Not that I know of."

He nods and takes my hand in his, bringing it up to his lips. "I'm so glad you're okay, Kendall. When I heard you were in an accident... Fuck, I was so scared."

"When did it happen?"

"Sunday morning."

Normally, we spend the day together. Even with his busy schedule, he makes it a point to spend time with me during the weekend. We go to dinner Saturday night, and then I spend the night. We spend all day Sunday together, and then I go home Sunday night so he can do some work before he returns Monday.

"I was on my way home on Sunday morning? From your place?"

Like earlier, Kyle flinches, and the hairs on my arms rise. "What aren't you telling me?"

"We, uh..." He clears his throat. "We got into an argument Saturday night. I was supposed to meet you for dinner, but I got caught up at the office. We didn't spend the night together Saturday night. You don't remember any of this at all?"

"No... So where was I coming from Sunday morning?"

Kyle shrugs. "I don't know. I was texting you all night, asking you to talk to me, but you wouldn't respond. And then your brother called me and said you'd been in an accident."

Something niggles in the back of my mind, but I can't quite grasp it. "Are we… okay?"

"Yeah." He bobs his head. "Of course. I shouldn't have stayed at the office, and I'll forever regret it. Had we gone to dinner and then back to my place, you would've been in bed with me instead of getting hit by a piece of shit criminal."

"People fight. You can't blame yourself for that." My head pounds, and I wince in pain. "I don't mean to be rude, but I'm exhausted."

"I can stay…"

"No, it's okay. Go sleep in a comfortable bed."

"I'll be back in the morning."

"What's today?"

"Wednesday."

"Then you have to work…"

"They know what's happened."

"I'm okay," I tell him, needing some space but not wanting to say that to him. "Go to work. You can't do anything for me here, and you heard the doctor. They'll be running tests tomorrow."

"If you need anything…"

"I'll let you know."

He stands and leans over, kissing the corner of my mouth. "I love you, Kendall, and I'm so sorry this happened to you." With his kiss, accompanied by his admission, I expect to feel a spark of some sort, for my heart to beat a little faster, for butterflies to take over my belly, to feel *something*—I'm engaged to this man and marrying him in a few short weeks—but I feel… nothing.

I smile up at him, unable to say anything back, and tell myself what I'm feeling—or the lack thereof—must be linked to my head injury. Once I'm back home, feeling better, things will get back to normal. I'm just feeling off right now.

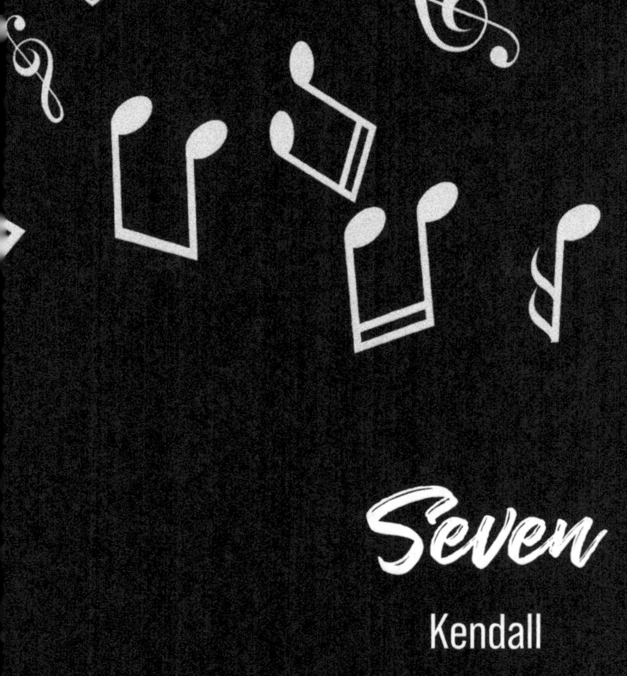

# Seven

## Kendall



"YOU'RE SURE YOU'LL BE OKAY HERE?" KYLE ASKS FOR THE TWENTIETH TIME. I WAS released from the hospital yesterday after several days of being monitored and every test coming back perfect. Aside from not remembering the past six weeks, I'm thankfully okay. The doctor warned me that headaches will be common, but if they become unbearable or lead to dizziness, vomiting, or blacking out, I should go to the hospital immediately. He also referred me to follow up with a neurologist.

My parents wanted me to go home with them, and Kyle wanted me to move in with him, insisting I'll be moving in once we're married in a couple of weeks anyway. But I turned them down, wanting to go home to my own bed. I know my parents mean well, but my mom will hover, and Kyle… well, I still feel off. I keep hoping I'll feel something with every kiss, every touch, but instead, I keep questioning why I'm marrying him. I must've loved him, right? Or I wouldn't be marrying him. And I didn't completely lose my memory, so I remember him proposing.

It was six weeks after we'd been dating. I had gone out with Kaylee, Layla, Bailey, and her wife, Cynthia, for a girls' night before Layla was due to give birth.

I stepped into my foyer, and the only sound was the humming of the refrigerator. I set my purse on the counter and stripped off my clothes, throwing them into the hamper before washing my face and changing into my pajamas.

After checking my social media accounts, I went through my photos from that night to make sure I could post a couple. As I was swiping through the pictures, I stopped on the one of Layla and me. She was glowing, her hand on her big belly. Instinctually, my hand went to my own, and I wondered what it would be like to be pregnant. To carry a life inside me for nine months and then after giving birth, hold a precious little miracle in my arms that I get to spend the rest of my life loving.

My thoughts went to my mom and how close we used to be. For the first several years, it was just me and her—and my aunt Naomi—against the world because my bio dad didn't want us. And even when Easton—the only dad I've ever known—came into our lives, and she had three more kids, she always made sure to make time for me. Our relationship had always been special, and we were always close, until I found out that my sperm donor was a piece of shit rapist who made her life a living hell for years. I don't know why finding that out changed things, but it was the start of me pushing her away. Maybe it was the guilt I felt for being the reason she suffered, or because I wondered if when she looked into my blue eyes—the same ones as my sperm donor— she saw him in me. If she would've had a better life if it weren't for her getting pregnant by him with me. She's never once made me feel that way, but it didn't stop me from thinking those thoughts anyway.

After that, I spent more time in LA than New York, insisting on going on long-ass tours and avoiding my family. I no longer felt like I was one of them, like I belonged. I felt like an outsider, dirty and tarnished.

And that's when it all started—me *stiffing* guys. At first, I didn't realize I was doing it. I would date someone, and when it didn't work out, we would break up. But with every breakup, the media speculated. I would write a song, and they would tie it to one of the guys. So I started paying attention, trying to figure out where it was all going wrong… I would nitpick them. They weren't neat enough, not ambitious enough, or they were too ambitious. I didn't see the same future they saw, didn't fall in love when they did. I didn't want to take the next step when they did. They would say I love you, and I couldn't say it back.

As I sat in bed, staring at the photo of Layla and me, I realized I was broken. I pushed everyone away, from my parents to my siblings to men. So instead of going to bed, I called Kyle and asked if he was up for company.

*"I'll come to you. I'm still at the office anyway."*

He showed up a little while later, and I clung to him, not wanting to be broken. Wanting to have what my parents have, what my siblings have. We spent the night together, and the next morning, when he shocked the hell out of me by proposing over breakfast, instead of running, I said yes.

"Kendall," Kyle says, snapping me out of my thoughts. "I can stay here with you. They don't mind me working from home."

Home… this isn't his home. This is my home. And in a couple of weeks, I'm supposed to give it up to move into his. The thought causes a bout of anxiety to rush up my spine and neck, landing in the dead center of my head, where I've been getting frequent headaches.

"I'm okay," I insist. "I'm just going to rest. I'll text or call if I need anything."

He frowns but nods. "All right. I'll see you later."

"Call first, please. In case I'm sleeping. I wouldn't want you to come here for no reason."

He looks like he wants to argue but just nods again. "Okay."

Once he's left, it feels like I can breathe again. I spend the morning resting, scrolling social media, and when the afternoon rolls around, I'm so bored that I take a shower so I can get out of the house. I'm not on bed rest or anything.

As I'm considering where to go, I spot my writing journal on the counter. I open it up and find the most beautiful lyrics. I remember writing some of this with Declan, but this song looks damn near complete, so we must've worked on it some more during the time I lost my memory.

I'm on a break, but I don't see why I can't go to the studio and mess around, maybe put some instrumentals to it. I text my dad, asking if there's an open studio, and he replies that there's always one available for me.

Thirty minutes later, I'm walking into Blackwood Records. Everyone knows who I am and what happened, so they all greet me with smiles and tell me they're glad I'm okay.

I go in search of my dad, but when I can't find him, I end up in an empty studio that the receptionist said he booked for me. Just being here, with the equipment and sound booth, makes me feel ten times better. I plop onto the comfy couch and am reading through the lyrics again when the door opens and in walks Declan.

He's dressed in a simple white Vans T-shirt that's taut across his chest, showcasing the hard body hidden underneath, ripped jeans that mold to his muscular thighs, and clean white Vans don his feet. His dirty blond hair is up in a man bun, and his midnight blue eyes are wide, having not expected me to be here.

"Shouldn't you be in bed resting?" His deep, masculine voice sends shivers down my spine, and I squirm in my spot, the apex of my legs clenching in… want. *What the hell? Since when do I get turned on by Declan?*

"I got stir-crazy," I say, inwardly cringing when my words come out breathier than intended.

"Gotcha. I didn't know anyone was in here. I'll just…"

He's about to back out when I blurt out, "You can stay… if you want. I was reading through this song I wrote. Actually, it's the song we worked on together. I don't remember finishing it, but it turned out so beautiful. I'm thinking of asking Johnny to help me put some music to it."

Walking over, Declan takes the notebook from me and reads the words before handing it back to me. "The song is already done."

"What?"

"We finished it… *together* and put the music to it."

"Really?" *Jesus, how much happened during the six weeks that I can't remember?* "Did we record it?"

"Kind of. We recorded it so you could pitch it to your dad, but we'll have to have it redone properly." He pulls out his phone and pulls up the file, then hands it to me so I can press play. The instrumentals start, and then I begin singing about finding myself and love. About halfway through the song, Declan's voice comes on, and I suck in a harsh breath at his words…

*I've been watching you all night*
*Memorizing your every move*
*Know exactly what you need*
*To cure that chaos in your heart*
*Hand it over, and I'll fix the broken*

*Turn the chaos into calm*
*Make that heart of yours mine*
*And you'll never feel alone*
*All you gotta do is say yes*
*And I'll handle the rest*
*Haven't touched a single drink all night*
*But I'm drunk as fuck*
*On your scent, on your touch*
*Hand it over, baby*
*And you'll never know what it's like to be without love*

Butterflies erupt in my belly, chills race down my spine, my heart… *my freaking heart* flutters in my chest as if it was dead inside and has been resuscitated. The song continues, but my focus is on Declan, on his words…

"This is a love song." I don't write love songs. I write about heartbreak. I knew it was a love song when I read the words in my notebook, but it didn't click until I listened to them.

"Yeah," he says, his voice devoid of all emotion.

"We wrote a love song together…" I glance at my notebook, reading the lyrics as I listen to the emotion bleeding through every word we sing. The song can't be about Kyle because we started it before I met him… *So who is it about?*

For some musicians, writing a love song isn't a big deal, but for me, it's huge. I think back to when we started writing the song. We were hanging out, and Declan was scribbling words. I read them, looked into his eyes, could feel every raw emotion in every word, and added words of my own. We went back and forth until our friends showed up, and we put the notebook away. At the time, I didn't realize we were writing a love song—not until I just heard it finished.

"It's just words, K," Declan says, snapping me from my thoughts. "Doesn't mean anything."

I glance up at him, confused, as he takes his phone back and turns off the song, but he won't look at me. It's as if he's looking *past* me. We wrote this beautiful, emotional song together, yet he's acting like it means nothing.

My thoughts go back to the day I woke up in the hospital. *"Kendall, you can do it. Wake up, sweetheart. Just open those beautiful blue eyes and come back to me."*

Something is off, but I can't pinpoint what it is, and the harder I try to reach into my brain and figure it out, the more my head hurts. I'm about to ask him, no, *beg* him, to tell me what's going on, but before I can get the words out, he says, "I need to get going." He leaves me alone, wondering what the fuck is going on and why it's suddenly freezing in here. It's as if he took all the damn warmth with him.

And I'm still sitting here, confused as hell, when my mom walks in. "There you are!" She sits next to me and wraps her arms around me. "I was texting you."

"Sorry," I say, sighing into her comforting embrace. "My phone is on silent."

"That's okay. You look good," she says, sitting back slightly to assess me. "How're you feeling?"

Confused, frustrated... "Okay."

"The seamstress called to confirm your appointment for your final fitting tomorrow. I was thinking we could make a day of it. Go to lunch, do some shopping. We had talked about buying you some bridal lingerie."

"How did you know Dad was the one?" I blurt out.

"Umm," she says, a bit taken aback by my change in topics. "Well, I think I knew he was the one when, even though I put up walls made of concrete, he tore them down like they were nothing more than paper."

When I don't say anything for a few beats, she takes my hand in hers, squeezing it softly. "What's going on, Sunshine?"

"I don't know," I admit. "Were you nervous when you married Dad?"

"Well, no…" She flinches. "But we're different."

*Yeah, I know…*

"Hey." She cups the side of my face. "Talk to me."

"I just feel different… *off*," I say, tears filling my eyes.

"Are you having headaches? Any vomiting or—"

"No," I cut her off. "I'm not talking about the accident. I mean, me. I know I can't remember the past six weeks, but it's more than that. I can't…" I sniffle back the sobs bubbling up. "I don't feel grounded, put together."

Mom's brow furrows, so I explain. "For a long time, I've felt like I was flying above the Earth on my own, lost and searching for something to ground me. I don't feel like I belong. I'm not like you or Dad or Camden or Bailey… I suck at love."

*Yet I wrote a damn love song with Declan.*

"Oh, sweetheart," Mom coos. "You don't suck at love."

"Yes, I do. I thought marrying Kyle would ground me and make me feel less… lost, but the thought of marrying him, living with him… *having kids with him* is doing the opposite."

"Maybe you're just having a moment," she says gently. "When I met your dad, I was lost. I was in school and working at the bar. Naomi and I were raising you the best we could. And then I met your dad. It wasn't love at first sight, but it was definitely lust." She smiles softly, probably remembering their first encounter, and my heart clenches, wanting to feel the way she looks—in utter love.

"We hooked up." She shrugs unapologetically since I already

know the story. She and my dad have shared it many times over the years. "And I ended up pregnant with your brother. When I found out I was pregnant, I was so scared, felt like you, like I was soaring above the clouds, lost, but Easton brought me down and grounded me. In the chaotic world, I found myself, my place, my calm, through his love."

My thoughts go to the lyrics of the song I listened to earlier:

> *To cure that chaos in your heart*
> *Hand it over, and I'll fix the broken*
> *Turn the chaos into calm*
> *Make that heart of yours mine*
> *And you'll never feel alone*

"What if... What if Kyle's not the one?"

Mom's eyes go wide before she quickly schools her features. "Only you can know that."

# Eight

## Declan



*"It's just words. Doesn't mean anything."*

I can't get the conversation with Kendall out of my head. The one where she was shocked we wrote a love song together, and I told her it didn't mean shit… even though those words meant everything. While we were writing it, I thought she would catch on and realize she was writing her first love song, but she never said a word if she did. She acted like the queen of heartbreak wrote love songs every damn day, when the truth was, she'd never written one before… until now.

And while one might say it's because of her relationship with Kyle, I refuse to believe that because when we started to write it, he didn't exist. It was just Kendall and me and a notebook.

Now, it's Kendall and Kyle… getting married. Fuck. When she finally woke up and was talking, I hung on to every word, hoping she would kick Kyle out and tell me that once she got out of the hospital, she wanted to pick up right where we left off.

But then, through the doctor's questioning, we learned she has no recollection of the past six weeks. Which means she not only doesn't remember saying she wants to end her engagement but she also doesn't remember the night we spent together.

"Dammit." I swipe the canister off the counter, sending it crashing to the floor. The only thing worse than spending the night with Kendall and her not remembering is knowing it will never fucking happen again. She might not be able to remember a damn thing, but I still remember everything. Every touch and kiss and fucking caress. The way she came on my fingers and cock over and over again.

And now, in two motherfucking days, I have to go to her wedding because it's still on. A reminder was sent to everyone, letting us know Kendall is doing better, completely healed, and the wedding will be taking place as planned. Two days. In forty-eight hours, she'll be married to a man who she can't remember not wanting to marry.

"It's such bullshit." I knock the other canister off the counter and grab the bottle of Jack I've been guzzling for the past hour since I got that stupid event reminder in the mail.

"Tell us how you really feel," Camden says as he and Braxton walk into the kitchen. Since Braxton used to live here, he still has a key and the code.

"What's got you drinking and cursing…?" He glances at the floor, where the shattered pieces of canisters are. "And throwing shit."

"I called Gage." I needed my friend, needed someone to vent to. "The receptionist said he's not accepting calls at this time. It made no sense. It had to be a mix-up, so I called your dad since he's Gage's point of contact, and he told me there wasn't a mix-up. Gage isn't accepting any phone calls."

Camden and Braxton glance at each other. "What do you mean he isn't accepting phone calls?" Braxton asks slowly. "Who the fuck is he trying to avoid? Because the only people who would be calling him are us, so why the fuck isn't he taking our calls?"

I shrug, at a loss. "I don't know, man." I've tried to think about why Gage wouldn't want to talk to us, but I can't think of one damn reason. We've always had each other's backs. Always. And when he agreed to get help, no one forced him.

"What are you guys doing here anyway?" Between Camden having a five-year-old and a four-month-old, and Braxton obsessed with Kaylee, we haven't hung out much, aside from the obligatory holidays or when we were all at the hospital visiting Gage and then Kendall.

When Camden's brows kiss his forehead, I realize I asked the question a bit too harshly, so I backtrack. "I just know you guys are busy," I mutter.

"What does that have to do with anything?" Braxton asks, taking the bottle from me and pouring it down the drain. "We've been trying to get ahold of you, and you haven't returned a single call or text."

"I've got a lot of shit going on." Like getting drunk and wallowing like a little bitch.

Camden picks up the reminder card and glances at it. I can already see the pity in his eyes, so before he can speak, I shake my head. "Don't go there."

"You saying the reason for you getting drunk has nothing to do with my sister getting married?"

"I'm saying it doesn't matter because like you've said on several occasions, she doesn't even know I exist."

"Not according to that song you guys wrote."

I snap my head up. "You heard it?"

"Was at the studio with my dad earlier. He needs the band to sign off on you releasing it with Kendall since it will be considered a solo, and it states in our contract if one of us wants to release without the rest of the band, we all have to agree."

"And?"

"Of course, we all agree. You think we'd hold you back?"

"No… I don't know." I shrug. "Just feels like the band's falling apart. Maybe releasing a song without you guys isn't the best idea."

"You know you saved his life, right?" Camden says, understanding what I'm upset about without me having to say it.

"And now he won't even answer my calls."

"We're going to get through this," Braxton adds.

"Yeah." I sigh. "So what were you trying to get ahold of me about?"

"Just wanted to check in. The ladies are, uh, doing a girls' night. Layla's mom is watching the kids, so Brax and I were thinking we could do a guys' night. Maybe play some poker and shoot the shit like we used to."

"Girls' night?" I raise a brow. "You mean they're at her bachelorette party? Why aren't you at your future brother-in-law's bachelor party?"

"He decided against one. Said some shit about not wanting to party." Camden snorts out a laugh. "I didn't question it since I can't stand the guy. I wasn't in the mood to party with him anyway."

"You don't like him?"

"He's a kiss-ass workaholic. One of those guys always looking for ways, or people, to help him climb the ladder. I honestly thought my sister would call this shit off before she made it down the aisle."

"So why the fuck haven't you said that to her?"

He raises his hands in a placating manner. "Ain't for me to

say. If you think she's making a bad decision, why don't you say something?"

I sigh and shake my head, debating if I should admit to them what happened between Kendall and me… at the very least, tell them what she said to me. Don't I at least owe her that much? What if what the guy did was something horrible, and now, she's marrying him.

"Before Kendall lost her memory, she told me something…" Camden's brow furrows, and he nods for me to continue. "She said she was going to end their engagement."

"When?" Camden asks.

"Right before she got into the accident." I decide not to mention what happened between us because it might look like I'm jealous. If she does decide to go through with the wedding, I don't want her knowing she technically cheated, especially since she can't remember ever being with me.

"Did she say why?" Braxton asks.

"No. Just said it was over."

"Probably just cold feet," Camden says. "Everyone knows my sister is afraid of commitment."

"Yeah, maybe," I agree even though that night it felt like a whole lot more than her being afraid of saying I do.

"C'mon." Braxton stands. "We need a night out. Shit's gotten too real lately, and we need a night to let loose, let off some steam."

Since I've been missing my friends and I'm down for drinking, I tell them to give me a few minutes to get changed, and then we head out. With our security detail tagging along, we end up at Lush, our go-to place. Instead of getting a table, we go straight for the bar in the VIP lounge.

The great thing about Lush is that the people here are just as wealthy, if not wealthier than we are, and many are famous in their own right, so we don't have to worry about being accosted. The bartender doesn't even bat an eyelash when she comes over to take our orders.

"I don't know what to do," Braxton says once she's dropped off our drinks. "Kaylee and I were supposed to get married, and then all that shit went down with Gage, and now…"

"You don't want to do anything while he's not here," Camden finishes for him, taking a sip of his drink. "I say you get married. You weren't planning a wedding anyway, right?"

Braxton shakes his head. "We just wanted something small, with just us, since our families suck. My brother said he'd be our witness." He shrugs. "But I don't know… It just kind of feels wrong, doing anything while he's… there."

"There's no way Gage would want you to wait on him. I mean, he could've changed since he left, but I can't imagine him ever getting upset over you wife-ing Kaylee up. He knows how much you love that woman. We all do," I tell him, patting him on his back.

"Yeah, you're right. I think after Kendall's wedding, we'll plan something. Maybe have a little dinner with everyone afterward. Since we're on a bit of a break, I'm going to surprise her with a trip to Paris. We talked about going there when we were younger."

"Nice," Camden says. "With spring break coming up, Layla and I are taking the kids to The Hamptons. Put the place we bought to use."

We're all quiet for a few minutes when Camden adds, "If you wanna go…"

"Bro," I say dryly. "I'm not about to play the fifth wheel with your family vacay. I'm good. I was actually thinking of taking off for a little while."

Both guys' faces swing toward me.

"Where?" Braxton asks.

"When?" This time Camden.

"I don't know. I just think I need to get away for a bit. Clear my head."

"You do what you need to do," Braxton says, putting his hand on my shoulder. "Just know that we're here for you. Any time. I don't give a fuck if I'm across the damn pond. You got me?"

"Yeah," I say, downing my drink. "I got you."

We spend the next couple of hours drinking and bullshitting. It's been a while since we've done this, so it's nice to spend some time with the guys, minus everyone else, even if it's bittersweet as hell since Gage isn't with us.

When it's late, and their women start to text that they're back from their girls' day/evening, we call it a night. We all grab separate cars since we're going in different directions. Instead of going home, I find myself at the studio. I text Easton to let him know I'm here so he's not confused when he gets a notification from his security company that someone's entered.

I assume the place is empty, and I'll have it to myself, but when I step into the room we tend to favor, I find someone already there, sitting on the couch, scribbling away in a journal.

"What are you doing here?" I ask from the doorway.

"Oh, my God!" Kendall jumps, clutching her chest. "You scared me. I thought this place was empty."

"It is… well, it *was*. I just got here, thinking the same thing." I step into the room and notice she's writing lyrics in her journal. "Shouldn't you be home with your fiancé? You're getting married in less than two days."

It's a dick question because I know she's refused to move in with him until after they get married, and she's mentioned on several occasions that she only spends the night on Saturdays because he works a lot.

"I've been with him since I got out of the hospital," she says. "I just needed a moment to myself."

"I'll leave you to it then."

I'm about to step out of the room when she says, "Or you can stay." She shrugs. "There's plenty of room in here for two."

I want to stay so fucking badly, but I'm torn because as much as I want to spend time with her, doing so only hurts, knowing I'll never have her. Knowing in less than two days, she'll bear another man's last name. She'll be his wife, one day give birth to his children, and the only thing that will be left of us is the memory of the night we shared—a memory she doesn't even have.

"Please," she says softly. "I'm writing a new song. Maybe you can… take a look at it."

Because I can't say no to her, I nod and walk all the way in, sitting down next to her and taking the journal so I can read what she has so far.

The words are both beautiful and heartbreaking, a story of a woman who's lost and begging to be found. She wants to love and be loved, but she doesn't know how to go about it. It's raw and gritty and so fucking Kendall. It reminds me of our conversation the night we spent together when she confided in me about her biological dad and how broken she feels. These aren't lyrics of a woman happily in love, excited about getting married and starting her life with someone. She might not remember that night, but it's clear in her words that she can still feel what she felt.

Maybe she just needs a little nudge to jog her memory.

"What do you think?" she asks, her eyes meeting mine.

"Are you sure you want to get married?"

Her eyes go wide, and I open my mouth to backtrack. That's not how I wanted to word what I wanted to say… at all. But

before I can think of what to say, she answers my question.
"I'm not sure."

# Nine

## Kendall

I'VE BEEN HIDING OUT, SPENDING MY DAYS AT THE STUDIO WRITING, DOING WHAT I DO best: getting lost in my thoughts while shutting out the rest of the world. Today was my bachelorette party, so I had to leave my bubble. I wanted to enjoy going to dinner and dancing with my friends and sisters and Mom, but the entire time, I felt too much like a fraud.

Every time they spoke of their own weddings, of them finding love, gushing about how beautiful of a bride I'll be, how perfect my day will be, how they're so excited to be there and share what will be the best day of my life—their words, not mine—all I kept thinking was that I'm making a mistake. I don't feel what they feel. I'm not excited. I'm scared and nervous and freaking the hell out.

I keep telling myself that it's just pre-wedding jitters, and once I say I do, I'll be okay. I'm overthinking things and overanalyzing. I was in an accident that injured my brain, for crying out loud. That's bound to mess a person up, right?

But then why was it that the second Declan appeared in the doorway of the studio—like when he sat next to me while I listened to the song that I don't remember recording with him—butterflies attacked my belly, and my heart pounded against my chest? Shouldn't I be feeling that way toward my fiancé?

"Kendall," Declan says softly, snapping me from my thoughts. "What do you mean you're not sure?" *Huh?* Oh, right! He asked me if I'm sure I want to get married, and I blurted out the truth instead of lying like I've been doing to everyone, including myself.

"I…" I almost lie, tell him I didn't mean it like that, but something inside urges me to be honest. I can trust him. He's not just Camden's best friend. He's mine too. We've written a beautiful, intimate song together, and that doesn't happen unless you're close.

"I think something is wrong with me."

His brows kiss his forehead. "What's wrong? Is it your head? Are you having headaches?" His eyes skate over my face and body, assessing my features.

"No, I'm okay. I mean, I still have occasional headaches, but I was checked out yesterday by the neurologist, and everything came back clean."

He sighs in relief, and my heart clenches. I know we're only friends, but is it possible he's feeling the way I am? Like there's something more between us, something I'm terrified to explore, both as Camden's sister and Kyle's fiancée?

"What's wrong?" Declan asks, moving a stray hair out of my eyes and tucking it behind my ear. My body acts of its own accord, shuddering in response. When Declan sees, the corner of his lips tugs into a sexy smirk, forcing my legs to tighten. I haven't once felt turned on since I got out of the hospital. I even told Kyle I wanted to wait until our wedding night to be together, hoping by then whatever is broken in me would be fixed, but sitting here with Declan, it's clear I'm not as broken as I thought.

"I… I feel different. Kyle has been so sweet and attentive since I woke up, but I can't conjure up any feelings for him. I must've cared for him enough to be engaged to him, but I… I don't feel it. When I look at him, I feel nothing."

"Then why are you marrying him?" His question comes out thoughtful and not at all judgmental.

"I spoke to the doctor about it, and he said what I'm feeling isn't uncommon. With memories come emotions, and I can't remember almost half of the time we've been together."

"Maybe you're feeling that way for a reason. Like something happened, and you can't remember." His statement is one I've thought about many times, but asking Kyle would raise a red flag, and I wouldn't even know if he's lying or telling the truth.

Before I can answer, my phone buzzes on the table, Kyle's name flashing on the screen. I've been avoiding him all day, so I should probably answer, but as I stare at the screen, I can't bring myself to do it. It stops and then starts up again, and I inwardly sigh, knowing I need to answer. He could be worried about me.

"I need to take this," I tell Declan, who nods. "Hey."

"You okay? I've called you a few times."

"Yeah, sorry. I'm in the studio writing. Phone's on silent."

"By yourself?"

"No." I clear my throat. "Declan's with me."

There's silence on the other end, and then Kyle says, "When will you be home?"

"I'm not sure. Did we have plans?" I know we didn't, but I'm not sure why he's asking.

"No, we haven't had plans since you woke up," he snaps, then sighs into the phone. "I'm sorry. I just miss you. I feel like I never see you. Your mom said the bachelorette party ended a while ago."

I should apologize, tell him I'll come over or offer for him to come over. Make plans for tomorrow since I don't have any. But as I glance at Declan, the only thing I want to do is hang up and write music… with him. So instead of saying what I should say and doing what I should do, I say, "I'm sorry. I'm really tired and wouldn't be good company."

"So what? I'm not going to see you until at the wedding?"

"You'll see me at the rehearsal dinner. Besides, it's bad luck to spend the night together before the wedding."

Kyle releases a harsh breath, and I wince, hating myself for what I'm doing to him, but I don't know how to fix this.

"All right, well, I guess I'll stay at work. I need to get ahead anyway since we'll be gone for a week on our honeymoon."

I don't realize how tense I am until I sag in relief. "Okay, sounds good."

"Text me when you get home, so I know you're okay."

"Will do."

There's a brief pause, like Kyle wants to say something, but instead, he sighs and says, "I love you, Kendall."

He's said those three words a few times since I woke up, but I've yet to say them back. I already feel like the worst person ever for living this lie, for being on the fence and not telling him how I really feel, that I can't bring myself to say it back. The truth is, as far as I can remember, I've never said those three words to any man, including Kyle. Maybe I said them during the six weeks I've lost, but I just can't bring myself to say them now. Not when I don't feel them.

"Good night," I say instead, then hang up, tossing my phone to the side and glancing over at Declan. "So what do you think about that song?" I nod toward my journal.

"I think you're living in a state of lies and denial, and the only truth is on this paper." He sets the journal down and takes my hands in his. "If you're not one-hundred-percent sure you want to marry him, you shouldn't do it. He'll wait if he loves you like he says he does."

He's right, I know he is, but the thought of letting everyone down makes me feel sick. My parents have spent thousands of dollars on this wedding, countless hours making sure everything is perfect. They're so happy I'm settling down and have found a man to start a life with. I know they were worried, with me jumping from man to man, refusing to get serious or commit. My mom mentioned how excited she is to have more grandbabies. And what about Kyle? Pushing the wedding back would hurt him, and he's been nothing but kind to me since I woke up.

No, this is just a moment. The effects of my brain injury. I'm going to feel again, and everything will be okay.

A text chimes from Kyle: **I really do miss you, Kendall.**

No butterflies. No sparks. But it's the confirmation I needed.

"I want to marry him," I tell Declan. "He loves me." I grab my phone and journal and stand. "I should probably go."

"Kendall—" He starts, but I cut him off.

"I appreciate you listening to me. You're a wonderful friend, and even though I don't remember us finishing this song, I know it's special. I hope once I get back from my honeymoon, we can have Blackwood hammer out the specifics so we can release it. I have no doubt it will be a hit."

Declan clenches his jaw. "I won't be here. I'm going away. But I'll let your dad know I'm on board with however he wants to go about it. If he needs me to fly in to record it, I can do that."

His confession rattles me. "Going where? Will you be at the wedding?" The thought of him not being there affects me more than it should.

"I'll be at the wedding. Then I'm taking off on a road trip. With the band on a hiatus and…" He clears his throat. "I just need to get away for a little bit."

I nod in understanding, but a huge lump fills my throat. "I'm sure they'll want to do a music video as well. How long will you be gone for?" I don't give a shit about the video, but I'm too much of a wuss to ask outright how long he'll be away.

"I'm not sure," he says, his voice hard. "I'll keep in touch with Easton, though."

"Okay." I bob my head up and down, trying to appear nonchalant, while I'm freaking out on the inside. Which is ridiculous since Declan and I are only friends, and him going away has nothing to do with me since I'll be away on my honeymoon as well. "Okay," I say again.

"Okay," he repeats.

He walks me out, keeping his distance, and when I get in the car, he mutters a goodbye before shutting the door and walking away. I have no idea what's going on with me, my thoughts, my chaotic mess of emotions, but as the car takes off from the curb, I can't help feeling as though my heart is being ripped from my chest—which is crazy because Declan doesn't own my heart. Kyle does. Right?

My intention was to go to Kyle's, but instead, I find myself back at home, alone, where I stay curled up in bed, writing lyrics and pouring my heart out, all while the words Declan said run on repeat: *I think you're living in a state of lies and denial, and the only truth is on this paper.*

"WOW," MY DAD SAYS, HIS EYES FILLED WITH EMOTION. "YOU LOOK LIKE A BEAUTIFUL princess."

It's Saturday afternoon, the day of my wedding. The morning has been spent with everyone getting their hair and makeup done and the seamstress ensuring everyone's dresses fit perfectly.

As I stare into the mirror, I have to agree with my dad—I do look like a princess. My makeup is flawless, my dress is elegant, and my glossy golden locks are up in a tight bun, complete with a diamond-encrusted tiara. But unlike the Disney Princesses, I'm unsure if this is where I get my happily ever after. My heart is pounding against my rib cage, and I feel as though I'm about to pass out.

The music starts up, indicating the wedding procession is about to begin. I'm hidden behind the door, but I can picture everyone walking down the aisle. We practiced it last night—who would walk when and where they would stand. Then afterward, we went out to dinner, where we ate Italian food, and I faked having a headache to be excused early, so I could spend the rest of the night writing more songs.

"I can still remember the day I married your mom," my dad says, placing his hand on my shoulder and gently turning me to face him. "As I watched her walk down the aisle, I knew I was the luckiest man in the world. She was carrying Camden, and she said she felt fat and ugly so many times, but when I looked at her, all I saw was the most beautiful woman, the love of my life. And I couldn't wait to officially make her mine."

As he recounts his memories from the wedding with a content smile on his face, I'm brought back to when I was a little girl, dressing up in my pretend wedding dress so I could marry my pretend fiancé, and begging my mom to retell the story of her wedding day. She would put on their wedding video, and we would watch, as my parents, with hearts in their eyes, promised each other forever. As a young girl, it would give me butterflies, imagining that one day I would fall in love and put on a pretty white dress and make the same promises to the man I wanted to spend my life with.

Only now, as I think about that, butterflies don't attack my belly. Instead, anxiety roils in my stomach with the fear that I'm making a mistake. That while I'm dressed like a princess, Kyle isn't my prince. I keep telling myself it's my brain injury, but shouldn't I feel something... *anything* toward him? Shouldn't I be excited that in a few minutes, I'm going to walk down the aisle, exchange vows with him, and start our lives together?

"It was without a doubt the best day of my life," my dad says, snapping me out of my thoughts.

"Of course, it was... because you married your best friend," I say robotically, knowing how the story ends. I've heard this same story a million times over the years, and both my parents always end it the same way.

"Well, that, of course, but also..." He softly palms my cheek. "Because it's the day I became a dad."

"Camden always has the worst timing," I say, rolling my eyes playfully. Only my brother would decide he was ready to join the world the night of my parents' wedding while they were attempting to consummate their marriage.

"That he does," Dad agrees with a chuckle. "And yes, your mother giving birth was definitely part of making that day perfect, but what I was referring to was you."

"Me?" I ask dumbly.

"Yes, you," he says with a light laugh. "In case you forgot, you made me a dad first. Before Camden was born, I signed the papers to legally make you mine. It was also the first time you called me Daddy." His lips curve into a watery smile. "Camden had just been born, and you were so excited. You looked up at me, and you said, 'Wow, today is the best day ever. I got a daddy and a brother.' And I swear, my heart swelled so big, I wasn't sure how the hell it still fit in my chest."

A choked sob escapes at his admission, and tears course down my cheeks. He thumbs a couple, smiling down at me. "I'm so proud of the woman you've become, K. You're strong and independent, and your heart… fuck, it's so big and full. I'm going to sound like a selfish asshole when I say this, but giving you away is probably the hardest thing I'll ever have to do, but if it means you have with Kyle, what I have with your mom, I know I have to be okay with it. Because that's all I want for you, sweetheart. To find love."

Something in me snaps at his admission. "I… I… I don't think I do."

His brow furrows. "You don't think you do, what?"

"Have what you guys have." My sobs strengthen, and it's hard to see through my tears. "I keep telling myself that it's in my head, it's because of my injury, but I don't feel anything. I don't think… I don't think I'm in love," I cry out. "Oh my God, Dad. I don't *think*… I *know* I'm not in love with Kyle." It's the first time I've said the words out loud, and while they suck, I know deep down they're the truth. I don't love Kyle. I'm not *in love* with him. He's not my best friend, and I can't imagine spending the rest of my life with him. "I'm broken, aren't I? I'm broken, and now I'm going to break him because I can't marry him."

"What? No… No, K. You're not broken." My dad pulls me into his arms and guides us over to the couch. "Sweetheart, why would you think you're broken?"

"Because I don't know how to love anyone. I fuck up every relationship I'm in. I wanted what you and Mom have so badly, but I'll never have it because I'm broken." I cover my face with my hands and cry, hating myself and wishing I wasn't so messed up.

"You are not broken. Hey… look at me." Dad lifts my face and forces me to make eye contact. "Just because Kyle isn't the one doesn't mean you aren't capable of love. You love me and your mother and your brother and sisters… And you're the best damn aunt to Felix and Marianna."

"But that's different. You guys are family."

"Love is love, K. And you have a huge heart."

"Then why can't I find what you and Mom have?"

"Oh, sweetheart." He palms my cheeks. "You just haven't met the right guy yet. One day, you will meet him, and you'll know he's the one. You'll look at him and see your entire life in front of you with him by your side."

"Or maybe I'm not meant to be with anyone. Maybe… it's not in me."

I regret the words the second I say them, but it's too late to take them back. My dad's jaw clenches. "Tell me you're not referring to your genetics."

"It would make sense, wouldn't it? The only thing *he* was capable of was destroying everyone around him. How am I any different?"

"Don't you ever say that," Dad says, his voice commanding. "You are nothing like that man. You might carry his DNA, but you are every bit your mother's daughter. And you are not broken. You are perfect just the way you are."

"You have to say that because you're my dad," I say lamely.

"Damn right, I am," he says. "You might not carry *my* DNA, but never, for a fucking second, doubt that you're not the best part of your mother and me."

He pulls me into a hug, and we both go quiet as the music in the background bleeds through the walls, reminding me that I'm supposed to be walking down the aisle. They must be wondering where we are. I'm honestly shocked nobody has knocked on the door yet.

"What am I supposed to do?" I whisper even though I already know the answer to my question.

My dad pulls back and takes my hand in his, squeezing it softly. "You're supposed to follow your heart."

# Ten

## Declan

Today's the day. The day I've been dreading since I received my invite almost four months ago. The day I didn't think would actually happen. Between Kendall being allergic to commitment, what happened with us, and then her getting into an accident and losing her memory, I honestly thought the wedding would be canceled at some point, but it's like a fireproof safe after a fire. The entire house has burned to the ground, but that damn safe is still standing.

I considered not going. It's not like I'm in the wedding. She probably won't even notice I'm not there. But something in me convinced me to go. Maybe it's my way of officially saying goodbye to the woman I've been pining after for the past decade. It's one thing to have feelings for her while she's jumping from guy to guy, but it's another to be crushing—for lack of a better word—on a married woman. And that's precisely what she'll be soon: *married*.

After I finish putting on my suit, I grab my suitcase and lock up since I'll be gone for several weeks. I don't have a concrete plan, but I'm thinking I'll drive down the East Coast and probably end up in the Keys. With it being March, Florida is the perfect place to chill for a little while. The beaches are beautiful, and the laidback vibe in the Keys is exactly what I need to lose myself for a bit.

When I get down to the garage, I pop the trunk to my Dodge Challenger I had shipped here from California and throw my bag in. She's not my favorite out of the vehicles I own, but she's the most practical to take on a road trip, and since I purchased her right before we moved to New York, I haven't put any miles on her.

I try calling Gage again on the way to the church, hoping something has changed, and he's now accepting calls. Only I'm told the same damn thing by the receptionist, who I'm sure is sick of hearing from me: *I'm sorry, but he's not accepting calls at this time.*

It's been over a month, and he still won't talk to anyone. Easton checks in with his doctor on a weekly basis, so we know he's okay, but fuck, if I don't want to talk to my friend myself. Hear him tell me he's okay. Since he'll be gone for at least ninety days, my plan is to be back by the end of April, so I'm back when he gets out. Until then, with the band on a break, there's nothing for me here right now.

I pull up to the church, and the parking lot is filled with vehicles. I check the time and see I'm about to be late, but instead of getting out, I don't move. I stay in the car, the engine rumbling under me, contemplating if I can do this. If I can sit in a pew and watch her promise herself to another man, one we both know isn't right for her. I have nothing against the guy. Don't even really know him. But from what I know, he works a lot, doesn't put her first, and for whatever reason, when she came to me that night, she was one-hundred-percent ready to end the engagement, which tells me all I need to know.

As I sit in my car, staring at the front doors where I'm supposed to walk through, I imagine how beautiful she'll look today with her hair and makeup done and wearing some expensive, gorgeous dress. Without a doubt, she'll be the most beautiful bride, but she won't be mine. Never will be. Because she belongs to someone else. She'll say I do to someone else, dance with someone else. Tonight, she'll go to a hotel room and make love to someone else. And tomorrow, she'll go on a honeymoon with someone else. Eventually, she'll give birth to beautiful blue-eyed babies, but they won't be mine. And she'll live happily ever after, like the queen she is, but it won't be with me.

Braxton sends me a text, asking where the hell I am, but I don't respond, unsure if I'm going in. I sit for a few more minutes, contemplating whether I should bite the bullet and just go in or say fuck it and take off.

I've almost convinced myself that the wedding has probably started by now, and I wouldn't want to walk in and disturb the service, when a blur of movement out of the corner of my eye catches my attention.

The window is open, and it looks as if a white blanket is being shoved through it. I turn the ignition off on my car and step out, wondering what the fuck is going on, when the white shit collapses onto the ground and then...

*What the fuck? Is that...?*

"Kendall?"

She pops her head up, exposing her flawlessly done-up face. Her blond hair is up in a bun, and a crown rests on top of her head. She huffs out a small laugh and shrugs, lifting her puffy dress and scurrying toward me.

"You, uh, going somewhere?" I ask, glancing around in confusion. The woman, who should be saying I do, just damn near fell out of a window.

"Yeah, away from here." She steps over to my car. "This yours?" Her eyes are wide and bright, a mixture of nervous and excited.

"Yeah, it's mine."

"Great. Mind giving me a ride? I didn't exactly think this part through."

"What part?"

"The getaway."

It takes me a second, but my brain finally catches up, realizing what she means. She's running away… from her wedding. And fuck me if I'm not going to help her.

"Hop in." I round the front and open the door for her.

"Thanks." She pops a quick kiss to my cheek and ducks in, gathering her enormous dress to fit in the vehicle with her. Once she's all the way in, I close the door, then click the fob to start the car while I head back over to the driver's side and get in. Music is thumping, my phone still connected, and when I get in, Kendall has already gotten her seat belt on and is changing the song.

"Does anyone know you left?" I ask, not giving a shit about Kyle but knowing her family will be worried if she just up and disappeared.

"Yep. My dad knows. He'll tell everyone."

"You told your dad?"

She nods, a giggle escaping past her lips, and fuck if it isn't the most beautiful sound in the world. "He told me to follow my heart." She glances over at me, her eyes filled with unshed tears. "So I did."

I know she isn't referring to me, her heart taking her straight to me, but I can't help but think about the fact that I was here when she escaped. I could've been inside that church, but I wasn't. And now, here she is, sitting in my car, in her goddamn wedding dress that she didn't get married in.

My screen lights up with a text from Braxton: **You wouldn't believe this shit. Kendall ran.**

"I think everyone knows."

"We should probably get out of here," she says, nervously biting the corner of her bottom lip.

"Where to?"

My phone goes off again with another text: **Enjoy your road trip, man.**

"That's right. You're going out of town." She flips her dress up, knocks her heels off, and plops her feet up on my dash. "Count me in. A road trip sounds perfect."

She looks over at me with a smile spread across her entire face, and I briefly wonder if I drank too much and am dreaming because… what the fuck? Did the woman of my goddamn dreams just agree to go on a road trip with me?

"We'll be gone for weeks," I warn. "Probably over a month."

"Perfect," she says. "That'll give everyone enough time to get over the fact I just left my fiancé at the altar." The door to the church opens, and Kendall's eyes bug out. "Oh, God, Dec, go!"

I put the car in drive and take off, dirt from the parking lot kicking up behind us as we peel out. The first few minutes are silent, but then her phone vibrates, and she pulls it out, cringing. "I better get this. It's my mom."

I turn down the music as she hits accept. It's a video call, so her mother's face takes over the screen. "Kendall Naomi Blackwood…"

"Oh, shit. All three names, Mom? Am I in trouble?" She sounds so adorable and apologetic, I want to pull her into my arms and comfort her, but I stay quiet, letting her talk to her mom.

Her mom sighs. "Of course, you're not, Sunshine. Are you okay?"

"I am," Kendall tells her with a soft smile. "I just couldn't… Dad told me to follow my heart and…" She sniffles. "I'm sorry."

"You have nothing to be sorry about," her mom says. "Your dad was right. You should always follow your heart. Where are you going?"

"I just need to get away for a bit. Clear my head."

"Okay, sweetheart. But please keep in touch so we know you're okay. I don't care how old you are, you're still our little girl, and we're always going to worry about you."

"I know. I'm sorry I left that mess for you to clean up."

"It's okay. Your dad handled it."

"And, uh… Kyle?"

"He's not too happy. I'm sure his ego is bruised, but he'll be okay."

Kendall nods. "I love you, Mom. Talk soon."

"Love you too."

She hangs up, and her phone goes off several times in quick succession. To give her some space, I turn the music up and drive while she texts everyone.

She sets her phone down a little while later and glances at me. "So, where are we going first?"

"The Jersey Shore."

She grins. "Nice." Then she looks down at her dress and frowns. "I don't have any clothes."

"We can pick some up once we get there."

"And where's there?"

"Not really sure. I didn't book any rooms, not wanting to be tied down to an agenda. I get enough of that with the tours."

"I feel that deep," she says, pulling something out of her clutch. It's a small silver flask.

I laugh as she opens it and raises it up into the air. "To road trips and freedom." She toasts the air and takes a quick sip before offering it to me.

"I'm driving." I shake my head.

"Just take a quick sip. It's like a contract. You have to drink to the road trip."

I do as she says, taking a sip of the vodka in it, and then hand it back to her. "To road trips and freedom."

She takes the flask back. "And whatever trouble we shall find along the way." After downing some more, she screws the top back on and drops it into her clutch. Then she turns up the music. "This is going to be epic."

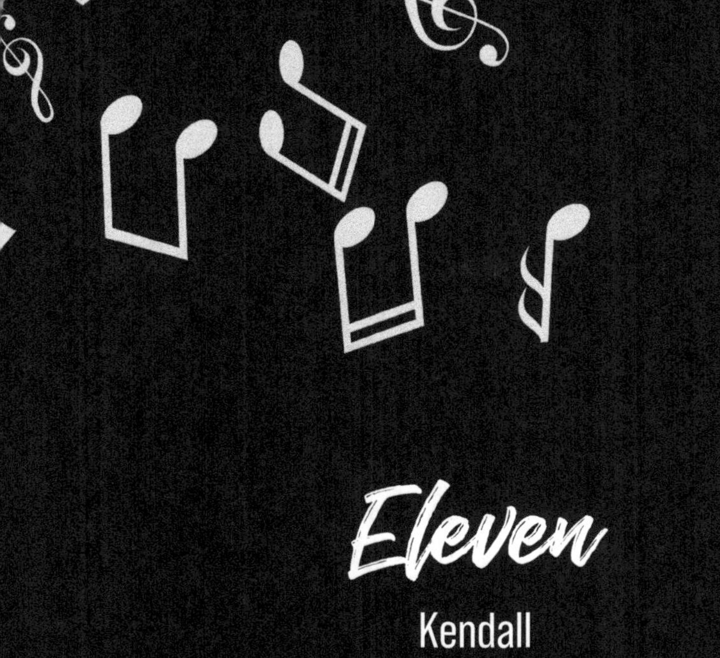

# Eleven

## Kendall

THE TWO-HOUR DRIVE TO JERSEY FLIES BY. THANKFULLY, DECLAN DRIVES IN SILENCE, giving me time to process what the hell just happened, and doesn't ask any questions. When my phone doesn't stop vibrating, and I turn it off, then turn up the music and sing the songs on his playlist at the top of my lungs, he only smiles, letting me let go.

At some point, I know I'll have to deal with what I've done. At the very least, I owe Kyle an explanation and apology, and I'm aware that running away is immature as hell, but right now, it's what I need to do. My dad told me to follow my heart, and I don't find it a coincidence that as I stumbled out the window, the person standing there was Declan. The guy I wrote my one and only love song with. The same guy I've been thinking about since I woke up in the hospital.

I've known him for years—he's been my brother's best friend for over a decade—and in recent years, we've gotten closer, hence us writing music together, but for some reason, it feels like more than that. There's an attraction there. A feeling I know I can't act on because he's too close to my family, too close to my brother, and I always fuck up the relationships I'm in. But maybe he's who I need right now. He was heading out on a road trip, and I was running away, so maybe in some crazy way, we were meant to be on this journey together.

We pull up to a gorgeous modern-looking resort, and when we step out of the car so the valet can take over, I inhale the salty ocean breeze.

"It's oceanfront," Declan says, taking my hand in his. "Let's go get our sun on." He waggles his brows playfully, and I can't help but laugh at how adorable he is. Don't get me wrong, he's sexy as hell, but he's also lowkey adorable, which is something you rarely see with rock stars. They're usually dark and broody and covered in tattoos. Braxton and Gage are the perfect example. My brother is more of a dark pretty boy. He's mastered the brooding, but his wife, Layla, brings out the softness in him. But Declan… he's always happy and smiling.

"I was wondering if you have a room available," he asks the woman at the front desk, proving what he said earlier, that he didn't book anything and was planning to just wing it.

"We do," she says, eyeing Declan in his suit and me in my wedding dress, which reminds me that I need to get out of this thing and into some regular clothes.

"We have the Presidential suite," she explains. "It's a two-bedroom, two-bathroom suite with an ocean view. It's the most common for honeymooners."

Declan's brow furrows, and then he laughs when he looks at me. "I forgot you're in your wedding dress," he says softly. To her, he adds, "That room will be fine."

"How many nights?"

"We're not sure," he says. "How many nights is this room

available?"

She taps away on her keyboard. "At least for the next five nights, but—"

"Perfect. Book it for all five nights, and if we leave early, it's no big deal."

"We, um, if we do all five nights, you'll be charged for all the nights."

"Of course." Declan hands her his credit card.

After she goes over the amenities and gives us our room keys, he has her point us in the direction of the resort shop, so I can purchase a bathing suit and cover-up.

I end up picking out a few different bikinis since their selection is good, along with a cute romper, a couple of cover-ups, a pair of sandals, some sunglasses, and a hat to help keep anyone from recognizing me. We also purchase a couple of fluffy towels since hotels—no matter how luxurious the hotel is—never have good towels.

Declan reserves the cabana by the pool for the next five days, and then we head up to the room to get settled in.

The moment we step into the room, the energy changes. Maybe it's because of the bottle of champagne sitting on ice or the fact that we're now alone, but suddenly, I'm nervous, unsure of what I was thinking when I hopped in the vehicle with him without having a plan.

"I'll take this room," he says, pointing at the room to the left and leaving the one on the other side for me. "Wanna get changed and hit the beach? I'm sure they have a bar down there where we can get some drinks and food."

"Sure."

Closing the door behind me, I take a deep breath as the heaviness of the morning drops onto my shoulders. I set the bags from the resort shop on the bed and pull my phone out to check my messages. My brother and sisters left several, telling me they love me, and if I need anything, they've got my back. One from my dad, asking that I let him know I'm okay once I get to where I'm going, one from my assistant, asking if I need anything, and a *What the fuck, Kendall?* from Kyle.

I text my siblings back, thanking them; let my parents know I'm okay and will stay in touch; tell my assistant that I appreciate it, but I'm good, and she's off the clock—paid, of course—until I get back; and then text Kyle back two words: I'm sorry.

It's a cop-out, but I don't know what else to say. He deserves an explanation, and once I have one, I'm going to give it to him, but for right now, I'm doing as my dad said and following my heart.

After I hit send, I throw my phone onto the nightstand, wanting to check out for a little while, and pick out which suit I'm going to wear. I go with the two-piece burnt orange ombre number and the matching cover-up, but when I go to take off my dress, I realize I can't. It's formfitting up top with several dozen buttons down my back holding it together. I couldn't even put it on myself this morning—my mom had to help me.

I try several times to get it off, but when it's obvious it's not happening, I head out to find Declan. He's standing in the living room, staring out at the beach with his back to me. I stop in my place for a moment, taking him in. His hair is up in his usual bun, and he's changed out of his suit and is sporting a pair of board shorts. But what has me staring, and maybe drooling, is his shirtless, muscular back. He's tanned and fit from years of living in California and working out every day. I always assumed he didn't have any tattoos, but in the center of his shoulder blades is a single tattoo. I can't see what it is from here, so I step toward him, but before I can make out what it is, he turns around.

"I'm not sure that's exactly pool attire." He smirks playfully, and I roll my eyes.

He sticks his arms through the holes of his shirt and is about to put it on when I reach out and stop him. "What's your tattoo of?"

His brow furrows, and he quickly throws his shirt on over his head. "Just a quote." He shrugs it off, which has me that much more curious. I've known him for years, and I've never known him to have one, so it has to be new.

"C'mon. Let me see."

"It's nothing. I thought we were hitting the pool."

I let it go for now since we'll be together for the foreseeable future. I'll find a way to see what he's got inked on his back when he least expects it. The guy can't keep his shirt on forever.

"I need help." I spin around and glance over my shoulder. "Unbutton me, please."

It takes him a second to understand what I mean, and once he does, his eyes go wide. "You can't do it yourself?"

"If I could, I'd already be in my bathing suit." I back up, so I'm closer to him. "Please."

With his big hands, one by one, he unbuttons my dress, exposing my back. Every once in a while, his fingers brush against my skin, and the craziest shiver races down my spine as I imagine what it would be like if, as he removed each button, he pressed a kiss to my heated flesh. When he gets to the last few buttons, leaving almost my entire back on display, I imagine my dress falling to the floor and Declan scooping me up into his arms and making love to me. Worshipping every inch of my body.

A moan escapes my lips, and I clear my throat to cover it up, praying he doesn't notice. This is what I wanted to feel with Kyle, what I *wished* I could feel for Kyle but couldn't, yet all Declan is doing is helping me take off my dress, and I'm fantasizing about him doing naughty things to me.

"There you go," he says, his voice gruff.

Holding my front up so I don't flash him, I turn around to thank him, but my words are caught in my throat when I realize how close we are. So close, I catch a whiff of his masculine scent—earthy and warm with a hint of comfort. His eyes lock with mine for a moment before his gaze descends slightly, landing on my mouth. My tongue darts out, wondering what it would feel like to kiss him. Would his lips be hard like the rest of his body? Would the kiss be heated, similar to the way he's staring at me, like with his look alone, he has the capability of setting my entire body on fire?

"Declan," I breathe, stepping forward and throwing all thought out the window, ready to find out.

Only my speaking seems to snap him out of the trance we're in, and he takes a step back, blinking rapidly. "I'll, uh…" He clears his throat, averting his eyes. "I'm going to call down to make sure our cabana is ready while you finish getting changed."

He flees the living room, and I'm left wondering what the hell just happened. Not with him… I don't blame him for not kissing me. I'm in my damn wedding dress, for crying out loud. No, I'm wondering what the hell is going on with me. When did Declan go from being a friend of my brother's to a man I'm sexually attracted to? Because that's exactly what I am… attracted to him. I felt it when I woke up to him sitting by my bedside in the hospital, when he walked in on me in the studio, when I listened to the song we wrote and sang together. And when I saw him standing outside of the church, my first thought was that it had to be fate. My dad told me to follow my heart, and there Declan was as if he had been waiting for me.

Now the question is, what the hell do I do with this new information? I could tell him. I could act on it. But then what? I'm just coming out of a relationship—even if I can't muster up a single feeling for him—and on top of that, Declan is, in fact, my brother's best friend and one-fourth of their band. And if my history is anything to go by, the only thing that will come from me acting on my feelings is me hurting Declan, and the thought of hurting him causes my heart to clench in my chest.

No… no way. Those feelings are staying bottled up, right where they belong. Declan and I are friends, and right now, what I need is a friend. I'm not going to risk losing him over some *feelings*.

When we get down to the pool where our cabana is set up, the server assigned to us introduces herself and takes our drink and food order. The cabana is so adorable, like a tiki hut but with three walls for privacy. A comfy-looking L-shaped couch stretches across two adjacent walls, and two equally comfy-looking lounge chairs face the crystal-clear infinity pool. There's a flat-screen TV hanging in the top corner, and directly underneath it is a mini fridge. If you want privacy, the front of the cabana can be closed.

After I spread my towel across the chair and remove my cover-up, I pluck the sunglasses and floppy hat out of my beach bag and put them on. Then I plop down, sighing in contentment. "I kind of feel bad," I admit as Declan removes his shirt, giving me another glimpse of his sexy as hell body. Unfortunately, he lies back quickly so I don't catch a peek at the tattoo, but I'm determined to find out what it is.

"About what?" he asks, crossing one ankle over the other. There's a portable speaker, so he sets his phone against it and clicks play on his playlist.

"I just left a guy at the altar with my family to deal with the fallout, and I'm relaxing at a beautiful resort"—the server sets my martini and Declan's scotch down and walks away, and I pick it up, taking a sip—"while drinking a delicious martini in a poolside cabana."

Declan takes a drink of his scotch, and I can't help but notice the way his Adam's apple bobs as he swallows. An image of me licking my way up his throat hits me so hard it's almost as if it's real. It can't be since I've never been with Declan, but the vivid picture—of my tongue gliding up his throat and across his stubbled jawline to his chin—has me squeezing my thighs together. I can't remember the last time I had sex or even got off. It was definitely before the accident since, despite him trying, I wasn't with Kyle at all from the time I was discharged and leading up to the wedding that obviously didn't happen.

I think I need to find some alone time to release some of this pent-up tension, and then maybe I'll stop fantasizing about Declan.

"Do you love him?" Declan asks, glancing over at me.

I don't even have to think about it. "No… I wanted to. I tried for weeks to conjure up some kind of feelings for him, but they weren't there. I don't know what happened, if it was the accident or what, but my heart wasn't in it." I sigh. "God, I'm such a shitty person."

"Nah, you're not. A shitty person would've gone through with the lie and led him on longer. You did the right thing by calling it off. Now you both can move forward."

"True, but my moving forward meant leaving my family to deal with everything."

"Your family loves and supports you, and Camden said your dad handled it all without issue."

"You told him I'm with you?"

"No." He quirks a brow. "But would that be a problem if I did?"

"I just think it would be best if no one knew we were on this trip together. They'll constantly try to check up on me and jump to the wrong conclusion. I don't want you in the middle of everything."

He nods in understanding. "I won't tell them you're with me, but if they ask…"

"You won't lie." I roll my eyes. "I get it."

"Where do they think you are?"

"I told them I needed to get away and promised to keep in touch. Honestly, they're kind of used to this." I take another sip of my drink, slightly embarrassed to admit what I just did.

"Used to what? You tumbling out of windows while running from your wedding?" He smirks playfully, so I know he's just kidding, but his tone is curious, asking me to explain.

"As you know, I suck at relationships." Everyone knows. It's not exactly a secret, what with my entire life being on display in the tabloids and on social media. "Whenever I break up with a guy, I tend to… escape. Well, hide. Let the media run me through the mud and then calm down."

Declan's lips tip down into a frown, and he swings his legs over the side of the chair to face me. "You don't suck at relationships." He reaches over and lifts my sunglasses, so I'm forced to look him in the eye. "You just haven't found the right guy yet. There's nothing wrong with dating until you find the person you want to spend your life with. You're not doing anything different than what most people do. The only difference is your life is on display for the entire world to see…*and*"—he chuckles softly—"you make a habit of writing music about your breakups."

"I don't write about *them*," I say with a huff, dropping my sunglasses back over my eyes and crossing my arms over my chest. "I write about my feelings. Anyway, my point is, they're expecting me to hide out for a bit, so they won't suspect anything."

"Unless we're spotted," Declan points out.

"If we are, then we are, but until then, please keep it between us. The last thing I want is to draw you into my circus of a life. One picture of us together and they'll be linking you to me, predicting how long it will take for you to get *stiffed*."

Declan snorts out a laugh and plucks my glasses off my face. "They can predict all they want, but it wouldn't happen." He pinches my chin and leans closer, so close I can feel his cool breath against my lips. "Those guys you dated got stiffed for a reason. They didn't know how to handle a woman like you."

His words cause my breath to hitch. "What are you trying to say?" I choke out.

"That if you were mine, I'd make sure you never had a reason to run."

# Twelve

## Declan


mean them—I do—but because I told myself I wouldn't go there. At least, not yet. Kendall just ended her engagement. Dipped out on her wedding. I meant what I said: she has no reason to feel bad. She did the right thing. Her brain might not understand it, but her heart knows, fucking *knows* she wasn't supposed to marry Kyle. I don't know why she planned to call off her engagement the night she came to me, but it was clear she had no intention of going through with that wedding. When she woke up and didn't remember, I thought for sure she was going to marry him, but the heart proved it's stronger than the brain, and even though she couldn't explain it, she knew the feelings were gone.

But even knowing that, she still needs time because I don't want to be her rebound. If I have it my way, I'm going to be her goddamn forever. I can see the way she's eyeing me with interest. Earlier in the room, I'm almost positive a part of her was hoping I would kiss her. Because that heart… it knows what she doesn't remember. That it opened up and let me in. I have a long way to go, but I'm okay with that. I've always been a hard worker. And having her here with me, just the two of us alone, will make it that much easier to show her that I'm the one for her.

I meant what I said. Those other guys didn't know how to handle Kendall, and none of them have what we have… what we've been slowly building for the past couple years—friendship. Kendall's going to be mine, but I have to walk before I can run. She's like a scared doe, and I have to approach her slowly, carefully, so she doesn't flee. And I will.

Which is why, even though I meant what I said—that if she were mine, I'd make sure she never had a reason to run—I shouldn't have said it out loud. The last thing I need or want is for her to get spooked and take off. Which is why I didn't kiss her earlier in the room. She might've wanted it, but once it happened, there'd be a damn good chance she'd freak out and run. And one kiss isn't worth the risk of her running.

"It's hot as hell out here," I say, standing. "I think we need to cool off." Before she can process where I'm going with this, I'm scooping her up and throwing her over my shoulder—her hat flying off her head and hitting the ground—then stalking toward the pool.

It takes her a second, but once all the dots connect, she shrieks, "Declan! No!"

"Shh, Kendall, don't yell." I give her luscious ass a quick smack. "We don't want to draw attention to ourselves."

At the edge of the pool, I slide her off my shoulder, ready to throw her in, but somehow, before I can complete the action, she clings to me. Her arms and legs wrap around me like a damn octopus, and instead of her going in, and me laughing, we both crash into the pool.

As we plunge into the water, she holds on to me, and when I come up for air, she's still wrapped around me, our bodies flush against one another.

"I can't believe you just did that!" She throws her head back with a laugh that rings out in the otherwise quiet area.

"That wasn't how it was supposed to go down." I mock glare, swimming us over to a private part of the pool tucked away in the corner with a large cluster of rocks. I push her against the wall, and even though she's holding me, I bring my hand down to grab her ass as if I'm holding her up.

With my other hand, I swipe a wet lock of hair from out of her eyes, tucking it behind her ear so I can get a good look at her face. It's free of all makeup—she must've taken it off while she was changing—showing off her sexy as hell freckles that are dotted across her nose. In the sunlight, her eyes are extra bright and filled with mirth. And her lips, full and pouty, are curved into a gorgeous grin.

"You look beautiful like this," I admit, unable to control the words spilling from my lips.

"Like a wet dog?" She laughs.

"Nah, you look… happy, carefree. I haven't seen you like this since—" I cut off my words, stopping myself just before I say *the night we spent together.*

"Since when?" she prompts.

"Since before the accident."

She nods even though she doesn't fully understand since she doesn't remember. "I feel different. I've been so frustrated lately, like someone trying to fit a square into a circle. I kept searching for the right size, trying other shapes, but this morning, I said fuck it and threw it all in the trash, realizing it didn't matter, and now, it feels like I'm free."

Kendall's legs tighten around my waist, and her center grinds against my crotch. Not wanting her to feel the hard-on that's undoubtedly to come, I back up and release her, thankful when she lets me.

"Wanna race?" I nod toward the other side of the pool.

"Sure." A small smile tugs at her lips, but I don't suspect she's up to anything until I count to three, thinking she's going to take off next to me, and she instead jumps onto my back.

"Giddyup!" she jokes, squeezing my sides and tugging on my hair like I'm a damn horse. "Let's go!"

"Keep it up, and I'm going to buck you off like a bull," I warn.

"Ha! What you don't know is, I've ridden one before and almost lasted the full time." She tightens her hold on me, and I twist around, determined to send her flying. When she doesn't budge, I hold my breath, submerging my body in the water to make her let go and swim to the surface.

Of course, her crazy ass never does what I expect, and she stays on while I swim from one side of the pool to the other. When I come up for air, she's still holding on for dear life.

"Better try harder than that to…" Her words trail off, followed by a gasp. "'Drunk on Your Love.'"

*Fuck. My tattoo…*

In her shock, she releases her hold on me, so I'm able to pry her from my back, but instead of getting off me, she slides around to my front, encircling her legs around me once again while she looks me dead in the eyes.

"You," she breathes. "You tattooed the title of our song on your body."

Since she didn't ask a question, I don't say anything.

"You don't have tattoos. All the guys have tattoos, but you always said…" She swallows thickly. "You said you wouldn't get one until there was one worth getting."

She still hasn't asked me anything, so I keep my mouth shut.

"Declan, say something."

"What do you want me to say?"

"Tell me why."

"It was worth getting."

"Why?"

I told myself I would wait and take it slow, but I'm not going to lie to her. Not when she's asking me a direct question. "Because the song means something to me."

"It's about two people falling in love…"

"It is."

"Are you… in love with someone?" she asks softly.

"I am," I admit truthfully.

Her eyes turn sad. "I didn't know." She shakes her head. "Do I know her? Is that why we wrote the song? For her?" Her brow furrows together in confusion, and for a second, I wonder what the hell she's talking about because everyone knows I haven't dated anyone in a long time. And in the past year, the only person I've hung out with is Kendall, but then I remember… *she* doesn't *remember*. She's heard the song, so she knows we wrote it. She can remember us writing the beginning of it, but she doesn't remember us writing the entire song together. She doesn't remember that when I wrote my verse, she was sitting across from me, smiling softly as I scribbled across the paper with only my feelings for her in mind. And even if she did remember, I never actually told her that every word I wrote and sang was about her.

She tries to scramble away, but I grip the curves of her hips, holding her to me. "There's no one else," I say, looking her in the eye. "There's only you."

Her eyes go wide. "Me?" she squeaks out.

"Yeah. Just you. Every word was written for you. There's only ever been you. You're the only person I see."

"You wrote that song for me?"

"*We* wrote that song together," I remind her. "You wrote about falling in love for the first time, and I wrote about falling in love with you."

"I…" She releases a harsh breath, and since I'm not ready to handle her rejection—where she tells me she had no idea, doesn't feel the same way, and only considers me a friend—I speak first.

"You don't need to say anything. It was a while ago, before you were engaged."

"Okay, but—"

"Please… Just drop it." The last thing I want is for our trip to be cut short because of this. I finally have her all to myself and a chance to show her what it would be like to be with me, but I can't do that if I send her running scared. I never should've taken my shirt off. I wasn't thinking.

I stare at her, silently begging for her not to reject me, not to cut me off before I've even been given a damn shot. I don't know what she sees when she looks at me, what's going through her head, but after several seconds, she sighs and nods. "Okay, it's dropped."

"Good. Because I'm starved. What do you say we eat and then head down to the beach?"

"Sounds good." I don't miss the way the corner of her lips tips downward slightly before she plasters on a fake smile.

"Hey," I say, feeling like something needs to be said before the trip is ruined, thanks to my damn tattoo and admission. "We're friends. We've been friends for years. Yes, I have feelings for you, but until you saw the tattoo, you had no idea. I promise I'm not going to attack you or anything. I know you just ended your engagement, and you're not looking to start anything new. I just want to have a good time and enjoy your company while you're here. Okay?"

She opens her mouth as if she wants to say something, and I internally flinch, hoping she isn't about to tell me she's out of here. But, after a few seconds, she simply nods in understanding before walking past me and up the pool steps. I stay where I am for several beats, watching as she saunters out of the pool, looking like a fucking wet dream as water slews down her tanned, toned body. My eyes land on her pert ass, which is barely covered by the scrap of material someone deemed to call a bathing suit, torn between enjoying the show and wanting to demand she cover her ass up—literally.

In the end, I tamper down the caveman in me and simply enjoy watching the woman in front of me own her beauty while mentally planning how to make every inch of her mine.

# Thirteen

## Kendall



WE'RE FRIENDS.

*I just ended an engagement.*
*He's my brother's best friend.*
*I suck at relationships.*

I keep repeating those four facts in my head every time I think about what it would be like to be with Declan, to get lost in him. When my brain goes haywire and tries to imagine how it would feel to be kissed by him, for him to be inside me. When I remember his confession—that he wrote his part of "Drunk on Your Love" for me… that he has feelings for me, it damn near throws those four truths out the window.

Since the night we talked all those years ago, I've thought about him. His words of wisdom—that we're all a little broken— took seed in my heart and have remained there, growing and flourishing, reminding me that it's okay if I'm a little broken. We've become closer the past couple of years, but I never allowed myself to go there… until now. Because now that he's confessed to having feelings for me, I can't stop thinking about him.

It's been several days since he told me he has feelings for me yet has no intention of acting on them. Every second of every freaking day has been spent with me thinking about him, watching him, and paying attention to every little detail regarding him.

Like when he wakes up, he walks out of his room all sleepy, his hair thrown into a sexy as hell messy knot, sporting no shirt and gray sweats—yep, motherfucking sweatpants—with his hand scrubbing his chest and abs lazily. I'm already awake, reading or writing on the couch. He glances my way with a sleepy smile and goes straight to the phone to order room service, his voice raspy in that sexy way from just waking up. He looks over at me when he's ordering to silently confirm I still want the same thing—coffee and French toast—and when I nod, he'll jerk his chin up in response, lifting his hand to his face and scrubbing his scruffy face that he hasn't shaved since the day we took off out of town.

Or when we're hanging out by the pool and beach and he goes into the water to cool off, swimming laps from one side to the other, his taut muscles flex in a way that reminds me of how strong he is—strong enough to pick me up and carry me like I weigh nothing.

And don't get me started on how well he knows me. It's clear that even though my paying attention to him is new, he's been watching me for a while. He knows how I like my coffee and what foods I love and hate. He knows I like a glass of wine at dinner and which ones are my favorites. He always orders dessert, knowing I won't do it but secretly want it, and shares it with me.

Every evening, after we both shower and are settled in for the night, we sit on the balcony together, writing and discussing music and life. I've written several songs for my next album, and he's written quite a few that he's said he wants to show the guys once he's back. He's worried about Gage since he still won't accept any of the guys' phone calls, and he's scared the band might not recover. For him, it's not about the money but the friendship. They've drifted, and he's not sure they will ever be the same.

Once I've had enough, yawning in exhaustion, we move inside and watch reruns of *The Vampire Diaries*. At first, Declan complained, but now he's as obsessed with the show as I am, wanting to know when Elena will finally figure out that Stefan is a vampire—which he only knows because he tricked me into telling him.

*We're friends.*

*I just ended an engagement.*

*He's my brother's best friend.*

*I suck at relationships.*

I chant the words again. I'm chanting them in my head as I watch Declan stalk out of the water with his board tucked under his arm, droplets of salt water sliding down his chest, with a huge grin on his face because he totally rode the hell out of the waves. I had no idea he could surf, but it makes sense since the guys spent several years living near the Pacific Ocean. I also had no idea how hot watching him surf would be.

"Damn, I'm beat," he says, planting the board into the sand and then dropping down next to me. Drops of cold water hit my warm flesh, causing me to jump and, in turn, make Declan laugh. Since he thinks he's hilarious, he shakes his hair like a wet dog and soaks my face and body.

"Stop!" I shriek, trying to get away from the water, which only has him laughing and shaking his hair and face harder. "Dec, I'm serious!" I try to push him away, but he grabs my wrist, and we both tumble over, his hard body landing on top of mine. For a second, our eyes lock, our faces so close all it would take is one of us to move forward slightly, and our lips would touch, but before I can contemplate if I'm brave enough to make the move, he backs up as if he's been burned, breaking the moment.

"I was thinking since it's our last night here, we could go check out the boardwalk," he suggests. "I know how much you love those carnival rides and games."

Of course, he knows because he knows everything about me. "And we can go on the Ferris wheel?" It's my favorite ride, and nobody ever wants to go with me because of how high up it is.

"Maybe…if you ask nicely." He winks, and holy hell, my lady parts tingle, wanting to know what else he'll give me if I simply ask nicely.

As if he can sense my thoughts, his eyes hood over slightly before he clears his throat and moves back slightly farther.

"So where are we going next?" I ask, not wanting it to get awkward. We haven't discussed anything other than whatever we're doing at the moment.

"It's a secret."

"What? Why?" I sit up. "Am I not part of this trip." I pout.

"You're a guest on this trip." He taps my nose playfully. "I'm in control, here. You're just along for the ride." His lips quirk into a sexy smirk, and I laugh, slapping his stomach, which hurts my hand more than it hurts him.

"Can I at least get a hint?"

"Nope." He rolls over onto his stomach and closes his eyes. "I'm going to take a nap. Wake me when you're ready to head up to the room to shower."

A few minutes later, he's snoring softly. I watch him sleep, wondering how much longer I'm going to be able to last without jumping his bones. Several times, I've considered making up an excuse to leave before I do something stupid like kiss him or, worse, have sex with him, but I can't bring myself to do it.

My phone pings with a text, and when I check it, I see it's my dad: **Hey K, just wanted to check in. I've been discussing your upcoming album with the team, and I think Drunk on Your Love would be perfect to promo the new album. I was thinking we could make it your first single. I know you're away and so is Declan, but I'd like to get the details sorted so we can get the ball rolling. Any chance you know when you'll be back? We'll need you here to finalize the song, make the video, and shoot the promo ads.**

I think about the best way to respond. On the one hand, I should admit I'm with Declan because otherwise, it's as if I'm lying by omission, but that will lead to questions I don't have the answers to, so instead, I snap a picture of the beach and go with vague: **Hey! I'm so glad you want to make it the first single. It might be my favorite yet. I'm good. Enjoying the sun. I'm not sure when I'll be back, but I'll ask Declan what his plans are, so we can figure it out. I've been writing a lot, and I think several songs will be perfect for the next album. I'd like to take it in a different direction. I was thinking I could call it: Falling.**

I hit send before I second-guess myself. I knew the title the second it came to me, but I know it will lead to questions… ones I'm not sure I'm ready to face yet.

Of course, my dad catches on and asks the hard question: **Falling… as in falling in love?**

And because I can't lie…

**Me: Yes, it's what I hope to do one day. Fall in love.**

You didn't really think I was about to admit I'm in love with Declan, did you? That would be crazy, right? No, I'm not in love with Declan. It's too soon for that, but as I watch him sleep, his lids fluttering every now and then and his full lips parted slightly, I can't help but admit to myself that, no, I'm not in love with

Declan, but for the first time in my life, I'm falling… hard. And it scares the hell out of me.

My phone pings with a new text from my dad: **You will, sweetheart. One day, you'll find the right guy, and you'll feel it. Your heart will beat a little faster, your smiles will get brighter, and butterflies will swarm your belly. And you'll know every wrong guy was simply leading you to the right one.**

As I read his words, I think about the past several days and how every action he mentioned I've experienced with Declan. From my heart picking up speed, to smiling and laughing more, to freaking butterflies attacking my belly—they all seem to happen more often when I'm around Declan.

I don't realize tears are leaking from my lids until Declan, who I didn't realize had woken up, asks, "What's wrong?" He goes from being asleep to wide awake, his features expressing his worry. He edges closer, and his thumb swipes across my cheek. "Kendall, talk to me."

"I…" I choke out. "I think…"

His brows dip in confusion. "You think what? Did something happen?" He glances at the phone in my hand. "Did Kyle text you?"

"No," I breathe. "I think…" *I think I have feelings for you.* I say the words in my head, but I can't make them come out because I'm a damn chicken. "I think I made the right decision by not marrying Kyle," I say instead.

Declan looks at me like I'm crazy for a moment, then he nods. "Yeah, I agree." He wipes another tear. "But why are you crying?"

Because I can't say what I really want to say, I give him a different truth. "I'm naming my next album *Falling*."

"*Falling*?" he repeats.

"Yeah, like falling in love. I've been doing a lot of soul-searching for the past few weeks, and I realized I said yes to Kyle because I didn't want to be alone. I wanted to prove I wasn't broken, so I went along with it when he proposed.

"Everyone in my family is in perfect love-filled relationships. And I wanted that... I *want* that. But Kyle wasn't the right guy, and coming to terms with that made me a bit emotional." *I'm also now realizing what it feels like to fall for someone, and the difference is like night and day.*

Declan smiles softly and tucks a wayward strand of hair behind my ear. "You just haven't found the one yet, but all the pieces will fit together perfectly when you do."

"I know that now. I think that's why the songs I've been writing recently all have a different vibe to them." Because every one of them is about how I'm slowly falling in love with the man lying in front of me.

"And those songs are amazing," he says. "*Falling* is the perfect title for your album, and I have no doubt it will be your best yet."

"It's so different...What if my fans don't like it?"

"They'll love it because every song you've written has come straight from your heart. I've watched you every night, putting your heart and soul into every one of those lyrics. They'll see that. See that you're evolving and growing, and they'll love that you're sharing your innermost thoughts with them. You've allowed them in, opened up every part of your life to them, which isn't something many people do."

"You're right," I agree, then change the subject, not wanting to risk blurting out that every song I've written lately has been with him in mind. "Speaking of which... my dad texted me. He wants to know when we'll be back so he can get things scheduled for the video and promo for 'Drunk on Your Love.' He wants to release it soon as a single and preview for my next album."

"You told your dad you're with me?"

"Well, no… I told him I'd speak to you, but he doesn't know that means in person instead of over the phone."

His lips tip down, but he quickly hides his displeasure. "I'm down for whatever. Since the band is on hiatus for the foreseeable future, my calendar's wide open."

"Well, not *completely* wide open," I say, shifting closer to him. "Right now, our calendars are marked as busy."

My eyes meet his before they dart to his mouth, wanting to kiss him, wanting him to kiss me. It would be a horrible idea to cross that invisible line. It doesn't matter that I'm falling for him. It would be irresponsible and selfish to act on my feelings. He's connected to my family, and with my track record, the chances of us working out are—

"Tell me what you're thinking about."

"How much I want to kiss you," I blurt out. "And how stupid I would be if I did."

He edges closer. "And why would that make you stupid?"

"The obvious reasons," I whisper. "I was just engaged…"

"And you said you never loved him." He sets his hand on my hip and squeezes softly. "Problem solved."

"You're best friends with my brother," I argue. "What if this ends badly?"

"You're worried about it ending"—he rounds his hand to my butt and pulls me closer, so our faces are only inches away from one another—"and nothing has even started."

He's right, but… "I suck at relationships."

He quirks a brow. "Who said anything about a relationship? I thought you just wanted to kiss me."

"I do, but—"

"Then kiss me," he says slowly. His lips are so close that all I'd have to do is lean in a little bit, and our mouths would connect. I want to, so damn badly, but I'm scared.

"What if—?"

"Kiss. Me." His warm breath carries a hint of the whiskey he's been sipping all day, and I wonder if he tastes how he smells.

He shrugs, his hand leaving my butt. His face starts to move backward, and I realize he's going to back away. The thought of losing my chance and not finding out what he tastes like, feels like, has me reaching over, gripping his neck, and pulling him toward me for a kiss.

Our mouths connect softly at first, our lips brushing against one another. I take his bottom lip between my teeth and suck on it gently, wanting to taste him, feel him. He groans, and the sound makes me gasp. He uses my action to slip his tongue past my parted lips, and in slow, methodical movements, his tongue caresses my own. He tastes perfect, sweet with a hint of spice, and something flashes in my head as if I've tasted him before. That can't be right since we've never kissed, but maybe it's because, unlike most first kisses, which can be awkward, kissing Declan is as easy as breathing.

When my tongue tangles with his, he sucks it into his mouth, deepening the kiss. As if his mouth is connected to an electric current, with every curve of his lips and every swipe of his tongue, my body is hit with the most delicious shock to my system, which goes straight to my belly, tightening my insides and then descending to the area between my legs. One kiss with Declan and my entire body is affected in the best damn way.

He ends the kiss, pulling back slightly, and I sigh at the loss of the connection, wanting to kiss him again. Wanting to strip him of his clothes and explore the rest of him. Wanting him to explore me.

"Did you feel that?" he asks, his lips brushing against mine.

"Feel what?"

"The connection… like your mouth was made for kissing mine."

*Yes, I felt it…* "Dec… I don't think—"

"No, don't think. Just feel."

And before I can argue, his mouth is back on mine, making me do nothing but just that…feel.

# Fourteen

## Declan

FUCK, THAT KISS. HER LIPS, HER TONGUE, THE WAY OUR MOUTHS MOVED IN PERFECT rhythm. Everything about her is addicting. Her taste, her scent. I want more. No, I *need* more. The last time I had her in my grasp, she slipped through the cracks. But not again. I can't go another month without kissing her, touching her.

Everything I tell myself, every decision I come to, I contradict. Since the day she showed up at the bar, and we spent the night together, I haven't been able to think straight. I keep telling myself to stand down, take a step back, and take it slow, but I can't help myself when I'm with her. I want her in every way possible.

So fuck it. I'm done trying to stay away. She's here, and it's clear she wants me, but she's scared. She has a dozen reasons we shouldn't jump, so my new plan is to show her how good it can feel to fly. No promises and no talk of the future. Once she sees how good we are together, she'll get on board. The risk will be worth the reward. She just has to feel it for herself. And she will. We have only kissed once, and I can see it written all over her face.

She wants more. And I'm going to give it to her. Right after I tell her the truth about us…

"We need to talk."

She places her perfectly manicured fingers over my lips. "No." She shakes her head. "Nothing good ever comes from someone saying, 'We need to talk.' And I am not about to let you ruin that kiss. So for now, no talking. Please."

Her big blue eyes plead with me, and maybe it's because I can't say no to her, or because the last thing I want to do is ruin the moment or… maybe it's because I'm scared as fuck that once I tell her about our night together, everything will change, but whatever the reason, I nod back, agreeing not to say what I was going to say.

"Thank you," she says, leaning in and swiping her tongue along the seam of my lips. "Now where were we?" Her mouth curves around mine, and that's all it takes for all thought to fly out the window. *Later*, I tell myself. *I'll tell her later.*

"THIS IS SO AWESOME," KENDALL SAYS, HER FACE LIGHTING UP AS SHE TAKES IN THE scene. As it turned out, the boardwalk is hosting a wine festival this week, so on top of us checking out the rides, games, and shops during our last night here, we'll also be tasting wine. Kendall couldn't be more in heaven.

She threads her fingers through mine and drags me over to the booth, where we purchase wineglasses to use during our wine walk. We spend the next hour going from booth to booth, learning from the different vendors about the types of wines they make: cabernet sauvignon, merlot, pinot noir… They all taste different, but I couldn't tell you which one is what. Kendall, on the other hand, discusses the various flavors and notes that she tastes in each sip, purchasing a few of the bottles of the ones she loves. So she doesn't have to carry them, they offer to leave them at the main booth with her info on them.

By the time we reach the end, she's tipsy from all the wine she drank, and she's smiling and laughing, looking so carefree and happy. Music plays from the speakers surrounding us, and when a song she loves comes on, she wraps her arms around my neck and says, "Dance with me, Dec."

It doesn't matter that we're in the middle of a busy boardwalk with people all around us, or that someone might spot us—despite me wearing a baseball cap and her wearing an adorable floppy hat—I pull her close and sway to the music. The song picks up, and I take her hand, spinning her out and then back into my arms. She throws her head back, laughing, as I dip her low and then bring her back up, tugging her body flush against mine.

We haven't discussed the earlier mini make-out session, so I'm sticking with my plan of taking action—showing her how good we are together. And I do just that by dipping her again and, when I bring her up, connecting our mouths in a searing kiss that I know takes her breath away. She gasps at first, then moans when I gently curl my tongue around hers.

"Dec," she breathes against my lips, her lids fluttering open, and her azure eyes looking at me with *more.*

I give her one more chaste kiss before I pull back and wrap my arm around her shoulders, tucking her into my side. "What do you say we go check out the rides and games?"

We spend the next couple of hours playing the overpriced games—I win her a stuffed unicorn and a goldfish we give to a kid who squeals in excitement while the parent glares—then go on several rides, including the Ferris wheel, where I make it a point to kiss her at the top. I'm shocked when she pulls out her phone and takes several pictures of us: smiling, cheesing, making crazy faces, and the last one… us kissing.

Afterward, we grab a couple of hot dogs, candy apples, and cheese fries at a local vendor and chow down while Kendall begs me to tell her where we're going next, and I refuse.

"Pretend it's a wrapped present for your birthday," I joke, making her pout.

"Don't remind me how old I am. We're going to pretend I'm turning twenty-five all over again."

"Pretend all you want." I shrug. "But you're still the sexiest almost thirty-two-year-old I know, and I'm not telling you where we're going because it's a birthday surprise."

I end my statement with a kiss, and she drops it.

Once we've experienced all the boardwalk has to offer, we stop by the wine booth to grab her bottles and then head back to the room. We shower—separately—and then crawl into bed to watch another episode of *The Vampire Diaries*. The suite has two bedrooms, but we've been sharing a bed since the first night and falling asleep while watching the show. Tonight, though, Kendall changes things up a bit, and instead of staying on her side, she lays her head on my chest, snuggling up to my body. I wrap my arm around her, feathering my fingers up and down her back, and within minutes, she's passed out, with me following shortly after.

"YOU'RE SERIOUSLY NOT GOING TO GIVE ME A SINGLE CLUE?" KENDALL POUTS FROM THE passenger seat of the vehicle. We've been driving on and off for almost twelve hours, and I swear she's asked this same question every hour.

"I'm seriously not," I say for the millionth time as I get off the highway. "What part of birthday surprise don't you understand? Besides, we're almost there." My original plan was to stop in North Carolina before heading to Florida, but when Kendall jumped on board, and I learned about her secret obsession with a certain show, my plans changed—and the fact that tomorrow is her birthday is the icing on the cake.

"We're almost there?" She looks around, trying to find a clue, but unless she knows what she's looking for, she won't get it. "What's in Covington?" she asks, scrunching her adorable, freckle-covered nose up in confusion when she spots the sign.

"You'll see."

We drive down a winding road leading to a bed and breakfast where I had to pull major strings to get a reservation. When we pull around and park, she still has no idea, but when we grab our bags—we went shopping while in Jersey and bought her some actual clothes—and walk around to the front, she eyes it curiously.

"This looks so familiar," she says, looking around. "It's beautiful." The bed and breakfast is a three-story colonial-style Southern mansion, complete with a second-story balcony, black shutters, massive, old-style pillars, and a wraparound porch.

"I'm surprised you don't recognize it." I pull out my phone and click on an image, then turn it around so she can see it. The moment she recognizes where we are, her eyes go wide, and she screeches so loud my ears ring.

"This is from *The Vampire Diaries*? Are you freaking serious?" She steps back and takes the mansion in with new eyes. "Oh, my God, Dec! This is the Lockwood mansion from 1864!" She walks over to the right side of the mansion. "This is where Damon and

Katherine walk and…" She rushes up the stairs and swings the door open, stopping in her tracks. "Oh, wow," she breathes. "This is where Stefan and Katherine danced. This is amazing." She turns around and jumps into my arms, wrapping her legs around my waist as she plants a kiss on my lips. "Thank you for bringing me here. This is the best birthday present ever!"

"Then you're going to love what I have in store for tomorrow." I grip the bottom of her thighs to hold her up, not giving a shit that we're standing in the middle of the foyer of a bed and breakfast, where other people are walking around.

"Better than staying where they filmed several scenes of *The Vampire Diaries*?"

"Yep."

"Tell me!" She encircles her arms around my neck and forces my face closer to hers. "Please."

"It's another birthday surprise." I kiss the tip of her nose and then set her down.

After getting checked in, we bring our stuff up to our room, which has Kendall freaking out since it was the Salvatore brothers' study. With floor-to-ceiling mahogany bookshelves surrounding a working fireplace, a queen-sized antique bed, and—according to the brochure—original tile, tub, and shower, it feels as if we've stepped back into the 1800s. Since it's getting late, we head out and walk around the property, checking out all the areas they used for filming. Because Kendall is obsessed with the show and has seen every episode no less than a half-dozen times, she tells me about each scene without giving away too many spoilers.

Once we've covered every square inch that we're allowed to see and explore, we go back up to our room to get ready for bed. Kendall showers first, and once I'm showered, I find her lying in bed, typing away on her phone.

"Whatcha doing?" I ask, climbing into bed next to her.

"Sending my mom pictures of the mansion. She's so jealous I'm here. Did you know they do—" Her hands still, and her head pops up to look at me. "Declan… Did you get us Vampire Diary tour tickets?"

Whatever facial expression I make must give me away because a second later, she releases a loud squeal, drops her phone, and then tackles me. "Did you?"

"It was supposed to be a surprise," I mutter. "You suck."

"I can't believe it! This is seriously the best birthday ever!" Straddling my torso, she leans down to kiss me. At first, the kiss is soft, a silent thank-you, but it quickly heats when her tongue slips into my mouth. As we kiss, she grinds her center—which I realize quickly is only covered by the barely-there material of her underwear—back and forth along my dick. It perks up, not having been given any proper attention in over a month, and I groan, knowing as much as I want to sink inside Kendall's warm, tight as fuck pussy, I can't. It's too soon. It's one thing to kiss her and show her how I feel about her, but it's another thing to have sex with her less than a week after she ended her engagement. I don't know the rule of how long I should wait, but it's got to be more than a week, right?

So I'm not tempted to say *fuck it* and fuck her, I flip us over to put her under me. She wraps her legs around my waist and pulls on the hair tie holding my hair up, making it fall and create a curtain around us as I kiss my way down her neck, peppering kisses along her exposed collarbone and shoulder. When she uses the heels of her feet to force me closer, I stop kissing her flesh and sit up.

"Why don't we watch an episode of *The Vampire Diaries*?" I suggest. There isn't a television in the room, but I have my laptop, and right now, I need a damn distraction before I'm balls deep in her.

Her brow furrows in confusion. "You want to watch TV?"

Taking her feet, I untangle her legs from around me, then drop onto my side next to her. I lift her leg over my thigh so we're still partially connected.

"Do I want to? Fuck no," I admit truthfully. "But you only just walked away from your fiancé…and"—I look her in the eyes, so she knows how serious I am—"I don't want to be your rebound."

"Dec…" She sighs, and my heart drops, knowing from her tone that whatever she's about to say isn't going to be in my favor. "I want you… I'm attracted to you, and even though I can't remember the past couple of months, I feel something between us. I wouldn't have written a song like 'Drunk on Your Love' with just anyone. But we can't ever be anything more than friends."

"Because you don't think you're capable of more?"

"Because you're best friends with my brother, close to my family, and when I mess it all up, they'll be forced to choose sides, and while you're like family, I *am* family, which means they'll choose me… even though I won't deserve it."

"So what is it you want?" I ask, already knowing the answer but hoping I'm wrong.

"Well…" She shrugs, and her cheeks tinge pink. "I was thinking while we're on this trip we could… you know…" She smiles shyly.

"We could what?" I push, wanting to hear the words.

She huffs. "We could have fun."

"We are having fun." Yeah, I'm giving her a hard time—I'm not about to make this easy on her.

"You know what I mean." She slaps my chest playfully. "I like you, and as I said, I'm attracted to you, but I can't be who you want me to be. You're Mr. Perfect, Mr. Romantic. Everyone knows that. Even the women you've dumped have nothing but nice things to say about you. But I'm just not capable of more, and I don't want to lead you on. So if you don't want to have fun while on this trip, I completely get it, but if you do, I'm down. But that's all it can be… fun."

Fuck, this woman. I don't get it. She's gorgeous, rich, and has the most amazing voice. She's the music industry's pop princess, not just because of all that but because she's also sweet and sexy and funny. She's the spokesperson for several charities that focus on various issues like domestic abuse and music education. She's a hands-on aunt with her brother's kids and a wonderful older sister to her siblings.

She might be flaky and all over the place, but if anyone needs her, she's there and would do anything for anyone. I've literally watched her take the jacket off her back and give it to a woman who was freezing on the streets of LA during a cold night without thinking twice.

But beneath the surface, she has such low self-esteem and thinks so little of herself. She has it stuck in her head that since she hasn't met the right guy yet, it means something is wrong with her. She doesn't see what everyone sees. She doesn't understand how goddamn lovable she is. And I'm going to make it my mission to show her, but in order to do that, I need time with her. If I push the whole making her mine thing, telling her I want her forever, she's going to run. It's what she does. This means I will have to go along with what she *thinks* she wants… for now. Give her, her fun while showing her how amazing we'll be together. And hope, when we return to New York, it's enough for her to give us a real chance.

"Okay." I say what she needs to hear. "We'll do it your way."

"Really? You're okay with just having fun?" she asks speculatively.

I grip the curve of her hip and pull her over to me. "Yep." I press a chaste kiss to her soft lips. "But I still think we should wait a little bit. We have our entire trip ahead of us, and you did just get out of a relationship… Besides, half the fun is the foreplay." I shoot her a playful wink that has a shy smile stretching across her face.

"Just so you know," she says, hooking her arm around me and kissing my neck. "Kyle and I never had sex once after I woke up in the hospital."

I pull back slightly. "What?"

"It felt wrong. I knew he wasn't the one for me. He tried a couple of times to start things, but I pushed him away. I don't remember the last time we had sex since I can't remember anything before waking up, but it was before my accident."

If that's true, that means I'm the last person she had sex with. Knowing that—despite her being engaged to another man and almost marrying him—I was the last man she was with sexually has me smiling on the inside. And if I have it my way, I'll be the last damn guy she's with.

# Fifteen

## Kendall

"ARE YOU FREAKING SERIOUS?" I WHISPER-SHOUT AS WE WALK INTO *THE VAMPIRE DIARIES* museum to check in with the tour guide. "It's just us?"

"You wanted to make sure we're off the radar, and the only way to ensure that is to make sure no one is around us long enough to recognize us." Declan shrugs. "So I paid for a private tour."

"I take it back. Yesterday wasn't the best day ever… Today is!" I encircle my arms around his neck and my legs around his waist and kiss him hard, not giving a shit who's around. So far, nobody has recognized us—aside from someone our first day in Jersey, but we took off before it could be confirmed—and I might be getting lazy, letting my guard down, but I just don't have it in me to care. I'm having the best time on this trip, and if someone finds out, I can just tell everyone that Declan and I are on this road trip as friends, which would be the truth since he understands I can't give him any more and has agreed to just having fun on the trip and keeping complications like commitment out of it.

We didn't have sex last night, the mood a bit ruined by the

talk about my ex and such, but we did make out, which was hot as hell, and then we watched another couple of episodes of *TVD* before falling asleep. Tonight, I hope Declan will give in, but if he needs more time, I'm okay with that too. As he mentioned, we have an entire trip ahead of us.

"Hi, are you Johnny and June?" a woman asks. Declan nods and sets me on my feet, taking my hand in his. "Yes, ma'am."

I side-eye him in confusion, wondering who the hell he's talking about, but I don't comment until we're checked in and on the golf cart, ready to get the tour underway.

"Johnny and June?"

"Yeah, I gave her different names so she wouldn't put two and two together." Ah, duh. Makes sense, but… "Who's Johnny and—" And then it hits me. "Johnny Cash and June Carter?"

He grins and nods while I think about the fact that he picked names of one of the most iconic couples in the music industry. I can't think too long, though, because a minute later, Tonya, our personal tour guide, is taking off and telling us all the fun facts about *The Vampire Diaries*.

We spend the next few hours touring the area. We get to take pictures where Damon and Elena shared a kiss in the pouring rain—and I totally have Tonya take a picture of us recreating the scene, minus the rain.

We stop and take more pictures in front of Elena's and Caroline's house, and then do a walk-through of the Lockwood mansion, where I make Declan recreate the image of Caroline and Klaus drinking champagne on the bench while on their date—yes, we totally stopped and bought champagne and glasses because I'm extra like that. I had no idea that scene was filmed in the backyard of the Lockwood mansion! Declan hasn't met Klaus yet, but he doesn't care.

He goes along with everything I want, acting like he's having as much fun as I am. Our last stop is in the town center, where we get pictures with the famous clock tower and in front of the Mystic Grill. While we're there, Declan tells me we'll be having lunch there later, and I damn near pass out.

Once we're back where we started, we thank Tonya and then head back to town. There's a cute little store that sells everything *TVD*, and I swear I buy everything in sight—from blood bags to a diary that looks just like Elena's. We even buy and put on matching Mystic Falls hoodies and hats.

After we take several more pictures, I send a bunch to my mom since it's her favorite show as well, telling her we're coming back soon and she's going to love it here.

**Mom: I love these! You're with Declan?**

Huh? What? Oh, shit! In my excitement, I included pictures of Declan with me.

**Me: Please don't say anything to anyone. We're just friends. Nothing is going on. I needed to get away, and he was already going away. He surprised me with a trip here for my birthday.**

**Mom: I'm not judging, and I'll keep it to myself. Declan is a good man, and I'm glad you're with him. At least now I know you're safe and not alone on your birthday.**

**Me: Thank you, and yes, I am. Love you!**

**Mom: Love you more. Have a wonderful birthday. When you get back, we're having a belated birthday spa day.**

**Me: Sounds good!**

"My mom knows I'm with you." Declan's brows rise to his forehead. "I sent her pictures with you in them by mistake. She promised not to tell anyone. She's glad I'm with you. It makes her feel better, knowing I'm not alone, especially on my birthday." I'm sure she'll tell my dad since she doesn't keep secrets from him, but she'll make sure he doesn't say anything to anyone.

Declan nods in understanding, then changes the subject. "You ready to go have lunch at the Mystic Grill?"

"Hell yes!"

"OH, JEEZ... SERIOUSLY?" I SCROLL THROUGH THE COMMENTS, WISHING I NEVER WOULD'VE opened the app in the first place. I knew what would be waiting for me, but no matter how thick of skin I have, I'm never fully prepared for the nastiness that is social media.

Like an idiot, I read a particularly hurtful comment and choke up, letting my emotions get the better of me. When I glance in the mirror and see my eyes are red and filled with tears threatening to spill over, I swipe out of the app and throw my phone onto the counter, not wanting to let that shit ruin the amazing day Declan and I've had.

"What's wrong?" Declan's baritone voice has me spinning around, my hand clutching my chest. "Way to sneak up on a woman." I glare. "Next time, knock."

"Door was open." He shrugs, leaning his shoulder against the doorjamb. "What's wrong?"

"Noth—"

"Nope, try again," he says, not even letting me finish my lie.

"I went on Insta."

"And?"

"And since I haven't made an official announcement about

Kyle and me, he did the honors." I grab my phone and pull the image back up, showing it to Declan. It's a ripped-up picture of our wedding announcement with the caption: *Only give your heart to an ice princess if you want her to jab an ice pick through it.*

"He's an asshole." Declan hands my phone back to me. "And you don't owe anyone an explanation. It's your personal business."

"That I made public by picking the career I did. I need to post something, but I've been putting it off."

"I stand by my previous statement," he says, gripping the curve of one of my hips and pulling me toward him. He plucks the phone out of my hand and holds the side button down until it prompts to turn off, then he swipes it off and drops it back onto the counter. "When you're ready, if you choose to, then you make a post. But you don't owe anyone anything. Just because you sing music doesn't mean you're required to post about every personal detail of your life. The guys and I don't post shit. Aside from the overdose speculation, nobody knows what happened to Gage or where he is. Let them fucking speculate. It just makes them want you even more."

"Guys do that shit, and they're labeled as mysterious. Women do it, and they're frigid bitches."

"Fuck them," he says, lifting me into his arms. I wrap my legs around his waist and hold on as he walks us over to the bed. It's late, close to midnight, and I was in the bathroom taking a shower and getting my pajamas on. We spent the day in Covington, eating ice cream at the local place where the cast of *TVD* used to eat it and having dinner here at the B&B, complete with a cake for my birthday. Afterward, we explored more of the property since we leave first thing tomorrow to head to Oklahoma. For what? I have no idea.

With me in his arms, Declan climbs onto the bed, stopping

once my head gently hits the pillow. "You're so damn beautiful," he says softly, moving several strands of hair out of my face. "And not just on the outside, but on the inside too." He palms my cheek, and instinctually, I lean into his touch. "Anybody who matters knows that you ending the engagement was for a good reason, and anybody who doesn't know that doesn't matter."

I get what he's saying, and I love how he sees me, the way he never judges me. "But—"

"No buts," he says, cutting me off. "I'm tired of listening to you second-guess every damn decision because you don't see yourself the way I do. You're not a frigid bitch or an ice princess. You're a warm, loving woman who almost married a man you weren't in love with because you were *hoping* you'd feel something for him so you wouldn't hurt him. Because you care about others.

"Haven't you listened to your songs? They're about heartbreak, about wanting to fall in love, about not finding the right guy, but you never say anything mean about a single one of them. Every one of them is about you. How you wish they could be who you need them to be. You wish you could be who they want you to be. You're not a bad person, Kendall. You just want to love and be loved."

His words hit the deepest, darkest part of my soul. I both hate and love that he sees beyond the surface, and he understands me on a deeper level. That somehow, along the way, he's been able to clear the fog and see the real me. The woman who, as he just said, wants to love and be loved.

"Dec," I choke out, a lump of emotion clogging my throat. "I want…" I try to think of what I want, what I need, but my head is a mess of emotions, and my heart feels like it's been cracked open.

"Tell me, baby," he says, leaning forward and brushing his lips against mine. "Tell me what you want, and I'll give it to you. Any-fucking-thing."

"I want… to feel…" *Loved* is what I want to say. I want to feel loved. I want someone to make me feel like I'm their everything, be the center of their universe, the way my family has found love. I want someone to look at me with hearts in their eyes and not just want me, Kendall Blackwood, the pop star, but actually want me, the insecure, vulnerable woman who secretly just wants to be loved. To know I'm not broken. But because fear stops me from saying any of this, I go with the next best thing. "I want to feel wanted."

"Done." That is all Declan says before he crashes his lips against mine with such passion it feels as though he's making love to my mouth. Our tongues connect, swirling with one another, tasting, coaxing, devouring. I can't get enough of him. I've been kissed by many guys, but none of them… not a single one… ever made my insides tighten and my heart beat faster the way kissing Declan does.

He breaks the kiss, only to pepper kisses along my jawline and down my neck, suckling on my sensitive flesh. He lifts onto his knees and pulls my shirt over my head, exposing my naked breasts. Then he stops and stares at me, his gaze filled with heat and lust. "You're so fucking beautiful," he says reverently, taking one of my breasts in his hand and pinching my nipple with his thumb and forefinger while he strokes the beaded tip with the pad of his other finger. "So damn perfect."

He dips his head and takes the nipple he's not playing with into his mouth. His tongue swipes the tip, getting it wet, and then he blows on it gently, his cool breath sending shivers down my spine. He does it again and again and then shocks the hell out of me when he bites it *hard*. A zap of pleasure shoots straight to my center, and I lock my legs around his waist, grinding myself against him.

"Fuck, this tattoo." He lifts my arms over my head and pins them against the headboard. "Keep them right there," he demands, giving me a chaste kiss.

"Do you have any idea what this tattoo does to me?" He glances at me for a quick moment before he spreads my legs and slides downward so he's eye level with my tattoo. "*It's okay to be a little broken*," he reads, then kisses the first word inked into my flesh. "Every day, for the rest of our trip, hell, for the rest of our lives if you let me, I'm going to show you how perfectly broken you are," he murmurs, kissing each word. I ignore the *rest of our lives* part, refusing to think about what the idea of spending the rest of my life with Declan does to my insides.

Once he's kissed every part of my tattoo, he licks and nips my flesh as he works his way across my side, planting an open-mouthed kiss to my hip bones.

Taking the waistband of my boy shorts between his fingers, he pulls them off and then takes my foot, kissing the instep softly before he trails more kisses up the inside of my calf and thigh, stopping at the apex of my legs.

"I've dreamed and fantasized about this," he says, sucking his bottom lip into his mouth and releasing it. His tongue darts out, sliding along his lips as if he's about to consume his favorite food, and then he drops onto his stomach, parts my lips, and licks up the center.

"Oh, God." I moan loudly, not expecting him to just dive right in. "Dec…"

"Shh," he murmurs, blowing onto my center. "Just watch, baby." He glances up and licks his lips. "Watch me want the hell out of you." His face disappears between my legs, and a second later, the flat of his tongue is ascending up my middle again. He laps gently, from my hole to my clit, up and down, over and over again. He stops at my clit, flicks it softly, and then goes back to teasing me. My body is hot and needy, and with every flick and lap and lick of his tongue, he works me up higher and higher until I'm dangling off the precipice, begging for him to shove me off the edge.

"You taste so good," he mutters as he shoves a finger and then two inside me, stroking my walls. Between his tongue stroking my clit and his fingers fucking me, I fall off the ledge, getting lost in the strongest orgasm I've ever been given. My body trembles, and my pussy spasms in the most delicious way.

Declan continues his ministrations until I can't take it anymore and push his head away. He glances up at me with a sexy smirk on his face and his lips wet with my juices, and the need to kiss him hits me hard. I sit up and, gripping the back of his neck, run my tongue along his, tasting myself on him, before I press my mouth to his.

"My turn," I murmur, peppering kisses over his stubbled jaw. "I want you."

"And you will have me… soon, but not tonight." He places his hand gently against my chest, forcing me to lie back down. "Tonight is about you."

My eyes widen in a mixture of shock and confusion. He's already made me come. "But…"

"You," he repeats, crawling up my body and kissing me softly on the lips. "Only you."

And holy shit, he does exactly what he said he would do. For the rest of the night, Declan fucking Pierce shows me over and over again just how wanted I am.

# Sixteen

## Declan



She's referring to the two-story, four-thousand-square-foot log cabin I've rented on a lake in Oklahoma. Since Kendall wants to stay under the radar, I figured the best way to have a good time is by spending some time on a lake, where we can go on a boat, go swimming, or relax in the hot tub. There's also a ready-to-use bonfire in the backyard and wraparound porches on the first and second levels. This is the perfect way to go camping without dealing with all the camping shit.

"We have the place for a week, but we can leave whenever we want."

"Let's go see the house!" She squeals in excitement, grabbing her luggage and running up to the front door. I use the code I was given to open the door, and she gasps when we enter. It's identical to the pictures: an open floor plan with hardwood floors, walls, and ceilings. The furniture is rustic, giving the place a luxurious outdoorsy vibe, with a two-story brick fireplace used as the focal point.

"Oh, my God, Dec! Come look at this."

I already know where she is, what has her freaking out, but I join her, loving her excitement. When I find her, she's looking out of the floor-to-ceiling windows that make up the entire back of the house. Since it's late and dark outside, you can't see anything, but in the morning, no matter which room we're in or which floor we're on, nothing will block our view of the backyard and lake.

"I rented a boat for the week as well," I say, stepping behind her and wrapping my arms around her waist. She sighs into me, resting her back and head against my front, her hands landing on mine and threading our fingers together.

Ever since we've agreed to *have fun*, Kendall's allowed herself to let go and not overthink our closeness and connection. It probably also has something to do with the three orgasms I gave her last night. With each one, it felt as though I was cracking the hard exterior that she uses to keep everyone out, exposing little pieces of the softness she keeps hidden underneath. I know it was the oxytocin from the orgasms, but I'll use whatever I have to my advantage to break down her walls.

"That'll be fun." She turns in my arms, leaning against the glass wall. "Thank you for this. For making sure we're not in places where we'll get swarmed. I didn't realize how badly I needed this time away."

I dip my head and kiss the corner of her mouth. "Let's go check out the rest of the place."

"Or…" Her eyes lock with mine as she reaches down and rubs her palm along the front of my pants, waking my dick from its slumber. "We could stay right here, and you can fuck me against this glass wall."

With a smirk, she lifts her hoodie over her head and throws

it to the side. Then she bends slightly and pulls her cotton shorts off and kicks her sandals out of the way. She pushes me back gently, and I'm able to take her in. A royal-blue lace bra barely covers her breasts, her rose-colored nipples showing through the see-through material while the swells of her breasts spill over the tops of her cups. The matching underwear is thin, covering only the important parts, and I have no doubt that her peach of an ass would be on display if she turned around. It makes me want to turn her around and see for myself.

"What are you thinking?" she asks, making me realize I've been staring at her for several long beats.

"How sexy you look like this." I run the tip of my finger along the swell of her breast and down to her nipple. She shivers slightly, and her nipple hardens instantly. "And…" I go with the truth because fuck it, why not? "I was wondering if I turn you around, will I get a view of your perfect ass?"

She sucks in her bottom lip seductively, then twirls around. Her palms smack against the glass, and her legs part slightly as if she's under arrest. And holy fuck, the sight is better than I imagined. With only a tiny, *so fucking tiny* string running up her crack, her entire ass is exposed. And then, because she's a goddamn tease, she peeks over her shoulder and wiggles that ass.

Unable to help myself, I step over to her until our bodies are almost flush against one another. One hand goes to hers, which is still on the glass, and the other goes to her pert ass, giving it a squeeze. "Keep it up, and instead of fucking that tight pussy, I'll fill your ass."

"Don't make promises you can't keep," she sasses.

I step back and give her ass a quick, hard slap, which has her squealing in shock. "You ever been fucked in the ass?"

She shakes her head slowly, and in the reflection of the glass window, I see her suck her lip between her teeth, her go-to move when she's turned on.

Gripping her chin, I turn her face, making her look at me. "You wanna be fucked in the ass?"

She shrugs. "I read it can be good, but I've never been with anyone I trusted enough to try it with." She says the words so nonchalantly as though we're talking about what we want to eat for dinner instead of anal play.

"You want *me* to fuck you *here*?" I ask, dropping my hand from her chin and sliding a finger along her crack.

She nods, and she might not realize it, but that's a huge step in the right direction. She trusts me. Something that doesn't come easily for her. But her nodding isn't enough. "I need the words, baby. Tell me you want me to shove my dick into that tight hole of yours."

She groans, her eyes fluttering shut for several seconds before opening them, her gaze locking with mine. "I want you to fuck me in *every* one of my holes."

God-fucking-dammit. This woman is going to be the death of me.

I grip the curve of her hip and turn her around, pushing her back against the glass. My fingers wrap around her delicate neck, and my mouth crashes against hers, kissing and devouring her. I've been waiting for over a month to be inside her again, and now that I've finally been given the green light, I can't go slow.

"This will be hard and fast," I murmur against her lips, silently vowing to go slower next time, to take my time and worship every inch of her.

"Yes," she gasps into my mouth, clearly on the same page. "Fuck me hard."

Without the patience I usually have, I wrench the scrap of

material she calls underwear off her body, then quickly undo my pants and yank my already hard as hell dick out. In one fluid motion, I lift her and then enter her tight, warm pussy. Kendall's legs encircle my waist while her fingers delve into my hair, holding on as I fuck her deep and hard against the glass wall. Our heated bodies slap against one another, our mouths tasting and consuming. Our tongues duel as hard as we fuck, and despite Kendall's position, she gives as good as she takes, meeting me thrust for thrust, grinding her pelvis against mine.

She comes first, screaming out her orgasm, and when her walls grip my dick so tightly, I lose any remaining semblance of control. Letting go, I fill her pussy with every drop of my cum.

"Oh, wow." She sighs, dropping her forehead to my shoulder. "I need to clean up, and then I need you to do that again."

I bark out a laugh, loving that she's again on the same page as me. "You don't have to tell me twice," I say, kissing the side of her head. "If it were up to me, I'd spend the next week inside your perfect pussy."

"Sounds like a plan," she quips.

SINCE WE'VE BEEN SITTING IN THE CAR ALL DAY—DESPITE IT BEING LATE, NEITHER OF US is tired—instead of going to bed, we end up on the back porch, lounging on the comfortable bed swing. It's in the fifties tonight, so we're in sweats and hoodies with a blanket she found thrown over us. Without the city lights, the sky is dark, and only the moon and stars shine any light on us. But it's enough that I can see her face as she stares up at the sky, inhaling the fresh air as she sips her wine from one of the bottles we bought in Jersey.

"Does this taste weird to you?" she asks, scrunching her nose and putting the glass up to my lips.

I take a sip, a hint of fruit hitting my senses. "I'm not really a wino like you, but it tastes all right."

She sets it on the table next to her and snuggles up against my chest, stretching her legs out over mine. "This is nice… I enjoyed Jersey and *loved* the B&B, but this is really relaxing. It reminds me of Big Bear minus the snow."

"I love Big Bear." Big Bear Mountain is a ski resort in California where Kendall's parents and grandparents own cabins. They've been vacationing there every winter since I've known the Blackwoods, and since Camden and I became friends, I've joined them damn near every year.

"It's a shame we didn't go this year. Maybe I'll try to convince my parents to go before the snow dries up in May."

I sit up slightly and look at her, confused because we did go to Big Bear. And then it hits me. She doesn't remember. "We went in January, right after the new year."

Her brow furrows, and then she frowns, realizing she doesn't remember. "Well, that sucks. I went and can't even remember if I had a good time."

"We did," I tell her truthfully. Kyle was busy at work, so we spent the entire trip together, skiing and chilling by the bonfire.

"I guess I'll have to take your word for it." She pouts and drops her head to my chest, and I wrap my arms around her. "I can't remember like six weeks of my life, and it feels like forever. I can't even imagine how I'd feel if I had no memory. Who knows what else I can't remember? I could've received life-changing news, and I'd never even know I got it."

I tighten my hold on her, then hold my breath, praying she didn't feel it. I've thought about telling her about us so many times, even came close a couple of times, but fuck, how do you *tell* someone you spent the most amazing night with them, a night they don't even remember? I keep hoping maybe one day she'll remember. Eventually, if she doesn't, I'm going to have to tell her, but I don't want her to be told how amazing the night was. I want her to *feel* what I felt.

"Oh, look!" She gasps. "A shooting star. Make a wish!"

I do as she says, figuring it can't hurt, and wish for Kendall to be mine forever.

"Did you do it?" she asks, glancing up at me.

"Yep."

"Me too." After a few minutes of silence, she says, "I'll tell you mine if you tell me yours."

I chuckle at how adorable she is. "You go first."

"No way! I just wanted to see if you'd do it. I'm not taking that chance." She huffs and cuddles closer to me.

Wanting to take advantage of the alone time, I decide to play twenty questions with her. "If you could travel anywhere in the world, where would you go?"

"Hmm… I'm not sure. I've been to so many places while on tour and on vacations. Honestly, I'm kind of tired of traveling," she admits. "I'm loving this road trip we're on, but I think once we're back at home, I just kind of want to stay put for a while. What about you?"

"Indonesia. There's a surfing spot I've always wanted to check out." Aside from making music and playing the bass, surfing is one of my favorite pastimes. I've missed it since we moved to New York. "Favorite food."

"Crème brûlée."

"That's not food. It's a dessert."

"Does it enter my mouth, go down my throat, and land in

my belly? Then it's food, and it's my favorite. I know yours… empanadas."

Mmm… she isn't wrong. Her grandma's empanadas are the shit. When she comes to visit, she'll make double just for me. "They're the best. I miss Grandma Alicia's cooking."

"I know how to make them," she says with a shrug. "I can make you some one day."

My stomach rumbles at the thought. "I'm going to hold you to it."

"New York or LA?" she asks, catching on to my game and joining in. "And you can't say wherever the band is." Actually, my thought was wherever she is, but I don't tell her that.

"That's hard. I love both, but if I had to pick one, I'd go with New York. It's crazier, but people leave you alone there."

"True," she agrees. "But I'd want to live outside of the city in the 'burbs. That's one thing I love about Calabasas. The gated communities and a bit of property. One day, I'd like to live on a bit of land, maybe have some horses and four-wheelers."

"With a husband and kids?" I ask. As soon as the words come out and she tenses, I immediately regret it, thinking she'll retreat into her shell, but she shocks me by answering.

"Yeah, I'd like a husband and kids someday," she says softly. "At least two, so they have each other. And I'd want them close in age because as close as I am with my siblings, being so much older makes me feel like the odd one out sometimes. What about you? You're an only child. Does that make you want to have one or a bunch?"

"I want a few. I loved when I'd go to your house, and the place would be loud, filled with people. Growing up, I never had that. My parents are uptight and close-minded, so I always avoided bringing my friends over. I want my home to be open and inviting and for my kids to know everyone is welcome."

"Do your parents hate that you're in a rock band?"

"Of course. They're hoping this break means the end of Raging Chaos. They made sure to reach out and let me know that I have a job waiting for me if I want to go to school." I scoff. "I would rather do anything besides work for their hotel."

"They own a hotel?" she asks, sitting up and looking at me. "How did I not know that?"

"Because I keep it separate. The media knows about Pierce Hotels, but since it's not gossip, they don't really talk about it."

"Wait? What?" She gasps. "Pierce Hotels is your parents' hotel chain? They're huge."

I laugh. "No shit, and my parents feel their son playing in a rock band taints their pristine reputation." I roll my eyes. "It doesn't matter how successful the band is. They'll always view me as a failure. All they care about is money and their image. They're not even in love. It's all business.

"Growing up, I saw how fake their marriage was, and then every summer, I'd go visit my grandparents, who were in love. Even in their eighties, they couldn't keep their hands off each other. It gave me hope that I could have what they had and not be stuck in a loveless marriage like my parents. My grandfather died when I was sixteen, and my grandma followed shortly after. I believe she was so heartbroken without him that she followed him to heaven."

Kendall sighs. "I want that kind of love."

I said I'd give her time, but I can't help myself when I blurt out the following words. "You can have that." I tip her chin to look at me. "We can have that. You just have to stop being scared and give us a chance."

She swallows thickly, and I worry she's going to run. But

instead, tears fill her eyes. "I want to," she whispers so softly, I almost don't hear her. "But you're right, I'm scared. So many things can go wrong."

"Or they can go right."

"But if they go wrong, it can ruin everything."

"Or it can be amazing," I argue. "We still have some time left on our trip. What if, instead of being hell-bent on just having fun, you give me a chance to show you how good it can be? Let me woo you."

She chokes out a laugh. In her family, the men always talk about how they woo their women. It's an old-fashioned term, but they believe in the old-fashioned kind of love. The kind where the man treats his woman like a queen and always puts her first, reminding her every day how blessed he is to have her in his life. And that's exactly what I want to do with Kendall. I want to woo the hell out of her.

"All right," she says, shocking me. "I'll give you a chance to woo me. But I don't want anyone to know yet. Just in case."

This is another gigantic step in the right direction, so I'm not about to argue. I started this trip with the intent of getting away from Kendall since she was marrying someone else, and now, here she is, willing to give us a real chance. I'll take it, and by the time this trip is over, she's going to be shouting it from the rooftops that we're together.

"Deal," I tell her, standing and lifting her into my arms.

"What are you doing?" she squeals.

"I'm about to woo the fuck out of you… *literally*."

She throws her head back with a laugh. "Sounds good to me."

# Seventeen

## Kendall

THE MOMENT MY BRAIN WAKES, I FEEL HIM BETWEEN MY LEGS, LICKING HIS WAY UP MY slit and then sucking on my clit. For a second, I wonder if I fell asleep while we were in the middle of sex, but then I remember, after the third time Declan made me come, he carried me to the bathroom so I could clean up. Then he carried me back to bed, tucking me under the covers and spooning me from behind. I crack my eyes open and notice the rays of sunshine darting through the slats of the blinds, telling me it's morning.

Declan nibbles on my swollen nub, and I groan. He sucks harder, then massages it slowly. My orgasm creeps up on me, and before my eyes have even fully opened, I'm moaning out my release.

"Is this your way of waking me up?" I ask, lifting myself onto my elbows to look at him. "Because a girl can get used to this kind of wake-up call."

With lips glossy from my juices, he smiles wide. "By the time I'm done with you, you're going to need to go back to sleep." The corner of his lips curls into a sexy smirk, and then he flips me onto my stomach, giving my ass a slap. Grabbing the curves of my hips, he pulls me onto my hands and knees and thrusts a couple of fingers into my sensitive center.

"Dec," I groan as he fingers me slow and deep. I'm so wet from my orgasm, my pussy suctions his digits, making a sound that would be embarrassing if I wasn't so turned on.

"Fuck, this pussy," he murmurs. "This ass…" With my head against the pillow, I can't see anything he's doing, but when his fingers leave my pussy, dragging up my center and puckered hole, I don't need to see anything to know where this is going.

A few seconds later, my cheeks are being spread, and then Declan's tongue is sliding up and down my slit, stopping at the tight ringed hole and pushing inside. I've never let anyone near my ass before, so I have no frame of reference, but the way he's licking me from top to bottom feels so good. My juices are dripping down the inside of my thighs.

"You gonna let me fuck this sexy ass, baby?" Declan croons. "You gonna let me spread these perfect cheeks and stretch your tight hole?"

Jesus, his dirty talk. Most guys cut to the chase. Don't get me wrong, I've been with guys who aren't completely selfish in bed and make sure I get off first, but it's always as if it's a prelude. But Declan acts like making me come is the main act.

"Kendall, I need words," he says, reminding me that he asked me a question. "If you don't want me to, just say the word and—"

"I want you to fuck my ass," I tell him, cutting him off.

"You sure?"

"Yes." I push my ass back to drive my answer home. "Fuck my ass."

The sound of a bottle popping open echoes in the otherwise

quiet room, and then cold liquid lands on my ass, dribbling down the crack.

"Is that… lube?" I ask as he runs his finger down the same line as the liquid and then pushes a single digit into my tight hole, making me groan loudly.

"Yep, got it at the store while you were sleeping. Also picked up coffee and breakfast." He pulls his finger out slightly, then pushes it back in. It feels odd… but not bad. Not good, though. I read that if it's done right, it can heighten an orgasm, and a lot of women find it pleasurable, but I'm not expecting to enjoy it the first time. I remember how badly it hurt when I lost my virginity, and that hole wasn't half as tight as this one.

"I also picked this up," he says, just as a vibrating noise hits my ears and then my ass. I jump slightly as the object pulsates against the ring of my ass before pushing in. It's thicker than his finger, and as he pushes it into me, inch by inch, I feel fuller and fuller.

"You… got… sex toys?" I breathe, trying to focus on my question, but the intrusion in my ass feels too good. It's hitting my insides in the craziest way, and if he keeps doing what he's doing, I'm going to explode.

"The store has a female pleasure section," Declan says. "Damn, baby. I wish you could see this. The way your ass is sucking the fake dick in. If I weren't afraid of my phone getting hacked, I'd record it so we could watch it later." My insides clench at the thought of lying in bed later with Declan and watching him fuck my ass.

"You'd like that, wouldn't you?" he says through a soft chuckle.

"Yes." I gasp as the toy almost completely leaves my ass, only to be pushed back in even deeper. I never thought I would ever feel comfortable enough to let a man this close. There have been guys who've asked, but I always said no. Couldn't imagine putting myself in such a vulnerable position. But with Declan, I didn't even think twice. And I know why that is. I trust him. He's more than just a man trying to catch me so he can say he had me. He genuinely wants to keep me. And the more time I spend with him, the more I'd really like to be kept by him.

"One day, I'll record us, but not on my phone and not today. I need to focus on this ass." His fingers plunge into my pussy, and within seconds, I'm coming the hardest I've ever come in my life. My ass tightens, my pussy clenches, and juices… Jesus, my juices slide down my thighs like a waterfall, no doubt soaking the bed.

"Fuck, yeah."

Suddenly, the toy is gone, and the head of Declan's dick is in its place. I hold my breath, expecting him to thrust into me, but instead, he goes slow, filling me little by little. He makes me promise to let him know if it hurts or is too much. It stings and is definitely uncomfortable, but thankfully, it doesn't hurt.

"Holy shit, this feels so good. So tight. I'm never going to last," he murmurs once he's stuffed me full of his cock.

When he doesn't move for several seconds, I wiggle my ass, needing him to do something. My pussy is sensitive, and my clit is throbbing. I've already come twice, but with him filling me, I want more.

He takes it as his cue to move and begins to slowly and gently fuck my ass. One hand grips my hip, and the other reaches around and under, finding my clit and massaging it. Between the fullness in my ass and the pressure on my clit, my climax builds fast, and then I come hard, screaming out Declan's name.

"Fuck, fuck," he grunts, then pulls out. I'm about to ask what he's doing when he flips me onto my back. His muscular thighs trap mine, kneeling over me, as he fists his cock, pumping a couple of times before ropes of white shoot out all over my belly and breasts. He doesn't stop until he's completely drained himself.

He releases his dick and reaches down, smearing his cum across my flesh and over my breasts. He stops at my pert nipple and swirls the sticky substance around the tip. "This is the most beautiful sight I've ever seen," he says, smiling softly, reverently, as if he's looking at a masterpiece and not at me, covered in his cum. "I need a Polaroid camera, so I can take pictures and remember you like this."

He drops his hands to either side of my head and locks eyes with me. "Thank you, baby."

"For what?" I mutter in confusion.

"For giving us a real chance…" He kisses the tip of my nose, and my heart picks up speed. "For trusting me." He plants a soft kiss to the corner of my mouth, and my head goes fuzzy. "For letting me love you." His lips brush against mine, and I suck in a sharp breath at the word love. He loves me? Declan Pierce loves me? As I'm trying to wrap my head around that, he kisses me again, this time harder, his tongue dipping into my parted lips and tasting me. "If you let me, I'll spend the rest of our lives showing you every day how much you mean to me."

*The rest of our lives…* The thought of forever should scare me. That was my cue to run—and run fast—with other guys, but as he trails kisses along my jaw, butterflies erupt in my belly, reminding me of the words my dad texted me.

*One day you will find the right guy, and you'll feel it. Your heart will beat a little faster, your smiles will get brighter, and butterflies will swarm your belly. And you'll know, every wrong guy was simply leading you to the right one.*

My heart is beating faster… My smiles are brighter… and fuck, it feels like I have an entire army of butterflies in my belly.

"Declan," I breathe.

"Yeah, baby?" he murmurs.

"I think… I think I'm falling in love with you."

He stops kissing me so he can look at me, his eyes filled with shock and happiness. "Say it again."

"I think I'm falling in love with you," I repeat, shocked as hell that I can even say the words a second time. "I know it's only been a couple of weeks, but I… *I feel it.*"

Declan dips his face and plants a soft kiss over my heart. "Time doesn't dictate your heart."

"I'm scared," I admit, feeling as though I've been cut open and exposed for the entire world to see. Aside from my dad and brother, I've never told a single man I loved him until now. "What if—"

"Stop," he demands, cutting me off. "No what-ifs. We're living in the present. I'm here, and I've got you, Kendall. It's okay to be scared. This is new for both of us."

"Both of us?"

"Yeah, both of us because you're the only person I've ever loved. And not to scare the shit out of you, but these feelings have been going on since I was a damn teenager"—he chuckles—"so I'm glad you've finally caught up to me."

His words nearly take my breath away. I'm unsure what to say, but I don't need to say anything because a moment later, his mouth is on mine, kissing me passionately, as if trying to prove the truth in his words through his actions.

He pulls me into his arms and carries me to the bathroom, never once breaking the kiss. For the next couple of hours, as we shower and then find our way back to bed, Declan shows me over and over again just how much he loves and wants me while I pray to God that I don't completely fuck this up. Because for the first time in my life, I can actually see my future, my life with Declan, and the picture is everything I've ever wanted and never thought

I'd have.

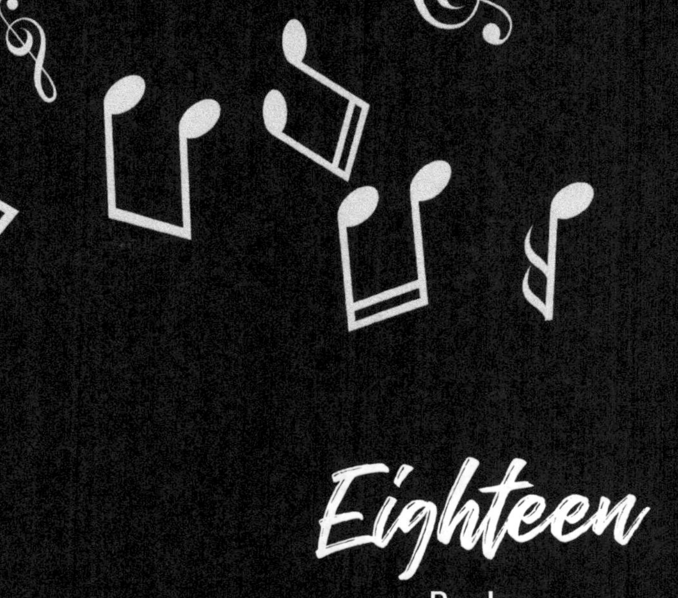

# Eighteen

## Declan

WE'RE SITTING AT THE TABLE, EATING THE BREAKFAST I PICKED UP EARLIER—EVEN THOUGH it's now lunchtime—and discussing what we want to do today when my phone rings. Kendall glances over and flinches slightly at the name on the screen—Camden.

"I'm going to take it in the other room," I tell her, standing and leaning over to peck her lips. I can see it in her eyes that she wants to tell me it's okay to take the call with her here, but I know she isn't ready to tell anyone about us yet, and I need her to know I'm okay with that. She needs time, and I'll give it to her. Knowing how she feels about me, that she's falling in love with me, is enough… for now. I don't want to overwhelm her with too much too soon. I'm still in shock that we went from being friends to giving a relationship a real chance in such a short amount of time. We have our entire lives, and if how long it took her to fall for me is any indication, she'll be ready sooner rather than later.

I step into the living room and click accept. Camden pops on the screen, along with Braxton, in a group video call. The only person missing is Gage.

"Well, look who it is," Braxton says with a smirk. "I was starting to forget what your ugly mug looks like."

I scoff. "Speak for yourself. What's up?"

"Hi, Dec!" Kaylee yells from behind, her head popping onto the screen and replacing Braxton. "How are you?"

"I'm good. How are you?"

"Perfect." She grins and holds up her hand, showing me her ring. "Braxton and I have some news… hence the video call. We got married! I'm officially Mrs. Braxton Lutz."

Fuck, I forgot they were planning to get married after Kendall's wedding. I left and haven't heard shit. Everyone's been giving me my space… Dammit, I should've been there.

She must see the look of guilt because she adds, "And before you think you weren't invited, we eloped. Went to Vegas and got married and then flew to Paris for our honeymoon. When we're all together again, we'll have a dinner to celebrate."

Braxton pushes her onto his lap so they're both visible and kisses her cheek. "We're in Paris now," he says. "Just arrived last night. We wanted you guys to be the first to know."

"Congratulations," I tell them both, happy that they found their way back to each other after all these years.

"Congrats!" Camden adds.

"Thanks," they both say, all smiles.

"Cam, how's the fam?" I ask.

"Good." He beams. "Marianna is trying to crawl and is stealing Felix's toys and driving him nuts. He said he's changed his mind and wants us to give him a brother instead. If she's this crazy at six months old, I can't imagine how she'll be when she's a toddler."

We all crack up laughing.

"Anyone talk to Gage?" I ask after a moment of silence.

"Nah," Camden says, his smile dimming. "My dad's been in contact, and he's still there but isn't talking to anyone on the outside. His ninety days are over at the end of the month."

"We'll be back before then," Braxton says.

"Same," I agree. There's no way I won't be there for our best friend when he gets out.

Camden nods. "Speaking of not talking to anyone. Have you heard from Kendall? Mom and Dad said she's contacted them, and they know she's okay, but she isn't posting on social media and hasn't reached out to anyone else. I'm worried. She's one of the strongest people I know on the outside, but deep down… " He sighs. "She's great at putting on a good front, but I think she's hurting and doesn't want anyone to see it."

"I haven't heard from her," Kaylee says with a frown. "But we're not all that close. She hasn't spoken to Layla? They're good friends."

Camden shakes his head. "Aside from a call to our mom and a few texts that she's okay, nobody's heard from her since she dipped out on her wedding."

"She's okay," I confirm.

"You've spoken to her?" he asks, his eyes wide.

"She's okay," I repeat, hoping he gets what I'm saying. I promised Kendall I wouldn't say anything, and I don't want to go back on that, but I can't just sit here and let her brother worry.

Camden looks like he wants to ask more questions, but thankfully, he doesn't.

We bullshit for a few more minutes, avoiding the topic of Raging Chaos since we've silently agreed not to discuss it until we have Gage back, and then everyone hangs up after saying we'll talk soon.

I throw my phone on the counter and go in search of Kendall, finding her lying out on a lounge chair on the expansive back deck. She's lost in thought, scribbling in her notebook, and doesn't notice I'm there until I drop down next to her.

"Your brother asked if I've spoken to you."

Her hand stills, but she doesn't look up.

"Said you haven't contacted anyone but your parents…" When she doesn't say anything, I continue. "I told him you were okay."

Her head pops up. "You—"

"Just said you were okay. Nothing more."

She nods.

"Why haven't you reached out to your brother and sisters?"

She shrugs, but I refuse to let her get away with that shit. Grabbing the notebook and pen from her, I drop them onto the end of the chair and then pull her into my lap so she's straddling my thighs. "Baby, talk to me."

Her gaze drops, refusing to look at me, so I lift her chin and kiss the tip of her nose. "Kendall…"

"I was embarrassed," she admits softly. "Still am… Bailey and Camden are both so perfect. They have the perfect relationships and make perfect decisions. They both told me I was rushing things, but I didn't listen. They probably think I'm such an irresponsible idiot."

"First of all," I say, meeting her eyes. "Nobody is perfect. And they might've said that to you, but it's only because they love you. You should've seen the look in his eyes. He's so damn worried about you. Nobody thinks you're irresponsible or an idiot. They only want you to be happy."

"I think this is the happiest I've been in a long time," she admits, making my heart swell. "I love our little bubble and didn't want to pop it."

"I love our bubble too," I tell her, kissing her pillow-soft lips. "But those people are a part of our big bubble, and in a few weeks, when we return, they'll be there because they're not going anywhere."

She nods in understanding. "How is he?"

"Good. Braxton and Kaylee got married in Vegas and are now in Paris for a few weeks on their honeymoon. Marianna is starting to crawl and driving Felix nuts. Camden said he wants to trade her in for a brother."

Kendall barks out a laugh. "I miss them." Her eyes water, and when a tear escapes, I wipe it away with my thumb.

"We can go home anytime you want."

"Not yet." She leans her head against my chest and wraps her arms around me. "I need a little more time with you. Is that okay?"

"Of course, it is," I tell her, kissing the crown of her head. "I just need to be back before Gage gets out."

We spend the rest of the day lounging outside. We write for a few hours, then hit the hot tub. When it gets dark out, we light the bonfire and roast hot dogs and s'mores.

One day at the lake turns into two, and before we know it, a week has passed, and we're packing up to head to our next destination.

"WHERE ARE WE GOING?" KENDALL ASKS AS WE DRIVE DOWN THE HIGHWAY TOWARD THE industrial airport, where a private plane is waiting to take us to our next stop.

"Surprise," I tell her. "Make sure you get everything of yours from the car."

"What? Why?" she asks as I pull into the airport.

"Someone's coming to pick it up and drive it back to Calabasas."

She glances around, her eyes going wide when she realizes where we are. "We're taking a plane?"

"Yep, it's too long of a drive where we're going." Technically, we could drive there, but with it being twenty-four hours by car, we'd have to stop a few times, and it's not worth it. Not when we have the money and means to get on a plane and be there in less than three hours.

The moment Kendall finds out where we're going, she squeals in excitement. "Big Bear Mountain?"

"You said you didn't remember skiing. Figured we could make new memories."

She wraps her arms around me. "Thank you, Dec. This has seriously been the best trip."

The ride from the airport to the mountain isn't too long. I hired a car service to pick us up and have security meet us there. The goal is to stay out of the spotlight, but Big Bear is filled with people, and anything can happen.

"There's a chance we'll get spotted when we go skiing," I warn Kendall as the SUV pulls up to the cabin I rented. I could've asked Camden or her parents to borrow theirs, but I didn't want to have to explain why. "We can hang back, stay at the cabin—"

"It's okay," she says, taking my hand in hers and lacing our fingers together. "If someone spots us, we can always say we're two friends spending time together. I'm planning to tell our family that we're together, but I'd like to keep our relationship out of the media for a little bit. Just in case..."

Her words trail off, but I can fill in the rest myself: *Just in case it doesn't work out.* I hate that she's so negative about herself and relationships, but over time, she'll see that I'm not going anywhere and what we have is forever.

We find the master bedroom and get situated. Kendall says she's going to shower the flight off, and while she does, I get Jose, our security, caught up to speed. He's just left—since we won't need him until we leave later for dinner—when Kendall walks downstairs in nothing but a towel, her hair wet and messy. Her eyes meet mine, and a seductive smile spreads across her lips.

"I was hoping you were going to join me." She reaches up to the knot holding her towel together and pulls it apart, the material falling to the floor and leaving her standing there naked and gorgeous.

"I had to speak to our security. He'll be back later so we can go to dinner."

"Or…" She saunters over to me. "We could have dinner here, and I could be your dessert."

"That would imply I have to wait until *after* we eat to eat *you*." I pull her into my arms, my hands landing on her plump ass at the same time as I crash my mouth down on hers.

We don't end up leaving the cabin, too lost in each other. Instead, I spend the rest of the day and night making her my dinner, dessert, and eventually my breakfast. The rest of the week pretty much goes by the same way. We never make it out of the cabin to actually ski. When we need sustenance, we order food and have Jose pick it up. Kendall has fast become my addiction, and while I want our relationship to be out in the open, I understand what she means about not wanting our bubble to burst. Because being in a Kendall-only bubble is the best damn way to live my life.

Unfortunately, that bubble can only stay intact for so long, and soon, we're going to have no choice but to pop it.

# Nineteen

## Kendall

 "MOM SAYS, A WATERY SMILE spreading across her lips. "Where are you? How are you doing? Are you still with Dec?"

My heart swells at her concern. It's been over a month since I've seen my family in person, and just as long since I've spoken to my siblings, and I'm missing them like crazy. After Declan and I spent time in Big Bear Mountain, we went to my place in Calabasas, where we lost track of time, getting lost in each other. We only came up for air when my dad texted Declan, letting him know Gage is due to return next week and that he's scheduled time for us to record "Drunk on Your Love" in the studio the following week, then the video after that. He also let us know that our publicists have set up promo for the single since it's going to be marketed as a preview for my upcoming album.

"I'm at home. I'm good. And yes, he's here with me." I can't help the smile that stretches so wide, my cheeks hurt, and of course, my mom immediately notices.

"Are you two…?"

I nod, biting my lip to try to contain a bit of my happiness. It's hard, though, when these past several weeks have been without a doubt the best of my life. I not only found myself on this trip but I also found love. Real butterfly-inducing, heart-thumping love. And it feels so good. I haven't told Declan that I love him yet. I'm scared. But once we're home, I plan to. I just want to make sure we can make it in the real world first. He has all the faith in the world, and I'm definitely on board, but I can't help the niggling feeling that I'm going to do something to mess it all up.

"You look so happy," Mom says. "When will you be home?"

"Late tonight. Declan is going with the guys tomorrow to pick up Gage, so I thought we could have a lunch date and see if Phoebe and Bailey want to join. We could invite Layla and Kaylee too."

"That sounds perfect. I'll call them. Have a safe flight, and I'll see you tomorrow."

"Love you."

"Love you more."

I close my laptop and stow it away in my luggage that contains everything I've purchased during our road trip, including a few gifts for my family.

"You ready to jet?" Declan asks, walking into the living room. He's dressed in a plain black T-shirt, a pair of ripped jeans, and is sporting a pair of black Vans. His hair is up in his signature bun, and the only thing I want to do is devour him.

"Not happening," he says with a smirk, knowing me too damn well. "Once we're home, you can have your way with me, but we'll never make it on that plane if you touch me now."

I shrug, not caring, and he frowns, mistaking it for me being scared about going home. "I told my mom we're together." His brows kiss his forehead. "And tomorrow, while you're picking up Gage with the guys, I'm meeting her and my sisters for lunch. Layla and Kaylee too, if they're available. I'm going to tell them that we're together."

Declan walks over and rests his hands on my hips. "You have no idea how much that means to me," he says, kissing my lips.

"I'm not ready for the world to know," I admit, "but I don't want to hide us from our family and friends. Just promise me that if things don't work out, we'll go back to being friends." I frame his face with my hands. "I care about you so much, and I can't lose you. And I don't want you to lose my family. I know how important they are to you."

"You're never going to lose me," he vows.

"Promise?"

"I promise."

He seals it with a kiss, and then we take off to the airport. Since the private jet we're on is my parents', complete with a bedroom, the flight is spent with him inside me—because apparently, we can't even go long enough to make it home before we attack each other.

When we arrive in New York, Declan insists I go back to his place with him, and I don't argue. We could probably use a bit of time away from each other since we've been together for so long, but I have no desire to part ways.

His place is spotless, and he tells me that he had Camden let a cleaning crew in to clean it while we were gone. He also did a search for drugs and liquor, so it'll all be gone when Gage gets home. Exhausted from the flight and sex, we fall into bed, tangled up in each other, and pass out immediately, not waking up until Declan's alarm goes off the following morning. We shower together, but nothing happens. I can sense Declan's nervousness about seeing Gage for the first time since everything went down, so I simply hold him and tell him I'm here for him.

Once we're ready to go, we call for a car since he's meeting the guys at my parents' place so they can drive together to pick up Gage.

"You ready for this?" he asks, standing outside my parents' door. He's referring to us walking in together with our hands entwined.

"I'm scared," I admit, knowing it's okay to be honest with him. "I've hurt so many guys in the past. I'm terrified it's in my DNA, and not even loving an amazing man like you will prevent me from messing up. The last person I want to hurt is you. You're perfect in every way and deserve everything."

Declan grins. "You love me?"

"What?"

"You said not even loving an amazing man like me will prevent you from messing up."

"That's what you took from all that?"

"That's the only important part," he says, his grin growing wider. "Is it true? Do you love me?" He pulls me into his arms, and I sigh.

"Yes, it's true. I've fallen in love with you, and that scares the hell out of me because, as you know, I've never truly loved anyone before, and I'm terrified of what will happen when we hit the concrete."

"Say it again."

I playfully roll my eyes. "I love you."

"Again."

"Dec!"

"Say it," he insists.

"Declan Pierce, I love you."

"I love you too, baby." He connects his mouth with mine for a heart-stopping kiss that makes me wish we were back at his place instead of on the stoop of my parents' house.

"Nobody's perfect," he says once the kiss ends. "And while having *everything* sounds amazing, the only thing I want is you because to me, you loving me *is* everything. So stop worrying about the what-ifs and focus on us. Because I'll never..." He kisses the corner of my mouth. "Ever..." The other corner. "Let you fall without knowing I'm there to catch you."

He kisses me again, this time softly, then pulls back, his brow furrowed. "Speaking of not being perfect...There's something I need to tell you." He tightens his grip on my hips. "Before your accide—"

His words are cut off by the door swinging open and my little sister exclaiming, "I knew it!"

I try to scramble out of his hold, but he holds me close, turning to face Bailey while wrapping his arm around my middle.

"Admit it," she says, raising a brow.

"Admit what?" Camden asks, coming up behind her.

"Can we take this inside?" I mutter, worried someone will be spying and catch us on camera.

Bailey moves to the side. "I'll let our sister tell you."

"Tell me what?" Camden asks, his eyes going to Declan's hand, which dropped from my waist so we could walk inside and is now holding mine. "Oh, shit. Is this where you've been? With my sister?"

Declan glances at me, leaving me to answer. "Yes," I admit to my entire family—including Layla and Kaylee—who're all now standing in the foyer, staring at us. "Declan and I are... dating."

I wince, ready for my brother or my dad to lose it, so I'm shocked when everyone starts hugging and congratulating us.

"Welcome back," my dad says into my ear when he wraps me

in his arms. "Happiness looks damn good on you."

"Thank you," I choke out.

"Dad's right," Camden says, hugging me next. "You look good, sis."

"You don't mind me dating your best friend and bandmate?"

"Maybe if he were anyone else," Camden says. "But I've known how much Declan cares about you for years, so I have no doubt he'll treat you right."

"You knew he liked me?"

"Everyone knew," Bailey says with a snort. "Everyone but you."

"Yep," Layla agrees. "While you were talking crap about me not knowing how Camden felt about me, you were completely blind to the crush Declan's had on you for years."

Everyone laughs.

"I didn't know."

"It's all good, baby," Declan says, kissing my temple. "It wasn't our time yet."

I snuggle into his side. "We're not telling anyone yet," I say to everyone. "I just want to keep this private for a little bit. It's only been a short time since I called off the engagement…" And a small—okay, maybe big—part of me is still scared, but some of my fear was tamped down by Declan's words outside.

My family and friends all nod in understanding.

"We better get going," Camden says. "Checkout time is noon."

The guys say bye to everyone, then take off, leaving the women and kids here. Instead of going out to brunch, Mom had food brought in so we could catch up in private. While we eat, I tell them about our trip. And once we're done, I spend some time with my niece and nephew, giving them the gifts I picked up.

Layla is about to take the kids home for a nap when Declan, Dad, Camden, and Braxton walk back through the door.

"What are you doing here?" Mom asks. After they picked up Gage, they planned to bring him back to his place and spend the afternoon making sure he had everything he needed.

"Where's Gage?" Kaylee asks. She and Gage are close, have been for years, and she hated not being able to go with them to pick him up.

Declan, Braxton, and Camden don't stop to answer, the three of them stomping down the stairs to where the studio is.

"What's going on?" Layla asks.

"Gage wasn't there when we arrived," Dad says. "He had already checked out."

"What?" Mom gasps. "So where is he?"

Dad shrugs. "We don't know. We were just told he checked out early."

"Oh, God." Mom tears up. "What do we do? How do we know he's okay? He has nobody. He needs us."

Dad pulls her into his arms to comfort her. Mom considers all of the guys to be her kids, especially since once they started coming around in middle school, they never stopped, practically living here. And when Gage aged out of the system, and the family he was living with made it clear they no longer wanted him, he moved in here, at my mom's demand. When Gage would have no one to attend his parent-teacher conferences, Mom would do it. And when shit went down at the end of their senior year, she and Dad helped him handle everything.

"There's nothing we can do," Dad tells her. "He's a grown man. We have to hope that wherever he's going, he's safe and will eventually contact us."

"IF YOU'RE NOT UP FOR THIS, WE CAN RESCHEDULE," I TELL DECLAN AS WE WALK INTO THE studio. It's been a week since they went to pick up Gage, only to find out he wasn't there. The guys needed some time alone but eventually came up to tell us that Gage sent a group text, letting them know he's okay but needs some time. He insisted they move forward with the band without him, not wanting to hold them back, but the guys agreed that there's no band without him and told him they'll be here when he's ready to come home.

Ever since then, Declan's been on the quiet side. Still attentive and loving, but I can feel his hurt and worry. I wish I could make it better for him, but the only thing that will help is Gage coming home.

"I'm good," he says, bending and kissing my temple. "This song deserves to be recorded for the world to hear."

"There they are," Johnny, the producer handling our song, says, giving Declan a fist bump. We recorded it a while back—though, I don't remember—to show it to my dad, but he made a couple of changes to the instrumentals, and we'll be finalizing it today. I also gave him all the songs I wrote while we were on our road trip, and he said there's enough for an entire album there. He's having one of his staff writers edit and tweak them, and then next week, I'll begin recording my album. I was set on the title *Falling*, but the more I think about it, I think a more apt title might be *Fallen* because let's be real—I'm not falling for Declan… I've completely and utterly fallen.

"You guys ready?"

"Always," Declan says, heading straight into the sound room. Since we're in public, albeit my parents' studio, we're not holding hands or touching, and even though it's only been a few minutes and my choice, I already miss him.

I put the headphones on to start my part, and once Johnny

gives me the go-ahead, I sing my heart out.

*I've never been in love before*
*Never knew what my heart was capable of*
*Until you walked in and turned my life upside down*
*Now my heart's racing, my body's vibrating*
*I should run the other way, protect you from me*
*From what I'm capable of*
*But you make me weak, make me someone I'm not*

*Because...*
*You've got me drunk on you*
*Drunk on wanting you*
*Drunk on needing you*
*You've got me drunk on your love*
*And I'll never be the same*

*The moment you walked in, everything changed*
*My heart is filled with chaos, my head fuzzy*
*I want to be the one who makes you happy*
*Who gives you the world*
*I've spent too long pretending*
*Wishing, hoping, praying these feelings would go away*
*This might be the biggest mistake I've ever made*
*But it will also be the best*

*Because...*
*You've got me drunk on you*
*Drunk on wanting you*
*Drunk on needing you*
*You've got me drunk on your love*

And I'll never be the same

I've been watching you all night
Memorizing your every move
Know exactly what you need
To cure that chaos in your heart
Hand it over, and I'll fix the broken
Turn the chaos into calm
Make that heart of yours mine
And you'll never feel alone
All you gotta do is say yes
And I'll handle the rest

Haven't touched a single drink all night
But I'm drunk as fuck
On your scent, on your touch
Hand it over, baby
And you'll never know what it's like to be without love

I'm handing my heart over to you
Keep it safe
Promise you'll never stray
I've fallen for you, I must admit
I'm flying high, not worried about the hit
That I'm going to take the day you walk away
Hoping and praying when I go down, you'll be there to catch me
I know it's a risk, but it's one I'm willing to take

Because…
You've got me drunk on you
Drunk on wanting you

*Drunk on needing you*
*You've got me drunk on your love*
*And I'll never be the same*

Declan and I spend the next couple of hours working with Johnny, perfecting the song, and with every word we sing, I wonder if deep down I maybe always knew how I felt about Declan.

My thoughts go to the day I woke up in the hospital. When I opened my eyes, Declan was the first person I saw, and all I could think about was how delicious and kissable he looked. I pushed the thoughts aside and told myself we were just friends, but the fact that I wrote my first true love song with him tells me that maybe it was more, and I just wasn't ready to admit it yet.

"What's going through that beautiful head of yours?" Declan asks, snapping me out of my thoughts. I look around and realize we're alone.

"Johnny said it's perfect," he says, giving me a chaste kiss. "He's going to finalize it after he grabs dinner and then send it to your dad and us to approve. Now tell me what's got you lost in your head."

"I was just thinking about when we wrote this song." I encircle my arms around his neck. "I think I knew you were the one for me back then, but I didn't want to admit it. I'm sorry it took me this long and almost marrying the wrong guy to realize my feelings for you."

Declan smiles. "It's all good. We're here, together, and that's all that matters. Now, what do you say we go home and celebrate 'Drunk on Your Love'?"

"And how do you want to celebrate?" I ask, knowing damn well how he wants to celebrate.

"By getting drunk on you, of course."

# Twenty

## Declan

"HOLY SHIT, IT'S COLD!" KENDALL LAUGHS THROUGH HER CHATTERING TEETH AS I PULL her into my arms, determined to warm her. We're on the set for the "Drunk on Your Love" video. It's been a crazy day, but we're in the final scene. The video starts off at the club, where I'm eyeing Kendall as she dances provocatively with a few of her friends, all for the purpose of seducing me. It goes to me asking her to dance and us spending the evening with her in my arms. When the night ends, she says goodbye, but I don't let her go. Instead, I follow her out into the night.

She tries to argue that the night is over, but I refuse to let her go, telling her that she's the one for me. While we're going back and forth, the skies open, and it starts raining. The water was supposed to be warm, but the water heater on the set is broken, so we had two options: wait for them to get it fixed, which won't be tonight, or finish the video tonight with cold as fuck water raining down on us.

"Don't focus on that," I tell her, rubbing her arms up and

down in an attempt to warm her flesh. "Just focus on me." She nods once, melting into my arms. I lean in and whisper, "When we're done, I'm going to warm you up… in the hot shower at my place, then again in bed."

Kendall shivers as a groan escapes past her lips. "You're such a tease."

Layla, our videographer leading this music video, yells at us to get dry so we can do it again, forcing us to separate.

The hair and makeup artists get us sorted, drying our hair and clothes, and then we head back out to try this again.

"Try not to laugh this time." I mock glare at Kendall. "If I have to dry off again, I'm going to be coming after you." I point my finger in her direction, emphasizing my threat.

She playfully rolls her eyes. "Is that a threat or a promise?"

I'm shocked she just said that in front of everyone since we're keeping our relationship on the down low, but she doesn't seem to notice or care, so I don't say anything.

The music starts, so we can make sure it matches once they put all the pieces together, and Kendall runs out of the club and is about to get into the cab, when—at my cue—I run out after her and pull her to the side before she can get in. The driver screams for her to get in or he's leaving, and then he speeds off without her, leaving only me and her.

My hand goes to the side of her face, and she leans into my touch instinctually. Since the music is playing, our parts are played through our actions, letting the music speak for itself. I tug her closer to me, my other hand palming her ass, and our eyes lock, everything and everyone fading away. It's just Kendall and me… and the ice-cold rain. But not even the iciness of the water falling around us breaks our spell. Maybe it's because she's expecting it this time, but she remains in character, focusing on me like I told her to.

I push her drenched hair out of her face, and her tongue darts out, licking across the seam of her lips. And then my mouth is devouring hers. She tastes like love and lust rolled together to create the most perfectly sweet addiction. My hand glides from the side of her face to her nape, deepening the kiss. She moans into my mouth, then nips at my lips before sliding her tongue along my top lip, then the bottom.

Needing to be closer to her, to feel more of her, I reach down and palm the backs of her thighs, lifting her into my arms. I'm about to walk us to the bed when it hits me... Fuck! We're not at my place. We're on set, with over a dozen people watching us make out. Yeah, we were supposed to kiss, but it wasn't supposed to be like this.

I break the kiss, and Kendall's eyes go wide, realizing the same thing I just did. I expect her to freak out and demand I put her down—the fake rain has stopped, the music has been silenced, and nobody is saying a word—so I'm shocked as hell when the biggest smile spreads across her face, and she says, "Oops," followed by the most adorable snort-laugh.

When a couple of people snicker, she drops her head into the crook of my neck to hide her embarrassment and laughter. A second later, she lifts her head and meets my eyes, and fuck if I don't want to finish what we just started.

"We done?" I ask Layla, who laughs.

"Yep, that's a wrap."

Without giving a fuck who's watching—and knowing they'll have signed NDAs and have no electronics on them since it's not allowed—without a backward glance, I carry Kendall off the set and to my dressing room, which has been vacated. Closing the door behind us, I lock it and walk us over to the couch, dropping her onto it.

"Oh God, I want you," she groans as I lift my shirt over my head and then drop back down on top of her, crashing my mouth against hers. We kiss, hard and rough, only stopping to remove her soaked shirt and bra, and then again to get our shoes and pants off.

Once we're both naked, she pushes me back and climbs onto my lap, lowering herself onto me. I let her ride me, enjoying her tits as they bounce along with her sexy ass. Her hips swivel from side to side, her pussy gripping me like a vise. I take one of her tits in my hand and bring her nipple to my mouth, wrapping my lips around the tightened bud and sucking on it.

"Oh fuck, Dec…" Her eyes roll to the back of her head. "Suck harder."

I love how responsive she is, the way she lets any and all of her inhibitions go when we're together. To the world, she's one person—a prim and proper pop star who's constructed a wall to keep her feelings in and everyone else out—but with me, she lets that wall down, exposing her real self and allowing every emotion to be front and center. She doesn't even realize she's doing it, but I see it… I see *her*.

I do as she asked and take her nipple farther into my mouth, sucking on it until her back arches, and a loud moan escapes her parted lips. As if there's a direct line from her breast to her pussy, she squeezes the fuck out of my dick, and I take over, needing to make her come before I do.

With one hand curled around her hip and the other stroking her clit, I move her up and down, massaging the inside of her walls with my cock until she's screaming my name in ecstasy as she comes hard, taking me along with her.

"Jesus," she mutters once she's come down. Her head drops to the crook of my neck, and she places a soft open-mouthed kiss on my flesh. "I can't get enough of you."

I smile inside as I lift her face and kiss her lips. "That's my hope," I tell her honestly. "That you'll always want more."

"PASS ME THE SALT."

Kendall reaches behind her and grabs the salt, handing it to me. Before I can take it, though, she pulls her hand back and leans forward. "Kiss first."

She makes the most adorable kissy face that has me chuckling as I step between her thighs and plant my hands on the countertop on either side of her. My mouth connects with hers, and my tongue delves in, capturing hers and sucking on it.

"Dec, you're going to burn the food," she says, pushing me away with a laugh. "And it smells too good to waste."

"Hey, you're the one who asked for a kiss," I point out, taking the salt from her and stepping back in front of the stove.

It's been almost two weeks since we've been home, and every night has been spent with Kendall at my place. When she's not at the studio recording her next album—where I join her most of the time—we're here eating, fucking, or watching *The Vampire Diaries*. We've created a nice little bubble—yeah, we love those damn bubbles—but it's about to be popped because tomorrow is Mother's Day, and my father has requested my presence at dinner. It's not that I don't want to see my mom, but every time we're together, it ends with them teaming up against me in some ridiculous and pointless effort to get me to quit my job. And with the rumors running rampant about Gage missing and the band and label staying silent, they probably think their chance of convincing me has increased.

Which is why I almost told her no when Kendall offered to go and play the buffer… but then she looked at me with bright and hopeful eyes, and I didn't have it in me to say anything but yes. She had mentioned once that Kyle rarely brought her around his parents because they would snub her career choice, and I didn't want to chance her thinking I was doing the same thing. So I called my parents and told them my girlfriend would be coming and warned them that she's a singer and if they so much as make a rude comment, we'll be walking out the door.

They were both so shocked I was actually dating someone serious enough to bring home that they agreed without argument.

"Eww, what's that smell?" Kendall asks, knocking me from my thoughts. I glance over and see she's referring to the garlic I minced earlier and just added to the pan.

"Garlic."

"I don't like that." She shakes her head and gags, jumping off the counter and walking over to the cabinet to grab us a couple of plates.

"It won't be as strong once it's all mixed in." I've been cooking while Kendall bakes because we're hiding out from the media until Kendall is ready to go public. We've spent weeks eating out while on our road trip, and we both actually enjoy eating at home. I've been cooking for the guys and me for years when our meals aren't cooked for us, and Kendall has always enjoyed baking.

"What time do you want to leave tomorrow?" she asks, pouring us each a glass of wine. "Brunch at my parents' place is at eleven, but I like to get there early to hang out."

"Whatever time you want." I take the food off the stove and plate us both a good-sized portion. One thing I've learned about

Kendall is that she loves to eat. In return, she busts her ass in the gym with her personal trainer, but she'd rather do that than miss out on all the tasty food.

I bring the plates over to the table and sit next to her, setting her plate down in front of her. I cut mine up and am just digging in when Kendall makes a gagging sound, then runs to the sink, throwing up whatever she had in her stomach.

"You okay?" I ask, grabbing a couple of paper towels so she can wipe her mouth.

"Yeah, I think it's the garlic. It's making me feel sick."

"Maybe you're coming down with something." I lift my hand to her forehead, and she feels a little clammy, but it could be from throwing up.

"Ugh, maybe." She groans. "Would you be super offended if I just ate a bowl of cereal?"

"Of course not. Go rinse off and take some vitamin C, and I'll bring it to you in bed in case you're coming down with something."

She smiles softly at me. "Thank you."

After putting the food away in the fridge for another night, I grab her a bottle of water, a vitamin C capsule, and make her a bowl of cereal—her go-to when she's not up for eating something heavy. I bring it to my room, setting it all on the nightstand for when she gets out.

While I'm waiting for her, my phone rings, and the name on the caller ID makes me hit answer immediately.

"Gage?" I breathe, walking out of the room.

"Hey, Dec." Those two simple words have me tearing up. The last time I heard his voice was months ago.

"Fuck, Gage. You okay?" I choke out, squeezing my eyes shut and praying the image of him lying in his room doesn't appear.

"I'm okay," he says back. "But..." he breathes out, and I hear the words he can't say. He's not ready to come home.

"It's okay. We're here whenever you're ready." I try to keep the emotion out of my words, but it's hard when all I want to do is beg him to come home.

"I just wanted to say thank you for saving my life."

Fuck, this guy. "Gage… You don't—"

"Yeah, I do," he says, cutting me off. "I need you to know how thankful I am for you. I'll never forget what you did. I… I gotta go," he chokes out. The line goes dead before I can argue and beg him not to end the call.

"Hey, what's wrong?" Kendall asks, framing my face with her delicate hands. She's freshly showered and smells like her signature scent. "Why are you crying?" She swipes a tear I didn't know had fallen, and I pull her into me, nuzzling my face into her damp hair. "Dec, you're scaring me."

"Gage called to thank me for saving his life."

She stiffens at my words. "Is he coming home?"

"He didn't say." I replay the quick conversation in my head, and it hits me. "He didn't say," I repeat. "He was calling to thank me, and it almost sounded like…" Fuck, no. It couldn't be. Gage wouldn't do this.

"Sounded like what?"

"Like goodbye."

Her eyes widen, on the same page, and I quickly call Gage back, only to be sent to voicemail.

**Me: Your call sounded like goodbye… Tell me I'm wrong.**

**Gage: If you're worried about me doing something like I did before, don't be. That will never happen again.**

His reply has me sagging in relief. He didn't say it wasn't a goodbye, but at least he's okay, and right now, that's all that matters.

**Me: I'm here always.**

**Gage: Thank you.**

"He'll come home," Kendall says. "He just needs time."

"I hope you're right." I kiss the corner of her mouth. "How are you feeling?"

"Better."

"Good, your cereal is in the room. Let's get you fed and full of vitamin C, and we'll spend the night watching some Damon and Elena."

Kendall rolls her eyes. "I can't believe you're Team Damon."

"What's that supposed to mean?"

"Nothing." She shrugs. "It's just… you're a good guy, so I figured you'd want the good guy to get the girl."

"It's not about good and bad," I tell her. "Damon is the right guy for her. Doesn't matter who he is or what he's done… When it's right, it's right."

# Twenty-One

## Kendall

"JESUS H. CHRIST." I GROAN AS I SUCK IN MY GUT, QUICKLY BUTTONING MY PANTS BEFORE releasing my breath. I've tried on several outfits, but none of them fit. And unless I want to go to my parents' place, and later, meet Declan's parents, in sweats, I need something to fit. I have a few dresses I could wear, but none of them are meant to be worn to Sunday brunch. The problem with living bi-coastal is that no matter which house you're at, the item you need always ends up being at the other one.

After I'm almost positive the button isn't going to pop off, I put on my heels, double-check my makeup and hair, and head out to meet Declan, who's been ready for the past hour—damn men have it so much easier than women.

"Ready?" he asks, standing and placing his phone into his pocket. Dressed in a white button-down shirt with the sleeves rolled to his elbows, a pair of gray linen pants that fit him perfectly, and a pair of white sneakers, he makes dressy-casual look so damn good.

"Women should really take a page out of a man's playbook." I shake my head. "Getting up, taking a shower, throwing on the closest items of clothing they can find, and dropping onto the couch, ready to go. This whole doing my hair and makeup and finding the right outfit takes up too much of my damn time. And after all that, I still don't come close to looking as sexy as you do."

With a lazy grin, he pulls me against him. "I love when you dress up in your tight little outfits and do your hair and makeup, but I can assure you, you're just as sexy when you wake up, with your hair a mess and your face free of all makeup."

On the outside, I roll my eyes, but deep down, I love every word he says. Especially since right now, I'm not feeling sexy at all.

"Thank you," I tell him, refusing to let my insecurities get to me.

The drive to my parents' place doesn't take too long, and when we arrive, since we're the last to do so, everyone is already in the family room chatting away.

"Auntie K!" my nephew Felix yells, running over to give me a hug. "I got the best dance! You gonna do it with me on TikTok?" Felix is almost six years old with the personality of a teenager and is one of the best dancers I've ever seen. He's appeared in several music videos and has millions of followers on TikTok—that his mom monitors and doesn't let him on, aside from doing the trending dances.

"Of course!" When I reach down to give him a hug, the button on my pants pops off, and the material attached to the zipper splits right open.

The button hits the hardwood floor with a clanking sound, and Felix grabs it. "Oh man, your pants just ripped!" he says, pointing out the obvious, loud enough for everyone to hear. "I bet my mom can fix it." He hands me back the button. "When I ripped my Justin Bieber Halloween costume, she fixed it."

"Thanks," I mutter. "Apparently, a couple of months of eating whatever I wanted and not going to the gym has caught up to me." I glance at my mom. "Can I borrow something?"

"Of course." She smiles sweetly. "Let's go to my room." She wraps her arm around me and kisses my temple.

"Happy Mother's Day," I tell her, leaning into her. "Dad spoil you?"

"Of course," she says with hearts in her eyes. I love that even after all these years, my parents are just as, if not more, in love than they were in the beginning. They are total relationship goals.

"You want another pair of pants?" she asks, turning on the light in her massive walk-in closet as we enter.

"Better go with a dress. We're the same size, and none of my pants are fitting." I groan. "Something Mother's Day appropriate since we're going to Declan's parents' place afterward."

"How about this?" She shows me a beautiful light pink flowy dress with wide sleeves. The neckline is a bit low, but it's the perfect mix of sexy and classy, and because it's loose, nothing should rip or pop open.

"Perfect. Thanks." I undress quickly and then grab the dress from my mom, unzipping the back and sliding it on over my head. "Zip me up?" I ask, giving her my back.

She attempts to do so, but when she gets to the top, it's too tight, and I wince at the way it adds pressure to my breasts.

"Dammit. I really should've been finding a gym while we were away."

"Let's try another dress," Mom offers as I take this one off.

After three dresses, we finally find one that fits me. I've just finished getting dressed when Bailey comes strolling in. "Hey, sis!"

She pulls me into a tight hug, and I gasp at my breasts' sensitivity. "Ow."

"What's wrong?"

"That hurt."

"Your breasts?" Mom asks.

"Yeah, I guess… a couple of months of eating whatever I want and not going to the gym, and I feel like I'm falling apart. Nothing fits, and my body is beyond sore. And I think I might be coming down with something because I threw up last night. We almost canceled today, but I woke up feeling a little better."

"Hey, Ken," Bailey says slowly. "When's the last time you had your period?"

"What?" I give her a confused look. "What does that have to do with anything?"

"Just humor me," she says with a tight smile.

I think for a second, but I can't recall. I never had one while we were away… and before that… Shit! "Not since the hospital."

"You had one while you were in the hospital?" Mom clarifies.

"No, I mean, not since before then. I can't remember." I think some more, and then it hits me. "In December. I had it the weekend of the Christmas parade."

"Sunshine," Mom says softly. "That was five months ago. Could you be pregnant?"

"No," I scoff. "I get the shot. You know this." I've been on it for years.

"When's the last time you got it?" Bailey asks. "It's every three months, right?"

I try to remember, but I can't because it would've been during the time I have no memory. But I had to have gotten it, right? I grab my phone and scroll through my calendar, finding where I input my last appointment: November 19th. Three months later would be… "Fuck! I should've gotten it in February."

"Do you know for sure you didn't?" Mom asks, taking my hand in hers and guiding us over to the loveseat. Bailey sits in the reading chair next to us.

"I would've put it in the calendar. I put *everything* in there." Oh my God. This can't be happening. It has to be some kind of a coincidence. The weight gain, sore breasts, feeling sick… It could be something else. Anything else. Right?

I dart my eyes back and forth between my sister and mom. "Between the accident and the non-wedding and then taking off, I didn't even think about it." Tears prick my eyes. "There has to be another explanation."

"There's only one way to find out," Mom says. "You need to take a test."

"Oh, jeez," I groan. "This is so crazy. Wouldn't I know if I were pregnant?"

"Everybody's body is different," Bailey says. "Cynthia didn't—" She slaps her hand over her mouth, her eyes going wide.

"Cynthia what?" Mom gasps. "Is Cynthia pregnant?" She and Bailey talked about using a surrogate. Bailey has no desire to carry a baby, but Cynthia wants to, so they were considering going to the sperm bank, but they haven't said anything.

"She is." Bailey's entire face lights up. "On the first try." Tears fill her eyes. "She's only eleven weeks, so we were waiting another week before we told anyone."

"Oh my God!" I leap into her arms. "I'm so happy for you guys."

"I'm going to be a grandma again?" Mom sobs, hugging Bailey next. "Congratulations, sweetie."

"What's going on?" Cynthia asks. "Why are you guys crying?" She walks into the room and closes the door.

"I slipped," Bailey admits sheepishly, making Cynthia laugh. "They know."

"Congratulations," Mom and I say, each giving Cynthia a hug.

"Sorry," Bailey adds, pulling Cynthia onto her lap. "Kendall was asking if she could be pregnant and—"

"What?" Cynthia gasps, her head swinging my way. "You're pregnant?"

"I don't know. They think I could be, but I feel like I would know if I were."

"Maybe not," Cynthia says. "I haven't had a single day of morning sickness." She reaches over and knocks three times on the wood. "Aside from my clothes not fitting, I haven't had any symptoms."

"You need to take a pregnancy test," Mom says again, giving me a sympathetic smile.

"Oh! I have one." Cynthia pops up. "I had a couple with us when we were traveling to test, and I never removed them. I'll go grab my purse." She scurries out of the room.

While she's gone, I scroll through my calendar. It's been roughly six weeks since the first time Declan and I had sex. It's enough time for me to have gotten pregnant, especially since we've never once used protection because I thought I was protected.

"Here you go." Cynthia hands me the stick. "It's digital, so it will read pregnant or not pregnant."

"Thanks."

I take it from her and head into the bathroom. Once I've peed on the stick, I wash my hands and then remain in the bathroom alone, waiting for the results to pop up on the blank screen. First, the word PREGNANT appears, but like an idiot, I keep watching and waiting for the NO to pop up as well. Only, after several minutes, it doesn't.

"Sunshine," Mom says through the door. "Are you okay?"

When I don't say anything, *can't* say anything with the ball of emotion clogging my throat, the door creaks open, and she comes in.

"You're pregnant," she whispers.

"Maybe the no just hasn't appeared yet," I croak out.

"Oh, sweetheart." She pulls me into a hug. "It's been enough time. If it were going to appear, it already would've. Do you want Declan here?"

"No." I shake my head, pulling back. "I don't want to get his hopes up. I can't be more than six weeks along *if* I'm even pregnant." Jesus, if my clothes are already busting at the seams at only six weeks pregnant, how big will I be at nine months?

"Does that mean he'll be happy?" Bailey asks.

"We haven't talked about me getting pregnant, but he said he wants a family." Although, that was just hypothetical. He never actually said he wanted to start a family *now*.

Oh, shit. He's still so young. What if he's not planning to start a family for several years?

"Kendall, you're breathing heavily," Mom points out.

"What... What if he doesn't want to start a family now?" I ask, my chest rising and falling in quick succession. I'm on the verge of having a panic attack, but I can't stop the freak-out that's building. "What if he freaks out like..." I swallow thickly. "Like Freeman freaked out on you. What if he doesn't want this baby the way Freeman never wanted me?"

Mom's eyes widen, and I immediately regret my words. She hates speaking about my sperm donor. "Don't you dare compare Declan to that monster. He might be shocked, but he would never treat you the way *he* treated me. Not every man is like that. Look at your father. When he found out I was pregnant with Cam, he was shocked but still excited, and he barely knew me. That boy has been in love with you for years."

Okay, yeah, that makes sense, but…

"What if I'm a shitty mom?" I blurt out, moving on to my next fear. Declan might not be anything like Freeman, but half my DNA matches that monster.

"Oh my God, Kendall, stop it," Bailey demands. "Take a deep breath." I try to do what she says, but I'm having trouble catching my breath.

"Sunshine, calm down," Mom adds. "Declan is going to be happy, and you're going to be an amazing mom."

She's right. I know she is, but I'm already chin-deep in freak-out mode, so I'm not thinking clearly. I'm drowning in what-ifs, and I can't come up for air. Suddenly, it all becomes too much. The room spins, and everything turns fuzzy.

"Mom," I mutter. "I don't feel so good."

And then everything goes black.

"THERE SHE IS," MOM SAYS WITH A TIGHT SMILE.

"What happened?" I rasp, my throat dry.

"You blacked out."

"What?" I gasp, my hand going straight to my belly. "Is the baby okay?"

Mom's smile widens. "It was only for a few seconds. You were sitting, so you didn't fall. You worked yourself up and passed out."

"You sure you don't want us to get Declan?" Bailey asks.

"No. I don't know for sure that I'm pregnant. I know the stick said I am, but I would rather have it confirmed by a doctor first.

Then I'll tell him."

The women all give me various looks that say they don't agree, but I'm sticking to my decision. If this is just a coincidence or something is wrong, I don't want to get him worked up for nothing. Once I know for sure, I'll tell him when we're alone.

"Can I ask you something?" Bailey says after a few minutes.

"Of course."

"Is it possible that the baby could be Kyle's?"

"What?" I shriek. "No! We haven't had sex since… I don't know when. At least since before the accident."

Cynthia quirks a brow, so I explain, "After I woke up, I felt off. I knew in my heart I wasn't in love with Kyle, so even though he tried, I never once went there with him. The only person I've had sex with is Declan."

"Okay, good," Bailey says. "I'm sorry. I just had to ask."

"It's—"

I'm cut off by a knock on the door, followed by Declan's baritone voice. "Kendall, are you okay?"

"We better get out there," I say, walking over to the door. "Please don't say anything."

My mom and sister both pretend to zip their lips while Cynthia nods.

I take a deep breath, then open the door, plastering on a fake smile. "Hey, sorry. Girl talk."

Declan rakes his gaze down my body. "That dress looks beautiful."

"Thanks."

"Breakfast is ready," he says to the four of us.

"Great," Mom says. "I'm starved."

The rest of the morning goes by without a hitch. Breakfast is delicious, and I make several TikToks with Felix. We watch the music video—since it's done and will be released, along with the song, on Friday at midnight—and my dad suggests Declan and I make our relationship public because, according to him, that video is way too hot. No way anyone in their right mind will believe nothing is going on between us.

After we give Mom our gifts, Declan and I say our goodbyes so we can head to his parents' place for an early dinner. Unlike the warm vibe at my home, Declan's parents are ice cold.

We spend the entire meal with them judging us while acting like they aren't. I try not to let it get to me—I'm used to public scrutiny—but it's hard when it's clear they don't approve of what either of us does for a living. I come from a home where the music industry is in all of our blood, and every dig they make feels like it's aimed at not just Declan and me but also my entire family.

Finally, Declan must have enough because he tells his mom we need to leave, using the excuse that I haven't been feeling well. She gets upset, saying we haven't even had dessert yet, but he insists we go, promising to see them soon.

The ride home is filled with silence, and I expect him to push me away, obviously upset over the way the dinner went, so I'm surprised when the moment we step through the door, he attacks me.

"Thank you," he murmurs against my lips as he reaches around and unzips my dress.

"For what?"

"For putting up with my parents' shit. I love them, but sometimes, I hate them so damn much. Thank you for being there today. It's the first time I've ever had someone in my corner, and it made it that much easier. It sounds crazy, but it would've been twice as bad had you not been there."

God, I can't even imagine. Your parents, your family, should be your safe place. You shouldn't dread going there. It's the one place where you can be yourself and feel accepted. Despite all my insecurities and hang-ups, I know without a shadow of a doubt my family loves me and supports me. Knowing Declan doesn't have that at home makes me so sad.

"I'll always be there." I cup the sides of his face and look up into his blue eyes filled with love and awe. "*Always.*"

"Promise?" he says, placing a soft kiss on my lips before backing away slightly.

"I promise. You and me… always."

"THANK YOU FOR SEEING ME ON SUCH SHORT NOTICE." I SMILE NERVOUSLY AT DR. Weisberg, the OB/GYN Layla recommended I use since my gyno is back in California. She mentioned she's the OB to many celebrities who require NDAs to be signed, so her office would handle it without any hiccups, and she was right. Not even twenty-four hours after calling the office, NDAs have been signed and sent to my assistant. I'm sitting on the medical bed in the small yet inviting room in only a cotton gown, my entire body buzzing with anxiety.

"You're very welcome," Dr. Weisberg says, sitting on the rolling stool in front of me. "You mentioned you were in an accident that—"

Her words are cut off by the sound of the door opening as my mom walks in. "Kendall Naomi Blackwood." My eyes widen at her using my three names, wondering what she's doing here and why I'm in trouble. Even though I'm thirty-two years old, it scares the shit out of me when my mom uses my three names.

"Mom, what are you doing here?"

She closes the door behind her and walks around the side to stand next to me. "Marcia told me you were coming here alone. Why wouldn't you tell me so I could come with you?" she chides in her motherly tone that has tears pricking my eyes.

"I don't know," I mutter. "I guess I'm scared and…" I shrug, unable to verbalize how I'm feeling. Ever since Bailey mentioned Kyle could be the dad, I've been freaking out on the inside. I wanted so badly to tell Declan I might be pregnant and that I'm scared it might not be his, but I couldn't do that to him. He might've become one of the closest people to me—the person I share my thoughts and dreams with—but I couldn't be so selfish to tell him there's a chance the baby I may or may not be carrying is his. So instead of saying a word, after Declan and I made love Sunday night and then again last night, I lay awake, watching him sleep, wondering what our future holds.

"Oh, Sunshine. You don't have to take on the world by yourself," my mom says, knowing me well enough that I don't have to finish my thoughts. "Whatever happens, you have an entire family who loves and supports you." She pulls me into her arms and kisses my cheek. "I love you, Kendall."

"Love you too, Mom," I choke out, feeling like shit for all the times I've pushed her away. It doesn't matter how many times I push because she always finds her way back in.

Once I've composed myself, the doctor greets my mom, already knowing her since she's Mom's gyno as well, and then I explain everything to her.

"Well, first things first," Dr. Weisberg says. "Based on your blood work, you have high hCG levels, telling us you are pregnant, but we want to do a scan to confirm and get an estimated due date. I'm going to have you lie back and cover you with this blanket.

Usually, I would try transvaginal first, but I believe you are far enough along to use a Doppler."

She hands me the blanket to cover myself and lifts my gown to expose my belly. My mom stays next to me, taking my hand in hers, and I've never been so thankful to have a mom who cares enough to know that I would need her today.

Dr. Weisberg explains everything she's doing as she does it, and then the loudest *woosh, woosh, woosh* fills the silent room. From going with my mom to her appointments when she was pregnant with my siblings, I instantly recognize the sound.

"That's my baby's heartbeat."

"It is," the doctor confirms. "A good, strong heartbeat at 141. And..." She moves the Doppler over slightly, the sound fading and then increasing again. "A second heartbeat. Also a strong heartbeat at 135."

"What?" I gasp.

Dr. Weisberg laughs softly. "You're pregnant with twins."

Mom squeezes my hand and leans over to kiss the top of my head. "Congratulations," she murmurs, causing me to choke up in the middle of my state of shock. Holy shit! I'm not only pregnant, but I'm pregnant with twins.

"All right, so based on these measurements," the doctor says as she moves the Doppler around and clicks away on the screen. "You're fifteen weeks along. Due November third."

Her words have my heart stopping in my chest, my lungs depleting of all my air. No. No. No, no, no... This can't be happening. I did the math a million times and checked several pregnancy calculators. In order for Declan to be the dad, I could only be, at the most, six weeks pregnant. Yet I'm...

"Are you sure?" I blurt out. "Could they be measuring big?"

The doctor explains each measurement and the weight of

the babies. Baby A is measuring at 6.47 inches and weighs 4.03 ounces, and baby B is 6.57 inches and weighs 4.12 ounces. They're not sharing a placenta, which means they won't be identical, even if they're the same sex. Everything looks good, and I'm in my second trimester of my pregnancy, missing the entire first one altogether. She shows my mom and me the hands and legs and head of each of the babies while my mom rubs my shoulder, and I push everything else aside, giving my precious babies my full attention.

"I can't believe I didn't know I was pregnant, let alone fifteen weeks along with twins," I say to no one in particular. Once she's done and has removed the Doppler from my belly, she hands me some paper towels to wipe the gunk off my stomach.

"It happens," Dr. Weisberg says, "especially if you don't have any morning sickness." She lifts the headrest and helps me sit up.

"I haven't had any," I admit, and then I remember something. "I've drunk wine…" Though, thinking back, I thought it tasted off and only had a sip. "Can that harm the babies?" My hand goes to my stomach, and now that I'm looking at it in a whole new light, it's protruding out and has been for a few weeks. I don't know if I was in denial or really thought I had just eaten too much, but now that my pregnancy is confirmed, my ill-fitting clothes make so much more sense.

"Everything looks good, and a little wine won't harm the babies. I want you to start on a prenatal vitamin as soon as possible, and we'll schedule your twenty-week checkup. It's an ultrasound, and generally, we can see the sex of the babies during that one, so if you have someone you'd like to bring, you can do so."

While she goes over a few more things and does an internal exam, I try to focus, but my emotions are all over the place: shocked, excited, scared, and the one I hate the most, heartbroken—because

I know what I have to do, and it hurts so damn badly.

Once I'm dressed, the doctor gives me several pictures of the babies, who are labeled A and B. I make my next appointment, and then we head out. Since I didn't drive here, instead of calling my driver to pick me up, I go with my mom in her vehicle. The ride to her house is silent. We stop at the pharmacy to get the prenatal vitamins that Dr. Weisberg prescribed and then swing by the deli to grab lunch to take back to her house. When we get there, the place is quiet.

"Phoebe is at school," she explains. "And your dad is at work."

I nod, setting the drinks on the counter. Ever since I found out how far along I am, and what that means, I've gone numb. My mom let it go since we were at the doctor's office and then in the car, but now that we're home, I know she won't let it slide for much longer. I swallow down the vitamin, and then we eat in silence. The subs are from our favorite deli, but it tastes like cardboard today. While we eat, Declan texts me a few times, asking how it's going since he thinks I'm in a meeting with the label regarding my upcoming album. It's the first time I've lied to him, and it makes me sick to my stomach.

"Kendall," my mom says once we're both done eating. "Talk to me." She takes my hand and guides us over to the couch. "Tell me what's going through your head. You were given a lot of information today, so it's normal to be a bit overwhelmed, but I'm mostly worried about one piece of information in particular. How far along you are."

"Declan's not the dad." Saying those words, despite my mom already knowing, were probably the hardest, most gut-wrenching words I've ever had to speak, and as the last word leaves my lips, the numbness that was temporarily holding me together disappears, forcing me to feel every heartbreaking emotion.

Tears fill my lids, blurring my vision, as a sob rises up my throat and forces its way out. My mom pulls me into her arms, and I bury my face in her chest, crying for everything I'm about to lose. Deep down, I always knew that the elusive happily ever after my parents and siblings have gotten with their significant others wasn't in the cards for me. It's why I always chose to sing about heartbreak.

But the hardest part is knowing I came so close to having it, only for it to be ripped out of my grasp. And what's even worse is that, while I'm devastated that I'm about to lose the man I love, I feel guilty because I can't regret getting pregnant. My babies, despite being Kyle's and not Declan's, already own my heart. The moment I heard their heartbeats and saw their tiny bodies fluttering across the screen, I fell in love.

And it's at this moment I finally understand why my mom was able to love me despite me having half of that monster's DNA.

"I get it," I choke out. "All these years, I've wondered how you could love me when half of me comes from such a horrible person. When I found out the things he did to those women, I started to push you away because I didn't understand how you could look at me and not see that evil monster…"

"Oh, Kendall," my mom murmurs softly, lifting my face and pushing my hair out of my eyes. "Why didn't you say something? From the moment I found out I was pregnant, you became my entire world."

"I get it now," I say, crying in her arms. "Because despite these babies being Kyle's, I love them so much, and even though it breaks my heart that they're not Declan's, it doesn't make me love them any less."

"Of course it doesn't," she says. "That's called a mother's love. We love our babies unconditionally."

"I have to break up with Declan," I tell her through a sob that has my entire body shaking. "And before you tell me I'm being ridiculous, I'm not. Declan is the best guy I know. He loves with his entire heart, and I know he'll accept these babies if I ask him to, but that's not fair to him. He deserves to find a woman he can love and create a life with. He's so romantic and wants it all—the marriage and kids—and it's not fair to force him into a situation where he has to play stepdad and deal with Kyle."

Fuck, Kyle… "Ugh, I'm going to have to tell Kyle I'm pregnant." I would never keep a man from knowing his children, but what a damn mess this is.

"When I met your father, you weren't his, but you'd never know it," Mom points out.

"Yeah, but you were also pregnant with Dad's baby, and he went into it knowing about me. I'm pregnant with twins by another man. He deserves to have babies of his own, and at my age, I have no idea if I'll have more kids. So I what, string him along and force him to take on two babies who aren't his? No, I won't do it."

Mom's lips purse together. "I don't think you're giving him enough credit, nor do I think you understand how unconditional love works. What if the roles were reversed, and he found out he was expecting a baby who wasn't yours? Would you want him to break up with you?"

"It's not the same thing. I could still get pregnant, and Declan isn't the kind of person to just sleep around with any woman. He takes relationships seriously. He wouldn't sleep with another woman and turn around and be with me a few weeks later." *Pulling stunts like that and messing everything up is more my style.*

"It's for the best," I tell her, sniffling. "He shouldn't be drawn into my shit show of a life. It's not like I deserved a man like him anyway. Fate has a way of reminding us where we belong in this world, and I don't belong with a man like Declan."

"Oh, stop with the self-deprecation," Mom chides. "You're hormonal, and your emotions are all over the place. Please don't make any rash decisions until you've thought this all through."

"There's nothing to think through. I'm not putting Declan in that position. He's a good guy and would no doubt step up, but I'm not going to let him do that."

"And where does Kyle fit in?"

"I won't be with someone just for the sake of the kids. Kyle deserves to be happy and in a marriage for love. I don't feel that way about him. I'll let him know I'm pregnant, and if he wants to be in the babies' lives, we'll figure it out."

Mom sighs. "Maybe you should move home."

"Mom, I love you, but there's no way I'm living with you and Dad again." I lean over and kiss her cheek. "I have the money and means to live on my own. But I would like to find a bigger place, and I'll need to look for help with the babies. I was supposed to go on tour for the new album, but—"

"Breathe. You have plenty of time. Take a deep breath."

"You're right," I tell her as items mentally get added to my list of things I need to do… starting with breaking up with Declan.

As if he knows I'm thinking about him, a text comes through from the man himself: **Dinner tonight at my place. Six o'clock.**

My heart drops out of my chest and into my gut. Tonight… Tonight, I'm going to have to break both his and my heart. **I'll see you then.**

# Twenty-Three

## Declan



Korean BBQ—her favorite—check.

Crème brûlée for dessert—also her favorite—check.

I reach into my pocket and open the box for the dozenth time…

Engagement ring—check.

When I had Braxton go with me to pick out the ring, I looked at hundreds, but only one caught my eye. It's an eight-carat oval-cut diamond with a micro-pavé band. It's simple and classic yet elegant, and when I saw it, I knew it was the one—the ring that will sit on Kendall's finger for the rest of our lives.

I light the candles and dim the lights and am about to text Kendall to see if she's on her way since it's a few minutes past six when the alarm indicating she's here sounds.

She walks through the door, dressed casually yet beautifully in a flowy dress. She's been down about gaining some weight recently since she's gone off her usual strict diet and workout routine, but I have to admit, the extra pounds look good on her. She was already the sexiest woman I've ever laid eyes on, but she's even sexier with the bit of thickness added to her. The other night when we were fucking, I flipped her onto her hands and knees and took her from behind, loving the way my fingers gripped her full hips.

I shake the visual from my head, not wanting to be stuck with a hard-on, and walk over to greet her. "How was your day?" I ask, leaning in for a kiss.

She dodges it, and my lips land on her cheek. And that's when I notice her face is splotchy, and her eyes are rimmed red. "You've been crying."

She answers by saying the four words every man dreads. "We need to talk."

"Okay, I have dinner in the kitchen."

"I'm not hungry." She averts my gaze, and when her eyes land on the table, all done up, she flinches. "Shit, I didn't know dinner was a *thing*. I'm sorry."

"It's fine. We don't have to eat." I try to take her hand to walk us over to the couch, but she pulls away. Fuck, this isn't good. I can feel it down to my marrow. Something is wrong.

"I've decided to move home."

*Huh?* I'm confused. While she's been staying here often, she hasn't actually moved in, so I'm not sure why she's telling me this.

And then she finishes her sentence, making it make sense. "...back to California."

"What?"

"The album is done, and most of the PR will be in LA, so it makes sense for me to move back to my house in Calabasas. This was never supposed to be my permanent home anyway."

"Okay." My head spins. "I was hoping to be here when Gage is ready to come home, but Camden and Braxton are here, and I can always fly—"

"I don't mean us," she says, cutting me off. "I'm moving back to the West Coast…alone."

"What?" I say again like a dumbass. But I'm so confused, I don't know what else to say. "Why would you move, and I stay here?"

The answer hits me at the same time she speaks the words. "Because it's not working out between us."

"What?" Jesus, can't I think of anything else to say?

"I'm sorry," she says, her lids turning a brighter shade of red as if her eyes want to cry but she won't let it happen. "I tried, but I can't do it. I care about you, but I don't want to be with you anymore." She turns her back on me, ready to bolt like the runner she is, but before she can make it out the door, I gently grab her elbow and spin her around. Her eyes are filled with liquid emotion, and I'm baffled as to why she's doing this when she's clearly so upset about it.

"What's going on? Why are you doing this?"

"I told you," she chokes out. "It's not working out. Please don't make this any harder than it needs to be," she pleads. "I'm sorry, but it's over. I have to go."

She runs out the door, and I follow, refusing to let her get away. I don't know what the fuck is going on, but I'm not about to lose her without at least knowing why. Since I've known Kendall, she's been a runner. When shit gets rough, she runs. When she gets hurt, she runs. When she breaks up with a guy, she runs. Hell, she ran from her wedding, climbing out a goddamn window, for God's sake. You don't get into a relationship with Kendall without understanding that she's going to run at some point. The difference is, I'm always going to chase and catch her. Every single time.

"Stop," I demand, covering the button to the elevator before she can press it. "You want to run? Fine. But first, tell me why you're breaking up with me."

She shakes her head. "Let me go. It doesn't matter why. All you need to know is that we're over."

"Did I do something wrong?"

She scoffs through her tears. "You're perfect, Dec. You could never do anything wrong."

I roll my eyes, hating that she sees me without faults and flaws. She puts me up on a pedestal that nobody belongs on, let alone me.

"Okay, so you did something? Talk to me, baby," I say, palming the side of her face. "Whatever it is, we'll get through it together. I love you."

For a split second, she leans in, her eyes fluttering shut, and I think maybe she's going to talk to me. But then her eyes pop open, and I see her resolve and determination. I know it will take more than me begging to get through to her.

"There's nothing to talk about," she says, her back going straight. "I'm leaving, and I would appreciate it if you'd let me go."

"Fuck that!" It's the first time I've ever raised my voice at her, but I'm so damn confused and frustrated. "Tell me what the hell is wrong so I can fix it! Please."

"You can't fix it!" she yells back. "Nothing you say or do will fix this. So please just let me go." She moves my hand from the button and presses it. The damn thing must've been sitting on this floor because it immediately opens, and she gets in. "I'm sorry," she mouths as the doors close, whisking her and my heart away.

I consider chasing her, but whatever's going on with her is something she isn't ready to talk about, so instead, I go inside and blow out the candles, throw the flowers and food away, and then go down to the bar for a stiff drink while I contemplate my next move. Because despite what Kendall thinks, we're not over, and if she thinks I'm going to let her get away that easily, she has another thing coming.

**Kendall: Congratulations on the release of Drunk on Your Love.**

I STARE AT THE TEXT, TRYING TO FIGURE OUT HOW TO PROCEED. IT'S BEEN FOUR DAYS since Kendall walked out the door. Four days since I've seen her beautiful face or heard her melodic voice. It's been four goddamn days since I've kissed and touched and sunk deep into the woman who I know without a doubt is my forever. And unfortunately, I'm not any closer to finding out why she's run across the damn country to get away from me.

Despite me texting her several times a day, telling her I love her and this isn't over, this is the first text she's sent me. It's midnight my time, and our song and video have been released. Blackwood's social media team has handled everything, so there's nothing for me to do but watch the music video on loop since it's my only way of seeing Kendall. The way she dances in my arms and the passion behind the kiss we share reminds me that she loves me and wants me. She's just going through something, and instead of coming to me, she's run.

The good thing is, I'm going to be on a plane to LA later this morning since we have a few appearances lined up to promote the song as well as Kendall's upcoming album *Fallen*. Yes, *Fallen* because despite the bullshit she's pulling, she's fallen in love with me. And once I remind her of that, I'll get her to tell me what's wrong, and we'll sort out whatever it is together because nothing could push me away or stop me from loving and being with that woman.

**Me: Congrats, baby. See you soon.**

Several hours later, I'm on the West Coast, sitting beside Kendall as we're interviewed on the *Late Night Show*. When a video clip finishes playing—the part where we kiss in the rain—the host, Steve Barkin, fans his face dramatically.

"So guys, I have to ask, because holy moly, the chemistry in that video…" His eyes widen for the audience. "Is there something going on between you two?"

I've already been told by the label that I'm not allowed to say there is, and honestly, I wouldn't anyway. When the world finds out about Kendall and me, it will be because she's made it happen. Because she trusts in us enough to know that we're forever, and she's comfortable letting everyone know.

"Have you seen this gorgeous woman?" I point at Kendall. "She's way out of this rock star's league." I shrug, laughing and making the audience laugh as well. Kendall's face falls for a second, but she quickly recovers, laughing it off. She looks like everything is fine to someone who doesn't know her. But because I know everything about her, I can see the faint black circles under the makeup, the tension in her shoulders, and the way she sits stiffly in her spot on the couch. Clearly, something is going on with her, and after we get out of here tonight, I'm going to find out what.

"Right, right, I can see that," Steve adds, moving on to discuss the song and how our collaboration came about. Then he talks with Kendall a bit about her upcoming album. Aside from the evident sadness she works hard to hide, she plays her role perfectly.

Once Steve thanks us for coming, and it cuts to commercial,

we thank him for having us and then head out. I follow Kendall, not about to let her slip away, and when we get outside where our security is waiting for us, I pull her to the side so I can talk to her.

"How've you been?"

She avoids my face. "I'm fine. I really need to get going, though."

"Get going where? To your house, to go to bed?"

She sighs. "Yes, to my house. It's late, and I'm tired and hungry."

"Let's go eat, and then you can go home and get some sleep."

"Dec, don't do this." The pain in her voice tears my heart to shreds. I don't know why she's doing this when it's obvious she's hurting as badly as I am.

"Do what? Ask you to get something to eat with me? You said if we broke up, you wanted to remain friends. This is me being your friend."

Her gorgeous blue eyes meet mine. "I appreciate that, but I'm not in the mood to go out."

"Then let me make you something," I offer, stepping into her space. "I get it," I tell her, saying what she needs to hear. "It didn't work out. Does that suck? Yeah, it does. But you were… *are* one of my best friends, so please don't shut me out. I'm trying to be your friend here, so let me."

I tuck a wayward hair behind her ear, and as my fingers skate down the side of her neck, I see her shiver from my touch. She wants to act like we're over, fine, but her body says otherwise.

"Please…"

After a long beat, she relents. "Okay, fine. You can come over and cook me something… as friends."

Since she had Gale, her housekeeper, restock the fridge upon her arrival, there's plenty of food for me to cook. While she showers and changes, I make a simple meal for the two of us I know she loves: breakfast for dinner.

I'm setting the plates of pancakes and bacon on the table as she walks into the kitchen, dressed in a pair of flannel pants and a loose pajama shirt that reads: World of Chaos—a shirt from one of our previous tours that she stole from me a while back. Her hair is in a messy bun on top of her head, and her face is free of makeup. She looks beyond beautiful, and it takes everything in me not to sweep her off her feet and take her to her room where I can get lost in her all night long. Not that she'd let me anyway since she's being all stubborn and shit and insisting we're over.

"This all smells so good," she moans, sitting at the table and grabbing a couple of pancakes. She snatches up a piece of bacon, breaks off a piece, and pops it into her mouth. The way she moans when the bacon enters her mouth has my dick twitching and begging me to reconsider taking her to the room.

Not wanting it to get awkward, I make light conversation about the numbers Easton sent us. The song has only been out for a day, and it is already topping the charts for being the most downloaded and streamed song in a twenty-four-hour period. The official video has over eighty million views.

"It wouldn't be what it is without you," she admits, forking a piece of pancake into her mouth. "Thank you for being a part of it."

I hate how formal she's speaking like we haven't been intimate, and I haven't stuck my dick into every one of her damn holes. But I bite the inside of my cheek and go along with it, hoping she'll say something that indicates why she's made this decision.

When we're both done eating, she insists I leave the dishes, then walks me to the door. "I'm really glad we can still be friends," she says softly, opening the front door. "I guess I'll see you tomorrow night for the interview with Larson?"

"Kendall…"

"Declan, don't… please." She shakes her head. "I don't have it in me to argue with you."

"Baby, I don't want to argue. I want to know how to fix whatever happened so we can go back to being us again." My eyes plead with her, but she doesn't give me a damn inch.

"I already told you it can't be fixed. I need you to leave, please."

"Ken…" I start to beg, suddenly feeling anxious. At first, I had it in my head that she was just freaking out, and as soon as I got her to talk to me, I'd be able to set her straight, but now, as I look at her defeated face, it hits me… It's really over. She isn't running or hiding. She let me in to her home and ate dinner with me. But she doesn't want to be anything more than friends.

For whatever reason, Kendall Blackwood no longer wants to be with me. The realization is damn near crippling, knowing the woman I want to spend my life with doesn't see or want the same future as I do.

"It's really over, isn't it?" I ask, needing her to say the words one last time.

"It is," she says softly. Her eyes flutter closed and then open, and a single tear slides down her cheek. "I'm so sorry, Dec," she says as more follow. "I'm so sorry for hurting you." She shakes her head, and I pull her into my arms, needing to feel her against me. Her signature D&G perfume hits my senses, and it takes everything in me not to break down.

Fuck! I don't know what to do. I'm at a loss. On the one hand, I want to lock her in the room and force her to talk to me, but that's not how this should be. It's not how a relationship should be. If she wanted me to know, she'd talk to me. Right? Deep down, I know she wouldn't. Kendall is sweet and funny and has the biggest heart, but she's also a little broken. There's nothing wrong with that. I stand by what I told her all those years ago: It's okay to be a little broken. But the problem is, whatever is broken inside her is preventing her from functioning, and I can't do it on my own.

"You don't have to apologize," I tell her, squeezing her a little tighter. "It was worth it… To have you in my arms, to be with you for that short time. It was worth the heartbreak."

She nods into my chest, then sniffles. "I agree," she murmurs. "I already miss you."

"Oh, baby. I'm here. I'm always here," I tell her, repeating the words she said to me not long ago. Needing her to understand that no matter what happens between us, I'm not going anywhere. "Always."

# Twenty-Four

## Kendall

"HAVE YOU SEEN THE POST FROM *THE GOSSIP GAZETTE*?" LAYLA TURNS THE SCREEN TO face me, and I cringe at the headline—"From doing bump to a baby bump?"

"Ugh. I hate them so much. They should be sued for slander." I've never done drugs a day in my life, but once, over a year ago, I made the mistake of attending an award show with a musician who did—and I had no clue. One party, where someone got a picture of him doing lines of coke while I was in the restroom— and when I returned and sat down and saw what he was doing, I had my security team escort me out immediately—and they've turned me into a damn wannabe druggy.

"Truth, but that photo they snapped of you… you can't deny you look pregnant," Layla says, popping a piece of bagel into her mouth. We're all at my parents' house for Sunday brunch. The guys—minus Declan and Gage—are helping my mom move around some new furniture she bought for the house and isn't sure how she wants them placed, while Layla, Kaylee, and I eat and drink our coffee as we watch Felix dance to a new music video. Marianna crawls around, chasing his feet and driving him nuts.

"I know." I sigh. It's why I've flown in from California this weekend—to handle something I've been dreading. I need to tell Kyle about my pregnancy, which I've put off all weekend. Since it's Sunday, and I know it's his only day off, I'm going to drive over there this afternoon. I'd call or text him first, but when I tried, I quickly realized he blocked me. Not that I blame him… if leaving someone at the altar isn't reason enough to never want to speak to someone again, what is? But that means I'll have to awkwardly go over there and deal with this.

"How are you holding up?" Kaylee asks, flashing me a look of sympathy. Since our family knew about Declan and me, I had no choice but to tell them that we broke up. I also asked them not to mention I'm pregnant. I want to be the one to tell him, but I need to tell Kyle first. I should've told Declan when I broke up with him, but it was too hard. My heart was too broken to go there.

"I'm hanging in there." I shrug. "I miss Declan so much, but he deserves so much better than what I can give him. Have you seen him?"

Layla and Kaylee both shake their heads.

"No," Kaylee says. "He's been MIA the past couple of weeks. I think between Gage refusing to come home and then…" She trails off and clears her throat. "He just needs some time."

My chest tightens, hating myself for what I've done and wishing I could change the facts.

"After I talk to Kyle today, I'm flying back to LA for the rest of my pregnancy so he can have some space."

"What?" My mom gasps, making me turn around. "You're leaving again?"

Dammit, this is not how I wanted to tell her. I'm just messing everything up with everyone lately. "LA is my home. And with Declan here... I don't want to rub it in his face. It's not fair to him."

Camden and Braxton both nod in understanding, and I knew they would because they care about Declan.

"But Kyle is here," Mom points out. "I can't see him being okay with that."

"And I'm planning to come back before I give birth if that's what Kyle insists. But if he's okay with me staying in LA, and him traveling to visit, I think that would be best. The last thing I want is for Declan to have to see me all the time."

"Or you could stop being stubborn," Camden says. "Tell him what's going on and let him make the decision for himself."

I stand, not wanting to have this conversation for the millionth time. "We'll agree to disagree. I'm going to head over to speak to Kyle. I'll come back afterward. I'm not leaving until tomorrow."

"I actually need to speak to you regarding some business," Dad says. "Can you come by the studio in the morning before you go?"

"Of course."

"You're taking security with you, right?" Mom asks. "I don't like you going to Kyle's by yourself."

"Yep. I'm going to text Evan now and let him know I'm ready to go." I give my parents a hug.

"I really hope you'll consider staying here," Mom says. "Your family is all here, and selfishly, I don't want to miss my grandbabies growing up. Bailey and Cynthia's baby is due not long after yours."

"I agree," Layla adds. "Would you rather be alone in California or with your family and friends?"

I know they're all right, but it's just so unfair to Declan. Not only is he about to be surrounded by his married friends, who are all happily growing their families, but he's going to have to be around the woman who hurt him.

"I'll think about it," I tell everyone noncommittally. "I better get going."

After saying goodbye to everyone, I head out with Evan. When we arrive at Kyle's place, I quickly find out that he's not home. Not wanting to leave without speaking to him, I have Evan drive over to Kyle's office. It's really the only other place he would be since he's such a workaholic.

Since I know the code to get into the building from when we were together, I input it into the elevator and take it up to the floor his office is located on, telling Evan to wait in the lobby for me. He isn't thrilled, but I think it'd be better to tell my ex-fiancé that he's about to be a father to twins without an audience.

Leaving Evan standing by, I walk down the hall to where I know Kyle's office is located. I hear a voice, telling me he's here, which isn't all that shocking. The man would live here if he could. He's probably making calls, something he often did on Sundays if I didn't demand he take the day off.

As I get closer, the voices get a bit louder, and I wonder if maybe he's not alone. That or he's on speaker. Regardless, since I'm already here, and he has me blocked, I should still proceed, so I can at least ask him to unblock me so we can talk when he's alone.

Even though the door is partially open, to be polite, I raise my hand to knock when my eyes land on the inside of his office, giving me the perfect view of Kyle thrusting into a woman who's bent over his desk, begging him to fuck her harder.

Her eyes meet mine, and something in me snaps as visions and images flood my brain.

*A little over three months ago*

**Kyle: I'm sorry I can't make it tonight. Ross gave me an important**

**project to work on. I'll make it up to you tomorrow. I promise.**

*I toss my phone onto the table, annoyed. This is the same excuse he's given me the past several Saturdays. I'm sick of his job coming first. I get that he's ambitious, but I'm not sure I want to be married to a man who's married to his job. I understand it firsthand, as I've spent years married to my music career, but at thirty-one years old, I'm ready to settle down and start a family. Do I really want to do that with a man who can't give me one night a week of his time?*

*Deciding that the only way for him to understand where I'm coming from is to speak to him, I head to his office. On the way, I stop at the deli we both like and pick up dinner since he's probably been too busy to eat.*

*When I get up to his office, the place is quiet, save for a couple of voices coming from Kyle's office.* I'll just knock and let him know I'm here in case he's in a meeting and will be a while.

*Only when I get to his door, I find it ajar, and the important project he's working on is Britney, his boss's daughter and colleague. She's bent over his desk as he fucks her from behind. In shock from the visual in front of me, I gasp, which has both of them looking up. Britney smirks while Kyle flinches.*

*"What the hell?" I shriek. "If you didn't want to be with me, why didn't you just say so?" I chuck the bag at them, and it breaks open, the food flying everywhere. "Fuck you!" Unable to look at him and not wanting to cry in front of her, I fly out of the office.*

*"Kendall, wait!" Kyle yells, but I'm already in the elevator with the doors closing.*

*I should've known… Deep down, I think I always did, but I was so caught up in wanting to have what my family has that I chose to ignore all the red flags.*

*Only once I'm safely in the car do I allow the tears to fall. I can feel my phone buzzing in my pocket, but I ignore it since there's nothing*

*Kyle can say or do that'll make this right. Honestly, he's done me a favor by saving me from entering a marriage that shouldn't be taking place.*

So then why am I crying?

*Because once again, I wasn't enough. I wasn't the woman Kyle wanted or needed. I tried to be everything he needed, even took time off work and put him first, but it still wasn't enough. I'm never enough. Just like I wasn't enough for my sperm donor. Because I'm broken. And unlike when you're little and can still play with the toys that aren't perfect, nobody wants to play with the woman who's damaged beyond repair.*

*Not wanting to go home, I have my driver take me to Declan's place. He's become such a good friend, and right now, I don't want to be alone. He's been down ever since Gage almost died, so I know he'll appreciate the company.*

*Before heading up to his place, I check the bar, where he seems to spend the majority of his time these days, and sure enough, I see him sitting there, throwing back a shot. "Drinking alone?" I ask, sliding onto the seat next to him.*

*"Got no one to drink with."*

*He downs his shot, then glances over at me with his hypnotizing blue eyes. He rakes his gaze down my body, and my heart goes haywire, something that's been happening more often. I ignore it because Declan is not only my friend but also my brother's best friend and bandmate. And while ninety-nine percent of the time, I make shitty decisions, I'd never do anything that would potentially jeopardize my brother's friendships or band.*

*"You okay?" he asks when his eyes land on my face—no doubt noticing my splotchy and tearstained cheeks. One thing about Declan is that he notices everything when it comes to me.*

*Not wanting to get into the details of tonight, I change the subject.*

"How's Gage?"

"Alive."

"Because of you."

"No, he almost died because of me."

When he reaches for the bottle, I pour it for him and hand him the glass. "You saved his life, Dec." I hate that he's drowning in guilt when he's the reason Gage is even alive.

"His life never should've needed saving in the first place." He downs the shot and slams it on the table, glaring at me. I don't take it personally since it's only because I'm the one who's here for him to take his guilt out on.

"It wasn't your fault."

"Yeah, it fucking was." He eyes me. "What are you doing here, anyway?"

I pour myself a shot. "Same thing as you…" I down it and cringe as the whiskey burns going down. "Trying to drown my problems at the bottom of a bottle."

I can tell he wants to ask questions, but thankfully, he pours us each another shot instead. "To drowning our problems."

"To forgetting the world exists."

We spend the next couple of hours pushing our problems aside and focusing on simply living in the moment. We drink and dance, and when the bar announces that it's closing, I'm not ready for the night to end or to walk away from Declan when all I want to do is get lost in him. This isn't the first time I've had these thoughts, but the liquor running through my veins is allowing me to go after what I want.

What about Kyle?" Declan asks when I tell him I want to continue the night upstairs at his place.

"We're over."

"What happened?"

"I don't wanna talk about it." I drag my nails up his neck, stopping *at his bun, and tug on it gently, loving the way his thick hair falls around his face. "I just…" I swallow thickly. "I just wanna forget." Declan just might be the only person in the world that I feel like I can be somewhat honest with, who I know won't judge me. Because he gets it. Gets me. "Please, Dec," I breathe. "Help me forget."*

*And that's exactly what he does… helps me forget, over and over again.*

I shake my head as several more memories hit me hard…

Declan telling me he's in love with me… and has been for years. Asking me to give us a chance. Me scared of hurting him, of tearing apart the band and my family. Scared of what people would think if I jumped from guy to guy.

But in the end, my heart wins out, and I promise him that once I get my shit together, we can see where things go. And Declan, the amazing man he is, tells me he'll wait however long it takes.

"Kendall, what are you doing here?" Kyle asks, forcing me to focus on him and the woman he was just balls deep in.

"You fucked her while we were engaged."

Kyle's eyes widen, realizing I know. Because of the accident and my memory loss, he thought he'd gotten away with it.

"Why would you continue with our sham of an engagement if you wanted her?"

"Because he pitied you," Britney snarks. "It would've looked bad if he dumped you after you'd just been injured."

"Can we talk alone?" I ask him, ignoring her. I should probably be more upset than I am about being cheated on, but honestly, I'm not. I realized a long time ago Kyle wasn't the one for me, and this whole time I felt guilty, thinking I was the one who hurt him. But now that I know the truth, that guilt has been washed away. But I do have some questions.

Against Britney's wishes, Kyle forces her to leave so we can talk. Once she's gone, I ask my first question. "Were you with her the entire time?" It doesn't matter now, but damn, if he wanted her, why go through the trouble of proposing to me? If he had just broken off the engagement, or hell, not proposed, it would've prevented us from wasting so much pointless time together.

"No. It just happened. She came onto me and…"

I roll my eyes. "Don't treat me like an idiot." I'm going to be dealing with this guy for the next eighteen-plus years. I'm not about to let him get away with that crap.

He sighs. "I fucked up. I wanted to make partner so badly. I bust my ass for this firm, and sometimes, it feels like I'm not getting any closer to my goals."

"So you slept with her, hoping to get an in?" It hits me that I really had no clue who this guy was. I was too caught up in wanting to settle down and prove I'm not broken that I didn't take the time to get to know the person I was planning to marry.

*You took the time to get to know Declan,* a voice in my head points out.

"I know it's too late," Kyle says. "But I didn't do anything with her again… not until after you left me at the altar and took off with Declan." He crosses his arms over his chest. "Speaking of which, why are you even here?"

I open my mouth to tell him that I'm pregnant when it hits me… I had sex with Declan the night before my accident— several times and without any protection. Which means… Holy shit! Declan could very well be the father.

I try to think back to when Kyle and I had sex, but my memories are spotty at best. I could ask him, but I don't want to raise suspicions.

"You know what… never mind. Coming here was a mistake."

Kyle tries to stop me, but I'm now on a mission to find the man who I spent—from what I can remember—the most amazing night with and never told me.

The moment I'm back in the SUV, I text him: **Where are you? We need to talk.**

**Declan: At home.**

**Me: I'll be there soon.**

This entire time, I thought we weren't together until the road trip, but he knew… fucking knew that we shared a special night together, when we made love. I told him about my tattoo, and he confessed his feelings for me. The next morning, we made love again, and then I was in the accident, and when I woke up, I didn't remember. Except my body and heart actually did. Because when I opened my eyes, I felt it… the pull, the connection with Declan, but I didn't understand it because I couldn't remember it. So I pushed it away.

Oh, my God! Declan knew my engagement with Kyle was over, yet he was going to let me marry him!

# Twenty-Five

## Declan

MY PLACE IS A FUCKING MESS, AND I STINK. I'VE SPENT THE PAST COUPLE OF WEEKS drowning my sorrows at the bottom of a bottle of Jack. Because I didn't want to see anyone, I canceled the cleaning woman who usually comes. And I can't remember the last time I showered because I haven't given a shit enough to.

After Kendall texts that she's on her way, I quickly jump in the shower and get dressed, then spend the rest of the time shoving garbage into cabinets to make it look like the place isn't as dirty as it is. Just as she knocks, I light a candle, hoping it will help the place smell a little better.

Figuring this is as good as it'll get, I head to the front door to open it, both nervous and excited to see her. I'm hoping she's changed her mind about us, but I'm not counting on it.

"Hey," I say when I swing the door open.

She glares and walks past me. "Hey yourself."

She stops in the center of the living room, and before I can ask what's gotten her so upset, she speaks. "When did you plan to tell me that we had sex *before* my accident?"

Oh, shit. Dammit, I knew I should've told her, but… "I wanted you to want me. To choose me. I wanted you to feel what I felt… what I feel. I didn't want to have to *tell* you that we spent the most amazing night together."

Her features soften slightly, so I walk over to her. "I tried to tell you a few times, but every time, I didn't know how. I mean, how do you tell the person you're in love with that the best night of your life is the same night she can't even remember?"

Kendall sighs. "You were going to let me marry Kyle, even after knowing I planned to end our engagement."

"Only because you never told me why, and when you woke up, you were acting like everything was fine. Again, how was I supposed to tell you that you shouldn't be with him because you told me you were going to end things? It was a shitty situation, and maybe I made the wrong decision by not telling you, but in the end, your heart told you, which is why you walked away."

"He cheated on me," she admits. "I caught him screwing a colleague of his. Walked in on them doing it again today, and it all came back to me."

"You went to go see him?" Fuck, if she tells me she planned to give him another chance, I'll lose my shit.

"Yeah, to tell him that I'm pregnant." She says the words so nonchalantly that I almost don't process them, but once I do, I stumble back.

"You're pregnant…with Kyle's baby?" Fuck. "You and him… after you broke up with me?" My heart feels as though it's been ripped from my chest, thrown onto the ground, and stomped on.

"What? No!" She bridges the gap between us. "No. I'm almost seventeen weeks pregnant."

I glance down at her belly that she's holding and see the bump there. With the baggy clothes she's been wearing, I couldn't see it before, but now, it's obvious.

"When I found out I was pregnant, I was scared and excited," she says softly. "I wanted to tell you, but I wanted to know for sure, and then Bailey pointed out that because of my memory issues and not getting my period since I woke up in the hospital, there was a chance the baby could be Kyle's. And since I couldn't remember the last time he and I had sex, I wanted to make sure I was pregnant and find out how far along before I told you…"

Her words trail off, but I can finish her sentence. *Before she told me Kyle's the dad…* Fuck, this sucks, and it also explains why she broke up with me.

"Kendall…" I pull her onto the couch and take her hand in mine. "Did you break up with me to be with Kyle because he's the dad?" She, of all people, knows that just because you have someone's baby doesn't mean you should be with them. Look at her mom and her sperm donor.

"No," she breathes. "I…" She swallows thickly and averts her gaze. "I broke up with you because I didn't want you to have to raise someone else's babies."

"What?" I heard what she said, but what the fuck. "Are you being serious right now? You didn't think I could love your ba—wait, did you say babies? As in more than one?"

She nods, and a smile lights up her face. "I'm pregnant with twins."

My eyes go to her slightly swollen belly. "Wow, twins? There are two of them in there?"

"Yeah." She laughs, and the melodic sound has me wanting to pull her into my arms. "You should've seen me when I found out."

My heart sinks. "I wish I could've been there." We're both silent for a beat before I continue saying what I had started to say a moment ago. "Did you break up with me because you didn't think I could love someone else's babies?"

She shakes her head, and tears fill her eyes. "No, I knew you could, but I didn't want to put you in that position."

"So, instead of coming to me and telling me you were pregnant, you decided for me?" The more I think about this, the more fired up I get. I understand Kendall has her issues, but to make decisions for me isn't okay. "Don't you think you should've asked me? Like 'Hey, Dec, I found out I'm pregnant, and it's not your baby. How do you feel about that?'"

Kendall's face falls. "I know. I messed up big time, but the thing is, based on the date of conception, there's a chance you could be the dad."

Wait, what? It takes me a second to wrap my head around what she said. I could be the dad…because we had sex during the time the babies were conceived. Holy shit.

"That's why you're here? Because you remembered our time together, and now there's a possibility I could be the dad?"

"No." She shakes her head, and tears fall down her cheeks. "Dammit, Dec. I suck at all of this. I'm sorry. I'm just all over the place. I thought I was doing the right thing. I love you so much, and I didn't want you to be stuck—"

"Stop saying that," I bark. "Stop thinking for me. Does your dad feel stuck? No. Does Camden feel stuck? Hell no. I get you have your insecurities, but instead of trusting how much I love you, you not only pushed me away but you also broke up with me. Had you not remembered what happened, you never would've come back here." I wait for her to disagree, and when she doesn't, I let out a frustrated sigh.

"So where do we go from here?" she asks, her eyes filled with tears. I want to pull her into my arms and tell her the only place we go from here is to the bedroom, so I can make love to her because I've missed the hell out of her. But I can't do that because I'm too hurt.

"Fuck, Kendall, I don't want to push you away, but I need some time." Her eyes flutter closed, and I hate that I'm hurting her. I palm her cheek, and she opens her eyes, sadness and regret filling them. "This all sucks. It feels like no matter what I do, it's never enough to show you how much I love you. That I want you, every broken piece of you, forever."

She chokes out a sob. "I'm so sorry, Dec. I know I messed up. I know you love me. I just… I really thought by letting you go, I was saving you, and I hear what you're saying, but I… I didn't see it like that. All I kept thinking is how you deserve better than this… better than me."

"I want to believe you, but at the same time, I think you used this as a chance to run. I know I fucked up by not telling you that we were together, but regardless, when you found out that you were pregnant, you should've come to me. Instead, you did what you always do… you ran.

"And I get it. Running is what you've been doing for years. But up until now, you were running from guys who weren't me. Who don't love you the way I do. We promised each other forever. You should've trusted in our love enough to know that no matter what, I would stand by you, and we'd make the decision together.

"The worst part is, you didn't just run. You left. I'm supposed to be your partner, your best friend. I chased after you, but you wouldn't let me catch you."

Sobs wrack Kendall's body, and I hate how upset she is. It can't be good for the babies. But I don't know what to do or how to handle this entire fucked-up situation.

"I guess I'll go," she says, giving me the saddest damn smile.

Even through the worst of times, she tries so hard to keep that wall up so the world thinks everything is okay. I'll never fully understand how a woman could be so strong yet vulnerable.

With her hand on her belly and her head hanging, she turns on her heel, ready to leave. But something in me screams to stop her from walking out the door. Yeah, she hurt me, but she's hurting too. And it's during the moments when we think someone deserves to be punished that what they really need is to be loved.

And if I want her to let me in, to stop running, pushing her away isn't the way to do it. I have to show her that she's safe with me. Safe to fuck up. Safe to make mistakes. Because no matter what, I'll be here. Always.

"Stay."

She stops in her place and glances over her shoulder. "What?"

"Stay with me tonight."

Her eyes widen. "Are you being serious?"

"Yeah. Stay here, please."

"Wha…What does that mean?" she asks, her words filled with nervous hope.

"It means that I love you, and I want you in my arms and in my bed. We can figure everything else out tomorrow."

Tears stream down her face as she cuts back across the room. I wrap her up tightly in my arms and kiss the top of her head, inhaling her scent. Fuck, I've missed her so much. Maybe I'm a sap for forgiving her so easily, but I don't care. All I want to do is love Kendall, and staying mad over shit isn't the way to go about it.

She grabs one of my shirts and changes into it, then crawls into my bed. "I need to call my mom. She called while we were talking." She puts the phone to her ear, and a second later, she says, "Hey, Mom… Yeah, I'm okay." I can't hear what her mom is saying, but while she listens, she chews on her bottom lip, telling me she's nervous. "I'm sorry. I was in the middle of talking to Declan." A soft chuckle. "Can we talk about it tomorrow? Okay, see you in the morning. Love you, bye."

She hangs up and eyes me. "The last she heard, I was going to tell Kyle about the pregnancy."

"How'd it go?"

"I didn't tell him. After I saw him banging Britney and remembered everything that happened, I left and came here."

I nod in understanding and open my arms for her, silently telling her to lie with me. She scoots down and snuggles into my side, then lays her head on my chest, her arm encircling my torso.

"It's not bedtime yet," she murmurs, pointing out the obvious since it's still the afternoon.

"Yeah, but there's nothing wrong with having a lazy Sunday in bed."

She sighs into me. "I agree."

With the hand that's wrapped around her, I run my fingers through her hair, knowing it calms her. Sure enough, within minutes, her breathing has evened out, and she's snoring softly.

While she sleeps, I use the hand that's not playing with her hair to pull out my phone and search all things pregnancy. Obviously, we're going to have to get a paternity test done. Even though Kyle's a cheating dick, he deserves to know if he's fathered two babies—but regardless of the outcome, I'm going to be in Kendall and these babies' lives.

I'm reading about the decreased chance of giving birth full term with twins when Kendall stirs awake, stretching her body against mine. She glances up at me, her blue eyes meeting mine.

"Hey," she says, her voice raspy from sleep.

"Hey back."

"I haven't slept that well in a while," she admits.

"I didn't sleep, but I get it. This is where you belong—in my bed and in my arms."

She sighs and lays her head back on my chest. "I like being here. If it were up to me, we'd never leave." Just as she finishes her thought, her stomach rumbles out loud as if to remind her that staying in bed forever isn't possible.

"How about I make us something to eat, and then we can come back to bed? We can stay here until tomorrow morning when we have to go to the studio."

She smiles up at me. "That sounds perfect."

While I make us a simple chicken stir-fry, I ask Kendall about her appointment, wanting to know everything.

"I really thought I was at the most six weeks," she admits. "When she told me I was fifteen weeks and there were two babies, I damn near died. Thankfully, my mom was with me."

I chuckle, imagining Kendall finding out and the look on her face she probably had. "When are you due?"

"November third. It's impossible to know exactly when the babies were conceived, but based on their measurements, the doctor said the estimated date of conception is February tenth."

"We spent the night together February twelfth." I know the date by heart. It's the night I confessed my feelings to Kendall, and the night before the accident.

"I can't remember when I had sex with Kyle, but if—"

"Hey." I set the spatula down and walk over to her, letting the veggies cook. "It doesn't matter. If he's the dad, we'll deal with it, but there's no point in worrying about what-ifs. I looked it up, and your doctor can do a paternity test that won't harm the babies." I lean over and kiss her lips. "The test will let us know, but regardless of the results, we're in this together, yeah?"

"Yeah."

After eating, we head back to bed, but instead of Kendall lying back down and snuggling into me, she climbs on top of me, straddling my thighs. With my back against the headboard, I grip her hips as she leans down and presses her lips to mine.

"I missed you so much, Dec," she murmurs against my mouth before darting her tongue out and silently asking for access.

"Missed you more, baby," I say, then part my lips, accepting her tongue into my mouth. I suck on the tip, which has her moaning and her thighs clenching.

"I want you," she whispers as she runs her hands down my chest and abs, then breaks the kiss to lift my shirt over my head. "I know we have things to figure out, but…"

"Kendall," I say, holding the side of her face. "Yeah, we've got shit to figure out, but do you want this? Us?"

"Yes." She nods emphatically. "I want you, always."

"Then you're mine, and I'm yours. *Always.* Which means you can have me any time you want."

I palm the nape of her neck and crash my mouth against hers, needing to feel her soft lips against my own.

She breaks the kiss again, this time to remove her own shirt, but when she does, exposing her bare breasts and stomach, I stop in my place because holy shit, she's a sight to behold.

"Baby…" I glide my hand over to the front of her swollen belly and admire the bump.

"I swear I popped this week," she says with a laugh. "I had to order maternity clothes because nothing fits. I can't even imagine how big I'll be when I'm ready to give birth." She smiles down at me, her eyes sparkling with happiness, and my chest expands. I love this woman so damn much, and in less than six months, we'll be having not one but two babies. I need to make her mine—

officially—as soon as possible.

I sit up slightly and tilt her back a little, then lean down so I can kiss the protruding area above her belly button, which no longer houses the navel ring she usually has. "I can't wait to watch you grow. When's your next appointment? I don't want to miss another one."

Our eyes lock, and hers are filled with raw emotion. "I want to say I don't deserve you," she says, sniffling back her tears. "After everything, you let me back in so easily when I don't deserve it, but I won't say it because I know what you'll say."

"And what's that?"

"You'll say I do deserve it, that I do deserve you."

"Damn right." I capture her mouth with my own and flip her gently onto her back. Without breaking our kiss, I tug her underwear down her legs, then inch downward so I can get reacquainted with her pussy. Trailing kisses down her growing belly, I settle between her thighs and spread her lips wide so I can lick up her center.

"Fuck, I've missed this. The taste of your pussy."

She moans, bucking her hips as I tongue her, stopping at her clit. With slow and methodical flicks to her swollen nub, I make her come so hard that she screams my name while fisting my hair and holding my face to her pussy. Only once she releases my face and pushes me away, shaking her head and telling me she's had enough, do I stop.

With one hand holding me above her, I take my shaft into my other hand, and guide myself into her tight warmth. She's so slick my dick glides right in. I stop once our bodies are connected, taking a moment to appreciate what this feels like: home. I'm finally home.

"No more running," I murmur against her lips as I start to

move in and out of her. "This is where you belong, with me inside you. Understand?"

"Yes," she pants, wrapping her legs around me.

"Say it," I growl, fucking her harder, deeper, needing to be as connected as our bodies will allow. I find her clit, and her body trembles as I massage circles, determined to make her come again.

"No more running," she breathes.

"Because you're mine." I suck on her heated flesh. "Always."

Just as she starts to repeat my words back to me, her orgasm rips through her, sending her over the edge and taking me along with her.

I drop my head into the crook of her neck, catching my breath, and she wraps her arms around me. "I'm yours," she murmurs into my ear. "Always."

# Twenty-Six

## Kendall


up for it, we can absolutely tell them no, but with you and Raging Chaos being in the running for several awards, when they asked, I wanted to at least run it by you guys."

"What do you think?" I ask Declan since the decision whether we play at the iHeartRadio Music Awards isn't only mine to make. While we're both supposed to be attending, since Raging Chaos is on a break and I was as well, we weren't scheduled to perform. But when another artist broke her leg, they called my dad to see if Declan and I would be up for performing "Drunk on Your Love."

"I think that's up to you," Declan says, squeezing my hand. "The show is next week, which will put you at eighteen weeks pregnant. Will you be up for that?"

"I don't see why not. Since you're not a dancer, we can have a tamer performance choreographed. Nobody will expect you to bust out with any moves."

Matty, my choreographer, snorts out a laugh. "That's true. We can play off the video. Have it set up like the inside of a bar. Then switch to the outside. Throw in some fake rain, some pyrotechnics, yada yada"—he waves his hand in the air—"and call it good."

"You okay with that?" I ask Declan, just to be sure since Raging Chaos's idea of a show generally includes them, their instruments, and at some point, them taking their shirts off while women beg them to impregnate them.

"I'm good with whatever you want to do."

He smiles at me, and Bailey makes a gagging sound. "We could just forget all the rain and pyrotechnics and have them dry hump on the stage. I bet the viewers would prefer it."

"Ha-ha." I glare at her. "Don't you have somewhere else to be?"

"Actually, yes, I do." She stands. "We have a week to get ready for a performance that we usually have months to prepare for."

"I want you both in the rehearsal studio as soon as this meeting is over," Matty says, standing as well.

"Actually, I have an appointment afterward. Can we start fresh tomorrow?" I bat my lashes at him, hoping it will keep me safe from his wrath.

He growls under his breath but agrees before stomping out. "Love you, Matty!" I yell.

"Love you too, *Stiff*."

I roll my eyes at his annoying nickname for me. "How long will we have to be together before that dumb name goes away?"

"I think in order for it to go away, people would actually have to know you're taken," Bailey says with a laugh before fleeing.

I glance at Declan, expecting him to say something, but he stays quiet, and I know it's because he respects my choice not to make our relationship public. Every step of the way, he's done nothing but respect my wishes and go along with my choices. It's time I stop thinking about only me and take us into consideration, which gives me an idea.

"Everything okay?" Dad asks once it's only Declan, him, and me in the room. When I give him a confused look, he adds, "You mentioned you have an appointment."

"Oh, yeah." I take a deep breath, needing to hype myself up to tell him my truth. "Declan is going to take a paternity test."

"Declan?" Dad quirks a brow up. "I thought Kyle…"

"*Might* be the dad… yeah," I admit, my skin heating in embarrassment. "But, um… there's a chance Declan might be as well."

Dad's eyes go wide. "How…? What…?"

I spend the next several minutes explaining how Kyle cheated on me and how I turned to Declan. I hate having to admit that there's a chance I slept with two different guys in a close enough date range that either of them could be the dad, but when I get done, like the amazing dad he is, instead of making me feel bad, he simply smiles warmly and says, "It will all work out, sweetheart. And no matter the outcome, I can't wait to be a grandpa again."

"And regardless of the outcome," Declan adds. "I can't wait to spend the rest of my life with Kendall and these babies."

Dad gives him an approving smile, and I sink into his side, falling more in love with him by the minute.

The next week and a half flies by. Between the grueling practices during the day and getting lost in Declan at night, the next thing I know, we're on a plane heading to Vegas for the award show along with my parents, Phoebe, Bailey, Cynthia, Braxton, Kaylee, Layla, and Camden. I was shocked to learn that they were leaving the kids with Layla's mom and making it an adult-only weekend getaway.

"Have you heard from Gage?" Declan asks my dad—a question he seems to ask almost every time he sees him.

"He's okay," Dad says, patting him on the shoulder. "I spoke to him a few days ago."

Declan nods, then turns his head to stare out the window. He doesn't say anything for the rest of the flight, and I know it's because he's lost in his own head. Gage is an intricate part of Raging Chaos, and without him here, it's as if the guys are all lost, unsure of where to go and what to do. I get he needs time, but I hate that it's leaving the guys in limbo since they're refusing to make any music or plans until he returns.

When we arrive at the MGM Grand, we get checked in. Since Declan and I are sharing a room and need to get settled, then head to the venue to get ready for the show, we tell everyone we'll see them later.

The show begins, and shortly after, we're announced. Our performance is perfection. My outfit covers the fact that I'm pregnant, and at the end, when Declan kisses me, instead of ending it after the three count we rehearsed, I wrap my arms around him and deepen the kiss. The crowd goes crazy when Declan lifts me into his arms, my legs encircling his waist, and walks us off the stage.

He doesn't put me down when we exit the stage, nor does he release me when he walks us through my private dressing room door and kicks it shut behind us, pushing me up against it. Our mouths devour each other as he shoves my panties to the side and thrusts into me from below. Unlike the way Declan usually takes his time, he fucks me with abandon, not stopping until we both find our release.

"Not that I'm complaining," I pant, trying like hell to catch my breath. "But what was that for?"

"That was because you kissing me the way you did in front of all those people turned me the fuck on." He drops his forehead against mine. "It was so unexpected, K, but fuck, it meant so much to me."

"I love you," I tell him. "And I don't want how I feel about you to be a secret."

"Did you get the results back?" he asks, knowing they were due any day.

"I did, and they're in my purse, unopened. I needed you to know that I want forever with you, regardless of what the test results reveal. You're my forever, Dec. Always."

Tears prick his eyes, and my heart swells in my chest that something so simple as kissing him in front of the world could make him so happy.

"I want forever too," he says, setting me on my feet. The warmth between my legs leaks out, but I ignore it as I watch Declan reach into his pocket and pull out a… Oh, shit! It's a ring. "I've been carrying this around with me since the day you broke up with me. I planned that dinner to propose, but things didn't work out that way."

My hands fly up to my mouth, hating myself for what I did. "I'm so sorr—"

"No apologies." He takes my hand in his and kisses the top of it. "It might've taken a little longer to get here, but I can't ever regret a single part of the journey I'm on with you. My reason for telling you that is so you understand that I wanted to ask you to marry me before I knew you were pregnant. Whatever it says in that envelope won't change how I feel or what I want. Since I was a teenager with a crush, I knew you were the one for me, and all these years later, I know without a doubt, you're the woman I want to spend my life with.

"So Kendall Naomi Blackwood, will you do me the honor of marrying me?"

For the first time in my adult life, there's not a single doubt, a single niggling of a thought that has me questioning if I'm making the right decision, when I squeal, "Yes," and throw myself into Declan's arms. Because for the first time, it feels like all those broken pieces of me aren't so broken after all.

"AND THE WINNER OF THE FEMALE ARTIST OF THE YEAR AWARD GOES TO… KENDALL Blackwood."

I jump out of my seat and hug my family and friends, who are all surrounding me. Everyone but Declan, since he's the one on stage. I had no idea he would be presenting an award, let alone one I was nominated for.

When I make it up to the podium to accept the award, he leans in and kisses my cheek. "Congratulations, baby." Butterflies erupt in my chest, and I can't help the grin I have splayed across my face as I turn to face the camera and audience. Unlike the outfit I wore on stage, the dress I'm wearing now shows my bump. People are going to speculate, but at this point, I don't even care.

"I'm not going to pretend I have a speech prepared," I begin, making everyone chuckle. "Most of the time, I don't know what the date is, what I'm doing, or where I should be. If it weren't for my amazing assistant, Marcia, and the team at Blackwood, I wouldn't even be able to function. My entire life has been about music, and because of my family at Blackwood, I've been able to follow my dreams. So thank you to everyone who makes it possible for me to do what I love.

"More importantly, thank you to my amazing listeners. Without you, I wouldn't be standing up here with this award in my hand. Your love of my music allows me to keep writing and singing."

I hold up my award, and everyone claps. "I would also like to thank my fiancé…" Gasps are heard throughout the stadium, and when I glance at Declan, he's shaking his head with a huge smile across his face. "*Go big or go home,*" I mouth to him before I finish my speech. "Declan is not only my best friend but he's also my inspiration for my upcoming album *Fallen…* because for the first time in my life, I've fallen in love, and I can't wait to share my journey with you guys."

Everyone claps as Declan escorts me off the stage, and we head to the back so I can take a few required pictures and then hand the award off to my assistant before finding my seat.

"You realize you just told over two million people you're engaged to me?" Declan asks, pulling me into his arms. "There's no going back now." He smirks playfully.

"I don't want to go back," I tell him seriously. "I just want to move forward… with you."

"YOU WERE SUPPOSED TO PROPOSE AT DINNER!" MOM LAUGHS, SLAPPING DECLAN playfully on the shoulder as we're seated at the table in the private room of the restaurant that Declan booked—to propose. "It's the entire reason we all came."

Declan flinches. "I'm sorry. It just kind of happened."

We find our seats, and the server immediately fills our glasses with iced water, then goes over the specials before excusing herself to give us time to look at the menu.

"How does proposing just happen?" Layla asks with a laugh.

"At least tell us how it went down. Was it romantic?"

The memory of Declan fucking me against the door and then dropping to one knee as his cum dripped down the inside of my thighs has me choking on and spitting out the water that I'm taking a sip of.

With a knowing smirk, Declan calmly pats my back as he says, "I think she was *satisfied* with it."

"Oh my God," I breathe, glaring at him. "He proposed after we performed," I tell Layla. "It was perfect."

Since Declan was supposed to propose at dinner, the table is filled with gorgeous flowers, and at the end of the meal, a decadent dessert and delicious champagne are brought out, along with a bottle of sparkling grape juice since I can't drink alcohol. We take tons of pictures and videos, and Declan and I both post photos on our social media announcing our engagement. As I thought, several people comment asking if I'm pregnant since the pictures of my bump are going around, but I ignore them. When I'm ready, I'll confirm the pregnancy. Until then, they can have fun analyzing every photo and angle of me.

Exhausted and knowing I'm close to crashing, we head back to our room after we're done eating dessert, telling everyone we'll see them in the morning for breakfast before we check out to go home.

While I know it has to be the same room we left our luggage in before the show, I do a double take when we walk in because it's been transformed into the definition of romance. Bloodred rose petals in the shape of a heart adorn the bed and are scattered along the floor. There's a platter of chocolate-covered strawberries on the nightstand, along with several candles placed along various surfaces.

"You did all this for me," I breathe, turning to Declan, who's standing behind me.

"I'd do anything for you," he admits, pressing his lips to mine. "I love you, Kendall. You and these babies…" His hand goes to my belly. "You're my entire world."

Tears prick my eyes as a huge messy ball of emotion climbs up my throat.

"What's wrong?"

"Nothing," I tell him. "Everything is perfect."

"Then why are you crying?" he asks with a laugh as he swipes a tear from under my eye.

"Because you love me."

"Yeah, I do." He laughs again, giving me a look of confusion as I try to figure out how to word the million different thoughts and emotions hitting me all at once.

"You did all of this without even knowing if the babies are yours," I choke out. "But it's more than just this—the engagement and romantic night. You planned to go to my wedding knowing that you were in love with me."

He nods.

"And when I climbed out of the window, instead of telling me to go fuck myself, you were my getaway driver, when the fact is, that road trip was supposed to be your way of getting away after my wedding because you were so hurt."

Another nod.

"And then you made the entire trip about me. The wine walk and *Vampire Diaries* tour… the lake and mountain…" I encircle my arms around his neck. "For years, I was so caught up on the fact that half of my DNA comes from the shittiest human that I allowed it to dictate my life. Every mistake, every failed relationship, I blamed him.

"Yet you come from a home where they only care about money

and reputation, and instead of allowing them to dictate your life, you love harder than anyone I know. And even if these babies aren't yours, I know you will make sure we're loved every day for the rest of our lives, just like my dad made sure I'm loved."

A sob escapes my throat as I realize I've had it all wrong this entire time. "I'm capable of being loved and loving someone else. My love might not be perfect, but it's okay if it's a little broken because we're all a little broken. The key is to find someone who can love all those jaded pieces."

Declan presses his mouth to mine tenderly. "And I love every single imperfectly perfect piece of you."

He loves me. Just the way I am.

"Marry me."

Declan laughs. "That's the idea, baby." He kisses the tip of my nose.

"No, now. We're here, in Vegas. Let's get married."

"You're serious?" he asks.

"Forever," I say. "Always."

# Twenty-Seven

## Declan

### THREE WEEKS LATER

"SHE BELONGS WITH STEFAN. THE FACT THAT SHE WENT TO SEE HIM INSTEAD OF DAMON says it all."

I roll over and hover above Kendall, giving her a peck on her lips. "That doesn't mean shit. She feels obligated to be with Stefan, but she wants Damon. Besides…" I roll onto my side, taking her with me so our bodies stay connected. "Klaus is the real MVP."

"What?" Kendall cackles. "He's a monster!"

"They should give him his own show." I shrug. "I'd watch that shit."

Kendall smirks. "He has his own show."

"What? Why aren't we watching it instead of this teen high school drama shit?"

She rolls her eyes. "You love this teen high school drama shit."

She isn't wrong, but I'll never admit it out loud.

"We have to watch them in order," she explains. "*The Originals* doesn't start until season five."

"Damn, that's like a million seasons away."

"Don't be dramatic." Kendall sits up. "We're almost done with season three."

"Does Klaus end up with Caroline?" That woman is without a doubt the most annoying character on the show, besides Bonnie, that is. "Maybe if she'd let Klaus hit it, she'd lighten up a little."

Kendall laughs. "I'm not giving you any spoilers."

I pout, hoping to get my way, but she isn't having it. "We need to get going so we're not late to my appointment." She edges off the bed and starts getting dressed while I stare at how goddamn sexy she looks carrying my babies. If I have it my way, I'll knock her ass up a couple more times, just so I can watch her belly grow.

"You going to stare at me all day or get ready to go?"

"I'd like to do more than stare, Mrs. Pierce."

Yeah, that's right. We not only got married the next day, at a small chapel in Vegas just off the Strip with her entire family there to witness it, but she also took my name—none of that hyphenated shit either—and I use every opportunity to call her by it—Kendall Naomi Pierce: my wife and soon-to-be mother of my children.

After we were married and celebrated with her family, we went back to our room, made love for damn near most of the night, and then opened the results, where we found out that I'm the dad—best wedding present ever.

"C'mon!" Kendall says. "I'm dying to see the babies."

Getting up, I throw my shirt on, then stuff my wallet, phone, and keys into my pockets. "If one of them is a boy, we should name him Klaus. That would be badass."

Kendall, who's walking toward the door, stops in her place and turns around to glare at me. "That's not happening. Baby-naming rule number one: no naming them after vampires… a horrible one at that."

"Klaus hater."

"BABY A IS A BOY!" DR. WEISBERG TYPES *BOY* ACROSS THE SCREEN AND CAPTURES A picture.

"Oh my God, we're having a boy!" Kendall chokes out, squeezing my hand while keeping her eyes trained on the screen. We've spent the past thirty minutes with the doctor taking measurements and making sure everything is on point with Kendall being twenty weeks. As she pointed and clicked, she explained everything she was looking for. I couldn't tell you half the shit she said, but what I do know is that there are definitely two babies swimming around and growing in there. They both have perfect arms and legs and spines. They both have strong heartbeats, and everything is progressing as it should.

"We're totally naming him Klaus, baby," I whisper, kissing her cheek.

She snorts out a laugh and looks at me with tear-filled eyes. "I love you, Dec, but that's not happening."

"We'll see." I shrug.

"And Baby B is… a girl!"

"Oh!" Kendall breathes, glancing back at me. "We're having one of each." The tears that were piling up fall like the most beautiful twin waterfalls down her cheeks. "Thank you," she chokes out. "I wouldn't have any of this without you."

I lean over and press my lips to hers, thanking God for everything good in my life. For years, I prayed to find a love like what my grandparents had—and nothing like my parents' marriage—and every time I'd pray, I imagined Kendall by my side, her gorgeous blue eyes filled with love and happiness. Recently, I thought maybe it wasn't meant to be. But now, as I look at my beautiful wife and our babies, I realize my prayers didn't go unanswered. It just wasn't our time yet. Kendall's and my path wasn't the shortest or the easiest, and at times, it's been total fucking chaos, but in the end, it led us to each other.

"It's me who needs to be thanking you," I murmur. "You've made me the happiest man in the world. Thank you."

Once the doctor finishes, she hands us several copies of the ultrasound pictures, then reminds Kendall to make her next appointment, and leaves us so Kendall can get dressed.

"I want to buy a house," she says, threading her fingers through mine as we walk out the back door of the office and straight to the SUV waiting with her security and driver.

"You already own a house."

"No, here. I want to live here, near my family."

"Then we'll buy a house here, near your family." I kiss her temple, then help her slide in.

"Can we buy a place before the babies come?" she asks.

"We can buy a place today if you want."

She beams up at me. "I'm so happy." Fresh tears fill her eyes. "I never thought I'd ever be this happy. I know our lives won't always be perfect, but I just want you to know, I'm really freaking happy, and it's because of you."

"It's because of you." I kiss the tip of her nose. "Because, despite being scared, you stopped running and let me in."

"I THINK THEY'RE TWO BOYS," FELIX SAYS, SIDE-EYEING HIS SISTER. "WE NEED MORE BOYS around here."

"I think one of each," Easton guesses.

We've just arrived at Kendall's parents' house for dinner, and we're going to announce the sex of the babies. We considered doing some gender reveal shit, but Kendall was too excited to wait.

"You're right!" Kendall squeals in pure happiness, not even waiting for anyone else to guess. "We're having a boy and a girl."

Everyone congratulates us while Kendall shows off the ultrasound pictures.

"We're going to need to go shopping stat," Sophia says. "I can't believe you're going to have twins."

"I know," Kendall agrees. "Declan and I are going house hunting soon. I'd like to be moved in before the babies come. I'm sure it's going to be crazy having two newborns, so I'd like to be settled, and neither of our places is big enough for two babies."

"Have you thought about what you're going to do once the babies are born?" Easton asks. "Your album releases soon. You planning on touring?"

I look at Kendall, wondering as well. Whatever she wants to do, I'll support, but we haven't talked about the logistics yet, aside from her saying she wants to live in New York.

"Actually…" Kendall glances at me, smiling softly. "I've been thinking, and this album is going to be my last. Every album has been about the journey of my life, and like the ending of a book, the last one is about me falling in love." She shrugs. "I've been searching for love for so long that I just want to enjoy it. I'm ready to settle down. No more touring. No more traveling. I just want to be a stay-at-home mom and wife." She sucks her bottom lip into her mouth and then releases it. "If that's okay with you."

"Baby…" I pull her into my arms. "I appreciate you asking for my opinion, but you never have to ask my permission to do anything when it comes to your future."

"I don't know how this all works," she admits. "I just wanted to make sure it's okay. Don't couples discuss it when one person wants to quit their job?"

I chuckle at how adorable she is. "Yeah, they do. And I love you talking to me."

"What about Declan?" Easton asks. "They're going to go back on tour once the band is back up and running."

"We can't even get Gage to talk to us," I mutter, hating the bitterness I hear in my voice, but fuck, it's been five damn months since we've seen Gage. "Is there even a band anymore? We all agreed not to record without him, and based on his actions, I think it's safe to assume he's done, which means the band is done."

"He's not done," Kendall says. "He just needs a little more time, and then he'll be back."

"Speaking of which," Camden says. "What are you going to do about the condo?"

"Gage asked us to move forward." I shrug. "And while the band isn't doing so, I won't put my life with Kendall on hold. I'll keep the condo until the lease is up, so if—"

"Not if," Kendall says, cutting me off. "*When…* he will be back."

I wish I had her confidence, but a part of me is scared Gage may never return.

"He'll be back," Kendall says again. "And as far as the band goes… I'm completely supportive of you guys touring. I've been doing this for over fourteen years, and I've loved every minute of it, but I'm ready to focus on being a mom and a wife now. It's your turn." She frames my face and kisses my lips. "And when you're gone, I'll visit and travel with you. Whatever it takes. But do not give up on Gage. Raging Chaos is not over. Not by a long shot."

FIVE MONTHS LATER

"WE NEED TO GET GOING TO MY PARENTS' HOUSE SOON," KENDALL SAYS, PLACING OUR son gently into his bassinet before climbing onto the bed and kissing the top of our daughter's head, who's drinking the last of her bottle, as her eyes flutter open and closed, barely awake.

"Just one more episode," I tell her, clicking into *The Vampire Diaries*. "I need to find out if Elena forgives—" My words come to a halt as I, for the first time since we've been watching this show, notice the information in the top left corner.

"Are you serious?" I mock glare at Kendall, who scrunches up her nose in confusion.

"What?"

"You're such a damn cheater!" I whisper-yell. "Nina Doprev? Really? Who is she? If you tell me she plays Elena…"

"It's a human name!" She laughs, startling Nina—our daughter, not the actress. "I named her after the human, not the vampire. And anyway…" She glares back. "Don't act like you didn't cheat too when you named our son Morgan… after Joseph Morgan, the actor who plays Klaus!"

Because she isn't wrong, I close my mouth and shrug. When Kendall and I agreed that we'd each name one baby, with the other person's final approval of the name, I thought I was slick. Turns out my wife had the same thoughts.

After propping Nina up against my chest and burping her, I give her the pacifier—or as Kendall calls it, her pluggy—and lay her gently in her car seat since we actually do need to get going soon. Today is Thanksgiving, and since my parents are opening a new chain of Pierce Hotels in Colorado, the only house we're going to is her parents'.

Kendall takes Morgan from his bassinet and puts him in his car seat, and then we load them up into the SUV parked in the garage. Once they're both covered with thick blankets, since it's in the low forties today, we head out of the house. Once we're out, I hang a left and then drive three houses down…to Kendall's parents' house. Yep, you understood that correctly. We found a house only three houses down from her parents, and Easton and Sophia couldn't be more thrilled. So much so, Sophia has decided to retire so she can focus on being a grandma. Between Layla and Camden's two kids, our two, and Cynthia due in December, she wanted to be around more often to help out. Something Kendall and I are particularly grateful for. It's only been a little over a month and a half since Kendall gave birth, and we're both beyond exhausted. I can't even imagine how we'd function if we didn't have our support system.

The second we walk in, Sophia, Layla, Bailey, and Phoebe are on the sleeping babies like white on rice. I find Camden, Braxton, Felix, and Easton watching football and drop onto the couch with a tired groan.

"It gets easier," Camden says with a smile.

"It better," I say back with a laugh. "I feel like I haven't slept in a month." The sound of Nina crying catches my attention, and then Kendall walks in, holding her in her arms. My sweet baby's eyes meet mine, and I sigh, knowing every hour without sleep is worth it. Kendall sits next to me, laying her head on my shoulder, and I situate Nina between my thighs, where she loves to lay.

"Where's Morgan?" I ask, turning my head to kiss her temple.

"He's still sleeping, so Mom put him in the guest room." She pulls the baby monitor out of her pocket and sets it on the table. "Would you mind keeping Nina so I can help with dinner?"

"Baby, you're supposed to be taking it easy." A few weeks before her due date, the babies went into distress and were delivered via C-section. They came out perfect and only had to be in the NICU for a few days, but because of the surgery, the doctor told Kendall not to do any strenuous activity for six weeks. Spoiler alert: she hasn't been following those orders at all.

"I will. Promise." She leans over and kisses my cheek, then scoops the monitor back up and takes off before I can argue.

With Nina sleeping safely between my legs, I close my eyes, needing a few minutes of rest. I don't know how long I'm asleep, but when I wake up, Nina is no longer between my legs, and Gage is standing in front of me. His hair is the same as it was the last time I saw him—chin length and curly—but that's the only thing that's the same. Unlike the last time I looked into his lifeless eyes, they're clear and lucid. His skin is no longer pale and pasty, and even through the shirt he's wearing, I can tell he's muscular and fit. He's been working out.

"Am I dreaming?" I ask groggily.

Gage chuckles. "As sweet as it is that you apparently dream about me… Nah, it's me, in the flesh."

I glance around but don't find anyone else in the room but Gage and me. "Where's everyone?"

"Giving us a minute." Gage sits on the couch next to me. "I wanted to say I'm sorry. I shouldn't have stayed gone as long as I did, but I needed time."

"What made you come back?"

"Your wife." He grins. "Congrats, by the way. Finally got the girl."

"Kendall?"

"Yeah, she came and saw me. Told me it was time to come home. Brought Kaylee as backup."

Fuck, I love that woman. "So where've you been? Why'd you stay away for so long?"

Gage drops back against the couch and turns his head to face me. "Where do I even begin?"

"How about at the beginning?"

# Epilogue

## Kendall

### FOUR MONTHS LATER

MY EYES POP OPEN AND I GLANCE AROUND, NOT HEARING A SINGLE SOUND. THERE SHOULD be sounds. With five-and-a-half-month-old twins, there are *always* sounds. And then it hits me… My parents kept Nina and Morgan overnight so Declan and I could have a night to ourselves.

"About damn time you woke up," Declan says, kissing his way up the inside of my thigh. "I was wondering if I was going to have to fuck you awake."

After dropping the twins off with my parents, Declan took me out for dinner and dancing. Since I hadn't had any alcohol for the past year, I passed out on the way home from the club, and Declan carried me inside, putting me to bed.

"I wouldn't be opposed," I say with a shrug.

With a light chuckle, he grabs the Polaroid camera I bought him for Christmas—since he always says he wishes he could take pictures without worrying about our phones being hacked—and takes a picture of me, shaking it until it appears.

"Fuck, you're so damn perfect," he murmurs. Since I purchased the camera for him, he takes daily pictures of us and puts them into a photo album I also got for him. I often catch him flipping through it, and as much as I want to be embarrassed that my husband has an entire album filled with naked images of us—well, mostly me—I love that he can't get enough of me.

After setting the picture and camera back on the nightstand, he places another kiss on my flesh, making my nipples harden from his touch.

Grabbing his shirt, I pull him up, so we're face-to-face, not giving a shit about morning breath. When you're raising two babies, you have to find time to be together, and in order to do that, you have to throw any and all perfect scenarios straight out the window.

Declan drops a sweet kiss to my lips before he drags his lips across my jawline and neck, trailing open-mouthed kisses along my flesh. Reaching between us, I pull his hard cock out and stroke it up and down, using the beads of precum to create the perfect amount of friction.

"I need you," I murmur as he lifts my shirt and takes one nipple in his mouth, sucking gently on the tip before biting down on it playfully.

"Careful, or you'll get more than you bargained for," I joke, referring to the milk he tends to get a taste of when he gets excited and forgets that I'm still producing and pumping milk for two babies.

"Eh." Declan shrugs. "Milk does a body good."

I throw my head back with a laugh, and he uses the opportunity to kiss the column of my throat. "I love you so damn much," he murmurs, working his way back up to my lips.

Since he already removed my panties while I was asleep, I

spread my legs and guide him inside me, needing to feel him. In one fluid motion, he thrusts into me, hard and deep, as he slams his mouth against mine, pushing all thoughts but him and me out of my mind.

I love the way Declan fucks me—rough yet gentle, hard but sweet. He worships my body, making sure I come before he lets go, filling me with every drop of himself.

"I don't think I'll ever get enough of you," he says, kissing me one last time before he pulls out.

"That's good because you're stuck with me for life." I stick my tongue out at him playfully and roll off the bed so I can get cleaned up.

He comes up behind me and swats my ass. "Keep up with the smart mouth, and I'm going to fuck it right out of you."

"Promises, promises," I say as I saunter to the bathroom, making sure to add some extra sway to my walk.

Of course, that leads to him doing just that: fucking me from behind under the water while we shower.

"What are you up to today?" he asks once we're both dressed for the day.

"Felix is on spring break, so we're taking all the kids to A Latte Fun. Wanna go?"

"Hell no." Declan mock shivers as he presses start on the coffee maker. "That place is nuts."

I bark out a laugh at his dramatics. He went there with me one time, and after seeing all the kids running around, jumping all over each other, and acting crazy, he swore he'd never be back.

"Whatever. What are you up to?" I ask, handing him my mug so he can make me a cup as well.

"Actually… the guys and I are going to the studio… to practice."

"What?" I gasp. "Seriously?"

"Yeah," he says, hitting me with a boyish grin. "I'm excited. All the songs are written, so it's time."

"I'm so happy for you!" I jump into his arms and pepper kisses all over his face. "The album is going to be amazing."

"Who's all going?" he asks, setting me down.

"Layla and Kaylee," I say with a laugh. "Bailey and Cynthia are home with Matthew. He's got a bit of a cold."

"Why the hell would Kaylee want to endure that shit when she doesn't have to?"

"Maybe because she's hoping she and Braxton will be pregnant soon."

Declan's eyes widen. "They're trying?"

"Yep, have been for a little bit. Don't say anything." I grab my coffee and pour it into a to-go cup. "I'm off to my mom's." I lean up on my tippy-toes and kiss Declan. "Let me know how it goes."

Before I can get away, Declan grabs my arm and drags me back. He kisses me tenderly, making my heart pick up speed and the butterflies soar in my belly. God, I'll never tire of that feeling. Ever.

"Give the babies a kiss from me," he says. "I love you."

"Love you too… Always."

"YAY! YOU CAN DO IT, NINA," I CHEER AS SHE ROCKS BACK AND FORTH ON HER HANDS AND knees, attempting to crawl.

"Don't encourage it," Layla says. "Once they start moving, there's no stopping them." She nods toward Marianna, who's jumping on the trampoline that's level with the ground. She bounces up and down, gaining height and then does a flip into the foam pit.

"That child is going to give me a heart attack," Layla says with a grimace.

"Hey, do you see that woman?" Kaylee asks, nodding toward where Marianna is. "The one with the blue shirt."

"Yeah," Layla and I both say at the same time. She's kneeling next to a little girl who's stacking a bunch of blocks.

"You know her?" I ask.

"I'm pretty sure that's Sadie."

Layla and I both whip our heads around to look at her.

"Gage's Sadie?" Layla asks.

"Yeah."

"I never saw her," I tell them. Shortly before Gage overdosed and then went to rehab, he was hanging out with some woman. I don't know the details, only that one day she was there and the next she was gone.

"Me neither," Layla agrees.

"Well, I have," Kaylee says, "and that looks an awful lot like her."

She pulls her phone out and snaps a picture of the woman, then types on her phone.

"Are you sending that to Gage? Do you think that's smart?" I might not have seen her, but I've heard about her, and I'm pretty sure Gage made it clear that he doesn't want anything to do with her.

"How old do you think that baby is?" Kaylee asks, ignoring my questions.

"Maybe eight or nine months," Layla guesses.

Kaylee's phone goes off and she curses under her breath. "I was right… It is her. And Gage is on his way here."

"What? Why?"

"Because if Layla's calculations are correct, that baby might be Gage's."

"Oh, fuck," Layla and I say in unison.

The Love & Lyrics Series isn't over!

Did you know Camden, Braxton, and Gage have books?
Check out the whole *Love & Lyrics Series*.

Want more of Kendall and Declan?
Find some sexy and sweet bonus scenes on my website.

Did you know Camden's parents have their own book?
Check out *A Chance Encounter*.

# About the Author

*Reading is like breathing in, writing is like breathing out.*
*– Pam Allyn*

Nikki Ash resides in South Florida where she is an English teacher by day and a writer by night. When she's not writing, you can find her with a book in her hand. From the Boxcar Children, to Wuthering Heights, to the latest single parent romance, she has lived and breathed every type of book. While reading and writing are her passions, her two children are her entire world. You can probably find them at a Disney park before you would find them at home on the weekends!